THE
SPACE
BETWEEN
THEM

The Space Between Them

Contact Information: lindsayjcampbell.com

Book Cover Designer: William Ntim

Editor: Jennifer Collins

Format Editor: Mirajul Kayal

ISBN: 979-8-9896973-0-4 (paperback)

979-8-9896973-1-1(ebook)

First Edition: December 2023

10 9 8 7 6 5 4 3 2 1

THE
SPACE
BETWEEN
THEM

A NOVEL BY

LINDSAY J. CAMPBELL

Dedicated to the family and friends who have supported me throughout all stages of my writing journey.

Especially to my mother. Without your unwavering support, I could not have accomplished this.
Thank you.

Prologue

Blood. There was so much blood that night.

It happened almost fifteen years ago. Normally I never remember the details from that haunting night. Yet, this time I do. It's as if a scalpel permanently carved the memory into my brain—it replays constantly like a broken reel.

The memory is a nightmare—feeling more like déjà vu on acid than anything. In it, I'm in my childhood home in Alaska; inside the little blue house. The only time I return here is when my head hits the pillow and my eyes close.

Everything is the same from that night, yet demonically and dramatically heightened. The hues of the living room are vibrant, shining like a social media filter. The smell of ashy smoke overwhelms my nostrils to the point where I wince—probably looking like I'm about to sneeze. The sound of the clock echoes in the empty room like a slow-beating drum, reminding me I'm alone.

I look down at my hands. They're tied tightly to the sides of a raggedy kitchen chair.

My throat tightens.

I push against the rope, feeling as if I'm an animal caught in a trap. The sound of the clock grows louder and picks up pace.

I give a final, aggressive push. Nothing budges, and I give up.

Then, to the left of me appears another kitchen chair. No one's sitting in it.

"Hello?" I call out.

My eyes scan the living room. I wait, pause, and then try again. This time, I call out her name. "Emma, where are—"

Immediately, I stop. My voice—the one that just spoke—doesn't belong to twenty-two-year-old me. It belongs to a child.

Drops of sweat slip down my neck towards the middle of my back.

Looking down again, I see a pair of two short legs instead of my adult legs. They don't reach the floor, and white tights and a red checkered dress cover them.

The ticking of the clock speeds faster.

I stare at the other kitchen chair.

Suddenly, a fiery heat engulfs me, the intense sensation overwhelming my body. It becomes more and more painful as each second passes, but my eyes never look away from the kitchen chair.

Then, everything goes black.

I'm awake—just like all the other times before. The covers from my bed fall to the floor as my gasp startles me, but then the relief comes.

"Thank God."

Upon hearing my everyday voice, I let tears fall from my eyes. Darkness overcomes me until my eyes adjust. Slowly, I lay back down in my bed, leaving the covers on the floor. I'm too hot, trying not to think of the fire from the nightmare. Placing a hand on top of my heart, it beats against my palm: it's the only noise in the room, and it reminds me of the clock.

Now, it's at this moment when I think of them again, even though I know I shouldn't. Emma and Victoria. Usually, I'm able to push the thought of them away and out of my brain. It's a survival tactic I learned during my brief time in therapy when I was in elementary school.

However, this time is different. This time, I allow them to manifest. Slowly and then quickly, the nostalgia of my childhood fills my mind as I stare at the ceiling. For many minutes, I'm in a trance as I think of both of them.

The clock's ticking returns.

It's when I start to sit up that I realize I can't. I'm frozen, as if straight-jacketed to the bed.

The ticking grows louder and louder.

My chest tightens, and I force words out of my mouth. I need to hear the reminder.

"Don't think about it." Only a whisper escapes me. "Don't think about it. You're stronger than this, Hayley."

But I do. I do think about it—just like all the times before when I've thought of either Emma or Victoria.

That's when *it* appears.

The shadow in the doorway.

And, suddenly, the ticking stops.

Chapter 1

MY ART STUDIO – MINNEAPOLIS, MINNESOTA

ME

While I'm usually annoyed on my way to work because of the morning rush hour, gratitude hugs me instead. The embrace feels similar to that of an old friend.

My productivity has been unstoppable. Even though the deadline for my most significant freelance project is fast approaching and deadlines make me anxious, my body is relaxed. Almost as relaxed as the moment you sit up after a massage. For weeks, I've been able to maintain a constant workflow, which is something I don't excel at because of my type b personality.

When I arrive at the complex where I lease space for my art studio, I park on the street and then grab my black artist bag. Jaywalking, I head towards the building and key my way inside.

I climb the five flights of stairs rather than taking the elevator. It's my only regular exercise for the day, which is embarrassing to admit. When I arrive on my floor, I turn the corner and reach into my pocket for the key, but it doesn't click when I place it in the lock. Suspiciously, I grab the handle, give it a little push, and the door opens immediately.

My eyebrows furrow as I stare into my art studio.

I forgot to lock up again last night?

Sure, I remember being tired, but was I *that* tired? This has got to stop happening.

I remind myself to check the lock before heading home tonight after work. Then, pushing the door open, I go inside and lock the door behind me.

While I've been in my studio hundreds of times, seeing it each morning always causes peace to wash over me. The space may be considered small by most people, but it isn't to me. The ceilings are tall, making it appear more spacious than it is, and I'm grateful for every square inch. There are more windows than walls in my studio, and natural light bounces in the room like bright confetti. While I'm a night owl, it's mid-mornings like this when I remind myself just how beautiful my space is. Plants with colorful pots make a home underneath the large windows. Dozens of twinkling lights hang strategically across the ceiling and in between shelves, looking like a milky galaxy when the sun sets.

On one side of my studio rests a wooden storage structure. Years ago, a former coworker designed and built it for me. Every penny I spent was worth the investment. It has flexible shelving, serving both as a sturdy storage space for my paintings and an opportunity for easy viewing. Next to it rests a bookshelf with old college textbooks and extra bottles of paint.

On the other side of my studio are canvases of various sizes stacked on the ground, my in-process canvas on a large easel, a mirror hanging on the wall, and several 10-drawer organizer carts.

I also have a kitchenette and a small futon which becomes my bed when I don't feel like driving back to my apartment. In the middle of my studio is a large, black desk. It serves as my paperwork station and a meeting spot when clients come in—particularly when I don't feel like meeting at a coffee shop or cafe.

There's a lot of stuff everywhere, but that's how I like it: things scattered like my thoughts, but deliberate like my intentions.

Lastly, hanging on the left side near the front door is a wooden decoration piece. I created it years ago, and it's in the shape of Alaska. While it may not seem important to others, it is to me. Though I've promised myself I'll never return home, it serves as a reminder of just how different my life is now compared to what it could have been.

After unpacking my artist bag, I head over to my canvas sitting on the easel. Shades of blues, whites, and golds are finally coming together beautifully on it. Looking up at the canvas reminds me of how thankful I am that I'm able to do what I do. Creating art is the most therapeutic and passionate thing I can spend my time on. Every color, pattern, and texture I create make a different song in my mind—ones nobody else can hear but me.

If I don't create, I don't function properly. I discovered this at a young age and during a difficult time.

Suddenly, I think of *her*. Her face and dark curly hair pops into my mind, but I shake it away.

No. Don't think about her.

A breath explodes out of my lungs and I pull my hair into a ponytail, staring at the canvas in front of me.

Her face tries to form in my mind again as I sit down.

I push her away like I always do.

Chapter 2

A WALMART PARKING LOT – ANCHORAGE, ALASKA

HIM

"You are just the kindest man. Thank you again, sir," says the seventy-something-year-old woman. She sounds grateful for even speaking to another human. He guesses she doesn't get out much.

A smile forms on his face as he drops the last bundle of groceries into her vehicle. "No problem, ma'am. I'm happy to help." His whiskers brush the bottom of his nose, making him feel like Santa Claus.

His voice is soft. Kind. For a man of his size, it doesn't make sense. He's now appreciative of it, even though it caused him to get picked on in middle school.

Less intimidating that way.

Less suspicious, which serves him well especially in this phase of his life.

4

He'd seen the older lady struggling when he'd been returning his own shopping cart. Most people hadn't noticed her, but he chose to go and help her. He had done the right thing.

Repeatedly, he reminds himself of what a good person he is—how he always does what's ultimately good. How he really tries to be a good person even if others aren't good to him.

"Have a good day, ma'am," he says.

He gives her one last smile before reaching for the shopping cart and pushing it away. With long steps, he returns it to the cart collector and then heads back to his Chevy.

Getting into the pickup, he thinks back to what he's purchased. Did he remember everything? He doesn't want to return to town for at least another ten days, so he can't forget anything. Quickly, he goes through the list in his head—vitamins, crayons, ibuprofen, a heating pad, and the usual list of food.

Yes, he got everything. Good because he's got a special work assignment coming up that'll require some backcountry foot patrol. He won't have time to come into town for at least a week. He works for the Alaska Department for Chugach State Park as a veteran park ranger and his role requires a little bit of everything: law enforcement, logistics, resource management, and foot patrols. Ironically, he's also called upon for emergency response to urgent public safety issues such as search and rescue missions and natural disaster response.

Starting the vehicle, he drives slowly out of the Walmart parking lot. With his sharp turn onto the road, the photograph pinned to his visor falls, but he catches it before it hits the floor.

With a nervous hand, he brings the photograph close to his face—staring at it solemnly.

He thinks of her, then. Her beautiful face. Ashy blonde hair and bright green eyes stand out like stars in a black sky, as was especially the case on the first night they met. To this day, he still remembers the exact shirt she wore—the same one he later made her wear the night he proposed to her.

Rage consumes him until he takes a deep breath, filling his lungs with as much oxygen as possible. He exhales sharply.

Shaking his head, he puts the photograph back where it belongs.

At the next red light, he whispers, "Soon. Soon, it'll be over."

After all these years, what he's been planning for is finally going to be executed. Finally, it's time for the much-needed round two.

Chapter 3

MY ART STUDIO– MINNEAPOLIS, MINNESOTA

ME

12:36 a.m.

After hours of painting, I'm standing in my studio's kitchenette, watching the second hand circle around the clock like a dog chasing its tail. It's not until exhaustion hits me that I snap myself out of it.

"No," I say, and then I chuckle. "Stay awake."

Shaking my head and looking away from the clock, I grab a bottle of Diet Coke from the mini-fridge before walking back to my canvas. I only have about an hour of work left for the evening, and then I can head home.

I'm excited to get back to my apartment. Hopefully, my roommates will still be up. Like ships crossing each other in the night, we only see one another briefly each day. Both Lillie and Catherine work early in the mornings, and I sleep in until ten or eleven. By the time they return from work, I'm usually only taking my lunch break, but I'm never home for that anyway. I'm at the studio.

As I walk towards the canvas, my reflection in the mirror catches my attention. While I don't normally stop and look at myself, I do this time.

God, I look tired.

I walk closer, continuing to stare. Besides the exhaustion on my face, what catches my attention is my eyes—more precisely, the color. It's no secret they're an unnatural color: icy blue. Most people who make comments about them ask if I'm wearing colored contacts. I always reassure them I'm not and sometimes I even have to bring up a baby picture to prove it.

What I notice next is my curly, dark brown hair. It's disheveled and pulled back in a high bun. My skin looks brighter than usual, but there are bags underneath my eyes. The faded burn marks on my neck are visible.

Naturally, I touch them. And then I look at my eyes again and think of *her*. Victoria Rossi, my mother. Immediately, my jaw clenches and my hand drops down.

From pictures, I know I've physically morphed into a clone of my mother, which has been the universe's cruelest joke on me. We have the same hair color, lean body frame, and chiseled facial structure. Most distinctly, our eye color is identical. What makes us different is our skin tone. Mine is an olive color while hers is porcelain white. The difference isn't much, but at least one part of my dad's genes made an appearance in me.

Who could guess that two people who look so similar are opposites? While I don't know Victoria anymore, she's given me my most important life lesson so far: Silence always says more than words ever can.

Frequently, I wonder how different my life would be if Victoria were still a part of it.

What if things were different?

What if that night had never happened?

Would Victoria be a good mom? Would we have been close?

For many years, journalists painted her in such an evil, damaging light.

Rightly so, but I can never tell if my memories of her are my own or if they're ones taken from news clips. As I continue to stare into the reflection, something eventually catches my attention. "What?" I whisper.

The face staring back at me in the mirror is not mine, but my mother's.

Victoria.

A gasp escapes my mouth and the Diet Coke bottle slips from my hand.

Blinking quickly, I refocus my vision. But she's still there, staring back at me.

She is me. I am her.

Dashing across the studio, I land back in my kitchenette. I work to get myself to calm down. Sweat pools at the back of my neck. My legs tremble and my heart beats like a prisoner against a jail cell.

I'm imagining this. Nothing is there besides my reflection. I'm just tired. "You're imagining this," I whisper. "You're imagining this."

It takes a few minutes, but eventually I walk back towards the mirror. I'll prove to myself that nothing is there besides my reflection. Not Victoria's. My steps are confident, but I'm still nervous as I get closer and closer to the mirror. I stop, taking a deep deep breath before looking into it.

My mouth drops open, but no sound escapes from it.

This isn't happening. This isn't real.

Staring back at me from the mirror is still Victoria. Her thin lips turn upward, giving me a lovingly smile as she looks into my eyes.

The scream mustering inside of me finally escapes. The sound is the equivalent of all of the glass in the world shattering at the same time.

* * *

IN THE WOODS– ANCHORAGE, ALASKA

HIM

Driving down the never-ending dirt road, he believes the woods surrounding him look like an alien planet. Everything is green this time of year—jungle green. The color reminds him of her bright green eyes, a beautiful shade only found in nature. He can attest to this as he's a park ranger. At least, that's what he would always tell her, and she'd giggle at his comment.

As he looks around at the thousands of trees, he thinks about how they will turn yellow soon. While it's only the beginning of Summer, Fall will come. It always comes quickly in Alaska.

His cell phone rings as he pulls into the driveway, and his eyes widen when he reads the name on the screen. "Hello?"

His friend answers, "I did it. I got inside and the camera is working."

Wow. He did?

The man raises a fist in the air, reminding himself of Judd Nelson in the Breakfast Club. "I'm impressed. How?"

"She left the door unlocked. Stupid."

A chuckle brushes against his whiskers. "That easy, huh? I'm surprised. So the camera is on right now?"

"Yes, you should be able to see it on the app."

His friend goes on to describe what he saw in detail in Hayley's studio. Then, they discuss the next steps, the ones needed before he flies to Alaska in a few weeks and starts his special assignment. He continues to sit in his Chevy as he goes over the details with his friend, and only when they finish up does he gather the grocery bags and carry them into the run-down old cabin deep in the woods of Chugach State Park.

Before putting the groceries away, he bolts through the cabin and walks towards the back patio. Sitting down in the chair, he logs into the app and suddenly, the video footage comes to life.

There on his screen is Hayley, with her back towards him, painting in her studio apartment.

An accomplished smile forms on his face as he watches her.

"There she is," he whispers.

Hayley looks so much older than what he imagined. While he can't see her face, her curly, dark brown hair is pulled back in a high bun. She's leaning forward, looking similar to the hunchback of Notre Dame as she intricately paints the canvas covered in shades of blues, whites, and golds. It all leads to the creation of a chariot and horses.

After spending some time watching Hayley from the app, he eventually heads back into the kitchen to put away the groceries and start dinner. The man leaves the vitamins, crayons, ibuprofen, and heating pad in a separate bin. Once he finishes making dinner, he'll bring these over to the other cabin.

Only a few dozen yards away is another old cabin–almost identical to the one he's in now. This one is the cabin where he mostly stays and it'll soon serve a bigger purpose. The other one is also a part of the plan.

Taking his time, he cooks grilled dijon chicken and prepares side salads in his limited kitchen. As he marinates the chicken with the limited seasonings in the cabinet, a notification dings on his phone. Taking the tongs with him, he opens his phone and on it, Hayley bolts across her studio, looking startled and frazzled. He ignores her for now, reminding himself he's got to stick to his routine and that he'll replay the footage later to see what happened.

Finally, the man finishes up dinner and packs everything up in a Yeti lunch box. As he makes his way over to the second cabin, the accomplished smile returns to his face. Again, he raises a fist in the air.

Chapter 4

I run away like a wild animal, bolting across my studio.

My breaths are quick, and my head starts to spin.

Victoria appears in my mind and refuses to leave even though she was just in the mirror. I'm in the kitchenette again, and I look at the mirror from afar. I remind myself over and over again that I need to calm down. Breathe deeply. What just happened wasn't real, and I need to believe that.

It takes a few minutes, but soon I'm moving closer to the mirror, staying out of the path of its reflection. I approach it where it hangs on the wall, my eyes are lowered, and in one swift motion, I lift it off and place it on the floor.

Quickly, I turn the mirror around and finally look at it again when I know the glass isn't visible.

My shoulders drop. "That wasn't real. You're just exhausted."

But it must've been real?

"It isn't," I whisper.

It's time to go for the evening.

I don't want to think about her. If I do, nothing good will come of it. I'll end up spiraling out of control mentally, and that's the last thing I need right now.

I push away my thoughts and walk towards my canvas, where I gather my used paint brushes and drop them in the sink. Then, I turn off the hanging lights and throw away the empty bottles of Diet Coke. All the while, I remind myself not to let my mind wander as I need to remain focused and thoughtless

Hurrying out of my studio, I almost forgot to lock the door.

Stop forgetting to do this!

Quickly, I lock the door. "You're just tired," I say. "You just need some sleep."

I turn and bolt down the hallway and then down the stairs. Desperately, I just want to be back at my apartment, away from the silence and be surrounded by people.

Eventually, I slow down my walk. As I exit the complex, the warm summer evening welcomes me. I'm working to remain calm by the time I drive through the busy Friday night traffic back to my apartment complex, which is near Uptown, Minneapolis. It's times like this when I'm thankful my friends are my roommates, as I have someone to come home to rather than being alone.

As expected, though, my mind reminds me of what just happened in the art studio. Victoria.

No. You were just imagining things. *She* wasn't really there.

For years, I've experienced hallucinatory moments like the one with the mirror. Stress causes them, or they come anytime I think about my past for too long. However, even with all of the hallucinatory moments, I've never seen Victoria in any of them. Why now?

I distract myself by focusing on finding the parking spot closest to my apartment complex. As I head towards the apartment complex, a train's whistle echoes in the distance and goosebumps mushroom onto my arms. I find a spot and then head to the building.

At the complex's door, I press the key fob against the black box and wait for the buzz before I'm let in. A yawn escapes my mouth as I climb to the second floor.

Please be awake.

When I unlock the door, I see that the kitchen lights are on, and hear sounds from the TV playing in the background. There is movement in the living room, and I sigh in relief. My two roommates are awake and lying on our hand-me-down couches. Pizza boxes and cans of sparkling water are on the kitchen island. Relief washes over me like starting savasana in yoga.

"Wow, you're both still up!" I call towards Lillie and Catherine, slipping off my shoes.

From the plaid couch, Catherine flings her head around. She stares at me with tired yet animated eyes. "Season two of Paradise Island premiered tonight. Come join us?"

Lillie keeps her head pressed against the floral couch, but waves towards the pizza boxes. "Help yourself to pizza."

I smile, grabbing a slice of pepperoni. As I take a bite, I remind myself that nothing healthy has touched my lips today. I'm going to need to get it together. I can't survive on just Diet Coke.

I sit down on the open armchair, pizza still in my hand. Grease droplets cover my hand, reminding me of dabs of paint. A few minutes pass and my eyes start to close.

No, I need to stay awake.

Before I doze off, I sense Lillie looking at me and turn towards her.

"What's wrong?" she asks, staring. It's as if she's gently challenging me, which is a usual thing for Lillie to do. She's alway so observant. Thoughtful. More of what I wish I could be.

"What do you mean?" I take a bite out of my pizza, trying to look innocent.

Lillie's head tilts. "You look…off.

"How so?"

"Are you okay?"

"Of course," I say. "I'm just exhausted. You know how it's been with all of these deadlines."

"Okay," she says with a nod, looking as if she doesn't believe me.

Thankfully, Catherine jumps into the conversation and changes the subject. It's her favorite subject: her. When the conversation starts to mellow out, the volume on the TV gets louder.

Even though a lot has happened this evening, my eyes easily close, and I drift to sleep. Unsurprisingly, I dream of Alaska. Like I always say, the only time I return to the land of snow and reindeer is when my head hits the pillow at night and my eyes close.

In this dream, I see beautiful scenes of the Alaskan terrain in Winter: knife tip, snow-capped mountains, the cascading colors of the Northern lights, and the delicately snow-covered trees.

It's a freezing fairytale of a land.

Who knew something so beautiful could hold such ugly memories?

Now, though, everything changes in the dream. The flowing river is a red color, resembling blood, with no hues of blue. Instead of a magenta and tangerine sunset, the sky morphs into a solid crimson color. The magnificent snow-capped trees collapse and wither into black ash.

Victoria enters my mind.

I gasp as I awaken.

Chapter 5

Carefully, Victoria Rossi runs a finger down her favorite photograph. It's an old photograph, from about twenty years back. The edges are wrinkled. Marks are imprinted on the back from Scotch tape holding it up on the wall for years.

Victoria smiles, reminding herself she has everything about the photograph memorized. She could quickly draw every line, shade, and curve if it were ever to get lost or taken away.

Art is what keeps her sane even in the most insane of places. Only days ago, the walls of her hospital room were covered with her artwork, telling and retelling the story of her life through beautiful colors and abstract designs. Hanging up her artwork was considered a privilege, as it had taken her many years to earn the allowance.

The walls are now bare.

Dust covers the chair which her sister Kate sits in during her visits. Victoria's twin bed is stripped of the covers—they're probably already in the washroom.

In the room, there isn't a trace of Victoria.

Gone.

Taking in a deep breath, Victoria continues to stare at the photograph in her hand. It captures one of her favorite memories: one spent with her identical twin daughters, Hayley and Emma. They're wearing matching pink one-piece swimsuits, the ones her mother got them for their second birthday. Their curly dark hair is pulled back in large pink bows. They hold onto each other tightly, smiling into the camera.

Victoria's body tenses up.

I prayed for so many years for them.

Her smile morphs into a frown, and she lowers the picture.

What if we'd never left California? Victoria thinks. *What if I had spoken up more?*

A quiet sigh escapes her mouth. Victoria brings the picture up again, focusing specifically on Hayley. Her throat becomes dry as she continues to focus on her daughter.

Will she forgive me?

For nearly fifteen years, Victoria watched her only living daughter grow into the woman she is today, doing so through a collection of photographs—ones she'd had to beg Kate to bring along with her to the hospital for her visits.

For years, Victoria wondered about Hayley's personality. Kate tried her best to describe it, but she never seemed confident—proving that she hardly knew Hayley herself. She'd use descriptive words like logical, cold, and assertive, yet none of them sounded right to Victoria.

Next, Victoria looks at Emma in the photograph. As expected, a burning sensation overwhelms Victoria's throat, and she forces herself to look away again.

There's a gentle knock at the door.

Quickly, Victoria slides the photograph into her jacket. She turns around, unflustered.

A nurse peers in through the doorway, giving her an 'I heard what happened, I'm so sorry' type of smile.

"Hi, Victoria. Ready to go?"

Victoria smiles and brings her hand upwards, pressing it over her jacket pocket. She feels the outline of the photograph.

"Ready is all I've ever been."

Chapter 6

MY APARTMENT– MINNEAPOLIS, MINNESOTA

ME

I fling my arms out when the dream ends, which startles Lillie and Catherine. It takes a few minutes to convince them I'm okay—especially Lillie. The dream was so vibrant, nothing could compare to it. Once they believe me, I excuse myself and head to the bathroom. Their eyesight follows me as I walk away.

Shaking, I close the bathroom door and avoid my reflection in the mirror. My body trembles as I undress. A bone-deep disappointment engulfs me. I distract myself from it by jumping into the shower and letting the hot water consume me. I'm a sponge, taking in every sensation and trying to focus on anything else besides the dream and what happened earlier in my studio with Victoria.

I'm fine. Everything will be fine.

When condensation fogs up the mirror so I can't see the reflection, I hop out of the shower. My eyes are lowered as I brush my teeth, avoiding looking in the mirror.

Tomorrow is a new day. I'll be asleep soon and I'll start over tomorrow.

Usually, my bedroom door is open when I sleep, but tonight it's closed. Why? Because just like clockwork when I'd think about Victoria for too long, I may see something. Something in the doorway if it's open. The creepy figment of my imagination that I imagine while growing up. For years, it would menacingly stand in my door at night each time I thought about the night of the murder, Victoria, or Emma for too long. Sure, I'm twenty-two years old now and surely I've grown out of seeing it. But you never know.

As much as I want to, I don't fall asleep. For the next few hours, I lay tossing and turning—afraid I'll think about the dream, the figure, or what happened in my studio. When my eyes eventually close, I am dreamless.

The following afternoon, I wake up to the sound of my cell phone ringing, blaring like toll bells. My eyes bolt open and then squint, trying to adjust to the light. I reach for my cell phone and at the screen. "Jeez, it's been a while," I say, brushing my hair back from my face. Sitting up, I slowly bring the phone to my ear, and then I hit answer.

"Hey, Kate."

"Hi, Hayley!" my aunt answers. "How are you?"

I smile weakly, closing my eyes. "I'm doing good. You?" Can she hear the exhaustion in my voice?

There's a three-hour time difference between Alaska and Minnesota, which reminds me she's calling me at around 9:30 a.m. Alaskan time.

There's a slight pause on the line—and her voice changes with her answer: "Oh, I'm fine, thanks. Am I interrupting anything?"

"No, why?"

"Well, it's Saturday morning. Just wondering."

"Well, you aren't," I say, trying to sound enthusiastic. "I'm just hanging out, at least until I head to the studio."

Lies. I haven't even gotten up.

"Oh, I see."

Silence bounces between us like we're two kids playing with a bouncy ball. Then quickly comes the awkwardness. Why do I always have to be the one running the conversation? *She* called *me*?

My eyebrows raise. "Hey, so, Kate. Are you calling for a specific reason?" As soon as the question leaves my mouth, I regret it. Before I can say anything to correct myself, Kate jumps in.

"Oh, no." Her voice is calm. "We're just really missing you here. I haven't heard from you in a while, so I wanted to check in."

Why don't I believe her? Her voice sounds kind of off.

I nod. "I miss you, too, Kate. Sorry about not being in touch. I've been really busy here, hence the lack of calls."

As much as I love and appreciate Kate—especially since she's the one who essentially raised me and still actively tries to keep our relationship alive—I can never give her what she wants, which is more time. More effort. More of everything. The act of even speaking to her on a weekly basis can be a lot, considering everything we've gone through.

"I understand," Kate says.

Does she, though?

Before I can reply, Kate continues, "Oh! I heard about your *New York Times* news. I can't believe they interviewed you!" She pauses, and then adds, "I mean, I can believe it. You know what I mean. That is so exciting."

I smile, remembering that the interview was earlier this year, not recently.

"Ah, yes. That did happen. Thanks, Kate."

"Well, congratulations. It's huge news!"

"Thanks. That means a lot."

She pauses. "I'm really proud of you, Hayley."

I hang onto her words—remembering how rare it is to hear compliments like this nowadays from my family. "Thank you," I tell her, trying to sound hopeful. "It's cool to see things starting to seriously take off."

The conversation changes. For the next few minutes, Kate shares updates about Alaska, the weather, and her family. She tells me a few stories about her daughter Natalie and all about the latest home project that my father David and his wife, Mia, have started.

There's so much distance between us, Kate's stories don't seem real. I feel so far removed from my former life, the one Kate still tries to keep me informed about. Instead of a side character in their life, I feel like an extra.

As much as I love being far away from Alaska, I'd be lying if I were to say there aren't moments like this when it's still challenging to hear about this life I'm no longer—and will never—be apart of again.

As I'm about to excuse myself from the conversation, Kate changes subjects again, and the tone of her voice changes as she continues, "So, Hayley. I, um, did actually call for another reason."

I knew it. I should trust my intuition more.

"Oh, yeah?"

"Yes. So, I'm wondering…are you planning on coming home sometime this Summer?"

My head tilts in confusion. She's kidding. When hell freezes over, I'll go. She knows I don't have any plans to return home.

"Like, to Alaska?"

"Where else would I be referring to?"

I want to laugh. Maybe even hang up the phone, but I won't. I promised myself I'd never return to Alaska. Again, Kate already knows this.

"Kate, you already know my answer."

"But it's been years since you've been home, Hayley."

"I'm sorry. That doesn't matter."

"But you haven't even met Natalie yet," she says in a higher pitched voice.

Here we go with guilt-tripping.

"Kate, you can't ask me to do this. You know why I don't want to be there."

"Do I?"

The silence is deafening. I pause, letting the silence sit between us. "Are you serious?"

"You know what I mean—" Kate says softly, but I interrupt her.

"I don't think I do," I say sarcastically, biting down on my teeth. "Why don't you explain it to me?"

"Well, it...it could be a great healing opportunity for you."

Healing opportunity? More like it would open up every sliver of family trauma.

I pause, taking in a deep breath. "I'm going to pretend I didn't hear any of this."

"Hayley—"

"No, Kate. You need to respect this boundary of mine. I'm not going to keep repeating myself."

Stand up for yourself. Kate can't keep doing this, trying to dig up the past and find every opportunity for me to come back to a place that I have no intentions of visiting ever again. It's offensive. Hurtful. Illogical.

"Hayley—"

"I mean it. Please don't ask me again, Kate. You already know my answer, and it's not gonna change."

"Okay." Her voice is barely a whisper.

I sigh. "I need to go."

"Just tell me you'll consider it.

"What? No, I won't."

"Even if I pay for your ticket?"

What part of 'please respect my boundary' doesn't she understand?

"Yes, even if you pay for my ticket," I say.

"Hayley—"

"If you ask me again, I'm going to hang up. Don't test me."

"I just don't understand—"

I press the end button, and the line goes dead. Then, I stare at the phone in my hand and sigh loudly, lowering it to my lap.

And this is why we didn't speak for almost two years.

* * *

DRIVING TO MY ART STUDIO–
MINNEAPOLIS, MINNESOTA

ME

As I maneuver in and out of traffic, my mind takes me back to yesterday. It's now later in the afternoon and I grasp onto the steering wheel as the memories of the previous night resurface. While I've experienced hallucinations for years, again, never have

I seen Victoria in any of them. Not once. So why now? Why all of a sudden?

Does it mean anything that I saw her? Sure, those hallucinatory moments I experienced always involved shadows and noises, but none of my mother. I inhale sharply, imagining the mirror in my studio, now backward and on the ground.

I grip the steering wheel more tightly. "No," I say. "Stop thinking about her."

Reaching for the music dial, I turn up the volume. Rock music plays in the background, drowning out my thoughts.

At the complex, I think of the mirror again as I breathlessly climb the five flights of stairs. Once I'm in the hallway, I head towards my studio. The key goes effortlessly into the lock, but I realize it's unlocked.

My heart sinks to my stomach.

"There's no way," I whisper, pushing open the door. "I locked this last night."

Cautiously, I walk inside my art studio. Nothing is out of place, thankfully. Everything appears to be just how I left it. Quickly, I search through my apartment just to make sure nobody is there.

My chest is tight as I think back to last night, remembering how I turned the key and pushed against the door to make sure it was locked.

"How is this unlocked? Did I imagine this, as well?" I ask myself out loud.

Walking back to the front door, I lock the door and stare at it—convincing myself over and over again that it is, in fact, locked. Turning around, my eyes gravitate towards the mirror, which is still backward and pushed against the wall.

My chest becomes tight as my mind tries to remind me of what happened here last night.

"You have work to do," I whisper to myself curtly. "You don't have time to be scared. You have deadlines to meet."

As I walk around the apartment to get set up for the day, every move I make feels staged, as if I'm an actor performing for someone—something. I push through my feelings because I have to. I don't have time to deal with this today.

Minutes pass, and I finally sit down in front of my canvas on the large easel. While I've been able to jump into work quickly, I now sit and stare up at the canvas. Sure, I take time to admire the beautiful colors, technique, and concept in front of me. However, I no longer hear the beautiful song in my mind that I normally do when working on art. Instead, sadness hums inside of me.

Eventually, I push through my feelings and my work day begins. The background music is louder than usual to distract myself, and eventually I'm able to get into a flow. As I work, my eyes look down at the mirror periodically, but I never give into my fear and leave the studio.

Hours go by, and the beautiful summer afternoon morphs into a chilly evening. I grab dinner at a nearby Italian restaurant, walking so that I'm able to enjoy some of the day outside. My order is to go, and I sit on my futon eating creamy pesto pasta and drinking another bottle of Diet Coke. As I eat, my eyes look back and forth between my cell phone and the mirror on the ground.

Stop it.

Don't freak yourself out.

Once I finish my pasta, I clean up after myself before heading towards the canvas for another few hours of focus work. Wrapping my hair back up in a bun, I sit down in the artist's chair and decide on which section of the canvas I'll start on next.

Lost in thought, I reach for a paintbrush. Then, a whisper tickles the back of my neck.

I freeze, and the hairs on the back of my neck raise like quills on a porcupine.

"Hayley," a voice says from behind me.

A scream escapes my mouth.

Chapter 7

MY APARTMENT– MINNEAPOLIS, MINNESOTA

ME

Knock. Knock. Knock.

I exhale sharply, swinging backward and falling from my chair. Its wheels irk against the hardwood floor sounding like an alarm going off. Goosebumps cover my body as I jump to my feet.

"What the hell?" I gasp, looking around the studio and thinking back to the voice. I expect to see someone, but I'm alone.

My hand reaches to touch the back of my neck.

Someone said my name. I know for a fact that I didn't imagine that.

"There's no way that was real," I whisper.

Again, there's another knock at the door. It only continues.

Hesitantly, I walk to the front door–wondering if what I'm hearing is real or not– and then look through the peephole. There, on the other end, is a woman.

Who is she?

I wipe sweat from my forehead and open the door, as the woman looks innocent enough. Suspiciously, I position my foot behind the back of the door—just in case.

"Hi," I say, trying to sound confident, normal.

The woman smiles brightly. She stands a few inches shorter than me with blonde hair and bright green eyes. A long floral dress hangs from her body and large earrings decorate her ears.

"Hi. My name's Rebecca but call me Beks. Sorry for interrupting you, but I thought I heard a scream coming from your place?" She sounds as if she's asking a question. "Well...I thought it was from your place. I live right next to you. I, uh, wanted to make sure everything was okay. That you were okay."

How did she get over here so quickly?

I smile awkwardly. "Oh, that? Don't worry, everything's fine. I...I actually saw a bug, a huge one, and it completely caught me off-guard."

Her eyebrows raise, and I can tell she sees right through my lie. She seems too polite to say anything.

I continue, "Thanks for checking, though. It's nice to know I have a neighbor who looks out for me."

"Must've been one big ole'...bug, then."

Yeah, she definitely doesn't believe me.

"It was." Quickly, I redirect the conversation. "I'm Hayley, by the way. I don't think we've met."

"No, we haven't." She smiles brightly again. "Maybe you've seen my son around before, though. His name is Matthew."

Her son? Why would I have seen him before?

I shake my head. "I don't think so."

Beks smiles again. "Well, you can't miss him. He's a big ball of energy."

"I'll have to keep an eye out for him."

Beks nods, shuffling backwards. "Well, I'll let you be. Please, if you ever need anything, I'm just a door down that way." She points down the hall. "Don't be a stranger."

Warmth returns to my body again. "Thank you, Beks. I appreciate it. A lot. I'm glad we've finally met. It's nice to know some of my neighbors."

She nods confidently, turning away. "Me, too. Have a good night."

"You, too."

Beks walks down the hall, and I close the door and lock it immediately.

Taking a deep breath, I turn around and look down at the mirror. A pit forms in my stomach. My shoulders drop, tears filling my eyes as I stand in fear, thinking about Victoria in the mirror and now hearing my name. Slowly, I lean against the door and slide down it until I'm on the floor.

What is happening to me?

Chapter 8

DAVID AND MIA ROSSI'S HOUSE– ANCHORAGE, ALASKA

VICTORIA

As Victoria lies in the king-sized bed in one of the many guest bedrooms, she stares up at the ceiling. The clock next to her reads 3:47 am. The bed's comforter is thick—a necessity for Alaskan Winters, but not for Summers like this. The sheets are buttery soft and the room is pitch black. But nothing helps her fall asleep.

She's not used to her new surroundings. *Any* of them.

Of course, Victoria never expected to feel at home—mainly because she's staying at her ex-husband's house with his new wife, Mia. Plus, how can she feel at home, considering she's still used to the life and conditions from the North Star Behavioral Hospital? *There's no trace of me anywhere besides what's online.*

At least, Victoria has her own space now.

Initially, Kate offered to let Victoria stay with her, but they both know Kate barely has enough room for her own family in their home and that they'd probably fight the entire time. Besides, it still painfully stings that Kate, Victoria's own sister, never believed Victoria.

All in all, Kate didn't have a guest room and sleeping on their couch seemed illogical when David lived in a home with five extra bedrooms, all on the opposite side of the master bedroom. At least they had distance from one another. Even though David never offered to let Victoria stay with them, his new wife Mia did. She was very accommodating and insisted after finding out about the news.

At least Mia has a conscience and a good head on her shoulders. Maybe it was the guilt she felt on behalf of David? Or maybe David did feel obligated—it's the least he could do considering everything— but made Mia be the one who offered? Either way Victoria is just happy to have her own space, even though it's unfortunately in her ex husband's home. Sure, it's strange. Really strange. But their family's story is stranger, so it doesn't make much of a difference at this point.

If Victoria and Kate's parents were still alive, Victoria knows she'd have been staying with them. Her life would've ended up so differently if they had been alive.

When Victoria first arrived at the house, Mia let her pick which guest room she wanted to stay in. Then, Mia filled a vase of colorful flowers and placed it on Victoria's nightstand. She also even brought in a basket of toiletries—everything from toothbrushes and toothpaste to shampoo and conditioner—and a giant, hotel-style robe.

How is Mia honestly doing with the news of me being released?

Does she see David in a different light? Has he even told her everything that happened?

Probably not.

Even if David hasn't told Mia everything, she can find a lot of it by searching online. Regardless, Victoria likes Mia. So far and that says a lot.

Mia is blonde and, ironically, looks nothing like Victoria. She more resembles Kate, who has lighter features like their mother, who was the stereotypical Scandinavian woman with blonde hair and blue eyes. Their father had dark German features, which is how Victoria got her beautiful features.

Mia is charming, loud, and feminine—everything Victoria is not. The only struggle Mia looks like she has is making it to her morning Pilates classes on time and keeping their beautiful house in order—especially with the renovations happening near their master bedroom. Most obviously, she's around fifteen years younger than David, and looks closer to Hayley's age than David's. Chuckling, Victoria thinks back to her and David's first date, and how he told her he liked older women.

The irony of their situation is that Mia is the only person actively trying to make conversation with Victoria. David has hardly said one word to her, and Kate has avoided most conversations, as well. She still came to the house every morning to check on Victoria, but the two of them would often sit in silence.

Even though nobody has been acting normal or are trying to make conversation, David has given Victoria a look one time.

The look.

A look from David that is full of empathy and understanding. When it happens, it's like he's actually seeing Victoria. The last time she saw that look was when Victoria was sentenced to the North Star Behavioral Hospital. No words between them were necessary during that time.

David gave her the look more recently when he first saw Victoria after the news broke only days ago. It was meaningful.

Impactful. And now he has hardly said anything to Victoria, as if nothing happened. She's not sure if she's more hurt or surprised by that. Either way, Victoria needs to move forward and continue to try and get Hayley here.

Victoria sits up, turns her side lamp on, and observes the space around her. The guest room is large enough for them to add in another queen bed. Tall, black bookshelves cover the entire wall in front of the bed. Medical journals and modern decor fill the shelves. A gold, abstract light fixture is hanging from the ceiling. It looks like a shape from a dream—nothing resembling anything man-made or from nature. The fireplace is off, but Victoria wishes it were on.

Even in such a beautiful room, Victoria sees no signs of memories. There's not a single picture frame in the room. Some hang in the hallway downstairs, but those are from David and Mia's wedding last Summer. Now, Victoria remembers how she and David filled their small blue home with dozens of pictures, reliving the stories of their lives on a daily basis through frames.

Memories are what make a house a home. Without them, a house is just a house.

Victoria swings her feet to the side of the bed and jumps off. Her feet are cool as they touch the hardwood floor.

I need some air.

In the few days since leaving the North Star Behavioral Hospital, she's gotten in the habit of sitting on the back patio in the mornings. While she's always enjoyed this, she especially loved sitting outside at night and wanted to make this a new habit, as well. She loved listening to the sounds of nature, taking a moment to be by herself, and reveling in the peace that surrounded her. It's been over a decade since Victoria heard the crickets and sat outside at night.

Years ago, David and Victoria would sit together on the back patio of their old home—always when he'd return from his shift and Victoria was up from breastfeeding the girls. They didn't see each other throughout the day, but at night they'd talk about their days and dream together, discussing all of their future family plans. Who would've thought their lives would end up like this?

Victoria slips on the robe and heads towards the bedroom door. She opens the bedroom door and sees a figure through the crack, standing in front of her.

She gasps, jumping back. The figure moves in closer, and it's David.

"David! What are you doing?" Victoria pulls the robe closer to her body.

He steps back from the door. "I'm sorry, I didn't mean to scare you." The sound of his voice has startled her. She forgot how deep it was.

Before responding, Victoria flips on the light and looks up at him.

Even nearing fifty, David still looks young. There's grayness in his dark hair and a sadness in his eyes, but he looks the same as she remembers.

"Wow, you finally said something to me," Victoria says.

He nods, but doesn't acknowledge her response. "What are you doing up?

"I could ask you the same thing. I could also ask why you're standing at my door in the middle of the night."

They continue to stare at each other in silence and David doesn't answer.

Victoria clears her throat. "Well, since you're not going to answer that, can you answer this? Have you talked to her since you found out?"

Victoria didn't need to say who she was referring to.

David shakes his head and looks down. "No."

Her stomach tightens. "Why not?"

"I don't know how."

"Have you tried calling her?"

He pauses but shakes his head. "It's not that easy."

Victoria sighs. "What do you mean? It's literally a phone call. Do you have plans to call her?"

"Yes."

"When, David?"

"I don't know," he says, rubbing his eyes and looking away. Victoria sees tears starting to form in his eyes.

"Well, I want to see her. I need to see her."

David shakes his head again, "Victoria—"

"I need to," Victoria says again, louder this time. "You're not going to continue to keep my daughter away from me."

"I'm not going to."

Victoria pauses. "When can you get her here? Or do we need to go to her?"

He looks at her, confused. "We still have a lot to talk about, Victoria. I'm not sure when we could even—"

It needs to happen now.

Too much time has already passed between us.

"Please, David. You of all people know how much you owe me this."

Chapter 9

MY ART STUDIO– MINNEAPOLIS, MINNESOTA

ME

A few days come and go, and nothing else strange happens. My front door isn't unlocked when it's not supposed to, silence fills the studio as I work, and the mirror remains on the ground still facing the wall. Thankfully.

Even though things seemingly have returned to normal, peace no longer washes over me as I step into my studio like it used to. The place that was once my oasis has dried up.

Should I let someone know what's going on?

Do I need to take this seriously?

I'm in my studio, sitting at my black desk with my computer in front of me. Nervously, I type in my symptoms and conduct research that should've been completed probably years ago.

Like I expected, my eyes pass over the word "schizophrenia" as I read through dozens of articles and disregard it. Another word "psychosis" also continues to pop up. This is apparently what happens when people are experiencing and perceiving the world around them differently than others. Well, I definitely fall into that category. Possible symptoms include delusions, hallucinations, talking incoherently, and agitation, which are some of what's been happening recently or what has happened in the past.

Do I really think I'm experiencing this, though? Not every symptom is happening now so that has to be a good sign, right? I've only seen Victoria in the mirror and heard my name. That's it.

Even though I'm reluctant to keep reading, I force myself and find potential treatments which include medication and talk therapy—neither of which I want to do again.

Taking a deep breath, I searched for the phone number for my primary doctor back in Alaska. Even though I haven't had an appointment in years, it may be worth it to still give her a call. But what would that realistically do? My doctor is all the way in Alaska. I'm in Minnesota now, starting my new life here. She's probably just going to recommend that I look somewhere that's not thousands of miles away since I have no plans to return to Alaska.

I begin to type the number on my screen, but I don't dial the number. Instead, my eyes remain on the number.

I don't have schizophrenia. And I don't have psychosis.

Slowly, I delete the number, set my phone down, and go back to work.

* * *

A PARKING LOT – MINNEAPOLIS, MINNESOTA

ME

It's been days since I searched for my symptoms online. While I have no current plans on doing anything medically about them, I'm instead taking control of what I can control in my life. I have to start somewhere and that includes improving my health.

Drastic times call for drastic measures.

Inhaling sharply, I close my eyes. Seconds later, I open them and see the building in front of me. It's a local fitness center in Minneapolis. A gym. Just a gym.

I grip the steering wheel. Embarrassment isn't my color, but I'm definitely wearing it.

This is going to be good for me. I need to do this and start getting healthier. Baby steps.

While already aware that my diet will be the most difficult thing to turn around, hiring a trainer seems like the best first step. If I pay for this, there's maybe a higher chance I'll actually follow through. At least that's what all the self-help books like to preach.

I take a sip from my water bottle and then get out of my vehicle. Hanging my gym bag on my shoulder and holding my car keys in my hand, I walk towards the gym. Inside, my nostrils are overwhelmed by the smell of disinfectant, body order, and chlorine. I skim the front area—feeling like the new kid in school—and then walk towards the front desk. I'm assuming that's what I'm supposed to do.

A middle-aged woman wearing a tight black shirt smiles. "Good morning." Her drawn-on eyebrows are lifted nearly towards her temple.

"How can I help you?"

I look lost, don't I?

"Hi, I have a session scheduled this morning at 7," I pause. "I, ugh, can't remember who I'm with, though. I called yesterday."

She nods enthusiastically and looks down at the computer. "What's your name?"

"Hayley."

"Perfect. I have you all checked in, and you're with Brandon this morning. It looks like you already completed your paperwork which is awesome. He should be out here shortly. You can take a seat over there until then."

Brandon?

He? Wait a minute, I specifically requested to work with a woman.

I stare blankly at her, but she doesn't return my gaze.

Before I walk away or say anything else, the receptionist says. "Your eyes. They're so beautiful. Are they natural?"

Here we go.

I smile. "They are, yes. Thank you."

Noticing her surprised reaction, I wait for her to ask about a baby picture but thankfully she doesn't.

Her eyebrows raise suspiciously. "Well, they are just so beautiful. I've never seen someone with such blue eyes."

"Thanks, I appreciate it."

I'm happy she didn't bring up the scars on my neck as many people have after complimenting my eye color. I'm not sure how they go hand in hand, but it's something I've noticed over the years.

Turning around, I walk towards the seating area. Before I sit down, two men walk out of an office and distract me. One is old enough to be my father while the other is probably around my age. My eyes open wider, immediately noticing their large structures. The younger man catches my attention the most—he's dressed entirely in black workout gear with a red stopwatch dangling from his neck. I mean, how could he not catch my eye? He's handsome. Scruffy, and with unruly light brown hair and olive skin.

My heart's already racing, and I haven't even worked out yet.

There's no way that's him. No way. Then, I realize I'm staring. Instantly, I look away—feeling my cheeks flush red as I pretend to look occupied.

I sit down and grab a hairband out of my gym bag. Then, from the corner of my eye, I see one of them walking towards me. My heart only beats faster as I continue to look busy.

The younger man approaches me then, beaming a smile. "Hey there. Are you Hayley Crowe?"

Well, shit. So, this isn't a joke? He's going to be my trainer?

I nod, my expression is a little too animated. "Yes, I am."

He extends his hand. "Hey, Hayley. My name is Brandon, and I'll be your trainer. It's nice to meet you."

I reach to return his handshake. A jolt of electricity runs through my body at the contact. "Thanks, it's nice to meet you, too." I pull my hand away.

After a few minutes of small talk, he eventually guides me over to an open area in the gym. There, he goes over some basics like stretching and the importance of warming up—things I already know, but I still listen. As Brandon speaks, I try to focus on his words, but he's distracting.

I remind myself that I can always change trainers. Or switch gyms if I really want to. Maybe just give Brandon a chance and then reevaluate. So far things are going well.

When we finish stretching, Brandon leads me to the line of treadmills near the gym's back wall. He stops at the first empty one and taps on it.

"Ready to get started?"

Not even in the slightest. "Wasn't the warm-up getting started?" I ask, jokingly.

"Not quite," he smiles.

I follow Brandon's instructions and hop on the treadmill. He continues to talk, and I walk briskly.

Just get through this first day. I can do this. They always say starting is the hardest part. I need to do this for my health and start taking things seriously. The last thing I want is for things to get worse.

For the next few minutes, Brandon and I chat as I walk briskly. He's still near my side, which surprisingly feels really nice.

The receptionist is back and she's heading towards Brandon. She approaches him, but he doesn't notice her at first. Hesitantly, she taps him on his shoulder.

"Hey, Brandon, sorry to interrupt you two. Do you have a second? Bart needs you."

Brandon doesn't answer right away. His silence causes me to look away awkwardly, nearly making me lose my balance.

He nods. "Sure, I'll be right there." Brandon turns towards me. "Hey, I'll be back. Continue at this speed until I get back. Or you can jog. I shouldn't be gone too long."

You better not be.

I nod, returning his smile. "Sure thing."

Brandon disappears, and I continue to walk on the treadmill and get lost in my thoughts. I wonder how long it's going to take for me to see any results? Does the gym have anyone who can create a nutrition plan for me? Or do I need to go to a nutritionist?

There's hanging televisions positioned above me and all throughout the gym. Playing on them are primarily sports channels that don't interest me. In a trance, I reach for my water bottle and take a long sip. My eyes look back at a television, now playing a commercial. In it, there are two little girls. They have red hair and are playing on a playground. I ignore the actual commercial, but I pay attention to the girls as they remind me of Emma.

Deeply, I inhale.

What would it be like if she were still alive?

While I don't think of my twin sister as often anymore, feelings of fondness appear when I do. For many years, I believed our twin connection was still alive—you know, the twin connection that everyone likes to think twins have. I convinced myself I sensed Emma even though I knew she was dead. Heartbreakingly, some of her body remains were discovered at Chugach State Park in Alaska a few weeks after the night of the murder. I can't remember what body parts they were, but it was enough for the murder trial to begin almost immediately.

In my opinion, this so-called special connection people think twins have with one another is a cliche. Creators, writers, and storytellers love to add a plot about twins and their telepathic abilities and connections. Sadly, I believed these stories for most of my younger years. Looking back now, I realize that was grief. I had convinced myself my twin connection with Emma was still there, even after her death.

I believed this until I didn't, which was right before high school, way before I had decided I was going to go to college in my late grandparents' home state, Minnesota. When I was packing up my belongings in Alaska, I realized that I needed to move on and focus on the new life I was carving out in the Midwest. Being emotionally tied to someone who was no longer coming back was pointless—no matter how tempting it was to think about her and the what ifs.

Sure, when someone brings up siblings, I'm reminded of her. Or if someone asks if I have siblings, I always say I'm an only child. It's easier than the alternative of saying my sister passed away. If I say the alternative, it opens the door for people asking what happened to her, and I'm for sure not saying she was murdered.

Plus, the last thing I want is for anyone to start connecting the dots and finding out who I really am and about my past. Even though I've changed my full name from Hailee Rossi to Hayley Crowe, which Crowe is my maternal grandparents' last name, one quick Google search and anyone can find my family's history online. In a time when everyone seems to be obsessed with true crime, it's almost a constant reminder.

Shaking my head, I return to reality and force myself to think of something else. Anything else as I can't keep thinking about Emma.

I have lots of work left on my main freelance project. Flashes of the supplies I need to reorder pop into my mind. Now is the time for me to start reaching out to prospective clients since I'm nearing the due date.

Still lost in thought, Victoria appears in my mind, not Emma. Her bright blue eyes shine into mine and she smiles at me lovingly.

My heartbeat races and I almost lose my balance.

No. Don't think about her. Of all places, this can't happen here in front of people.

I shake my head, focusing my attention on the line of treadmills in front of me as a distraction. Before my mind conjures any other memory of Victoria, I press on the increase-speed button on the treadmill.

This is my new life now. Victoria's not here and never will be here.

Unfortunately, I don't realize I'm holding the increase-speed button down for too long. Before I have time to look at the treadmill, suddenly, the speed catapults drastically. Distracting thoughts continue to overwhelm me, and then, in what feels like slow motion, my left foot fails to step quickly enough. I lose my balance, falling to my knees on the treadmill, and my body flings off the back of the machine. Wincing in pain, tears flood in my eyes as reality slaps me in the face as I'm laying on the ground.

Embarrassment is now my color, and I'm covered in it.

Chapter 10

DAVID AND MIA ROSSI'S HOUSE– ANCHORAGE, ALASKA

VICTORIA

Victoria's eyes flutter open.

It's daylight and days after catching David outside the bedroom. She's lying in bed, remembering how David made no effort to collaborate with her on getting Hayley to Anchorage the other night. Instead, he only made loose promises...ones he probably made out of obligation. Considering that he knows Victoria's been released from the hospital, Victoria can't help but wonder why he hasn't said anything about it. The night he was outside her bedroom would've been the perfect opportunity for him to talk to her.

But he didn't. He chose not to.

What was he doing outside of my bedroom anyway?

How would Mia feel, having him out of their bed and snooping on me?

While Victoria's grateful to be out of the hospital and finally have some more space, part of her is now starting to feel like a prisoner—a prisoner in a fancy house. In her ex husband's house.

David doesn't want me here. I don't want Kate to take me in. And nobody knows what's going on with the investigation.

Why does silence feel so deafening?

A wave of sadness rushes through Victoria—to the point where it feels like it's touching her soul. She looks around the bedroom sadly.

The what-if game starts. This could've been her life. This could've been her home with the girls. If it was, Victoria would first start by hanging up pictures. Then, she'd actually add some color to the house. Maybe shades of green and blue. Seeing neutrals everywhere reminded her of a hospital. Maybe that's just the style nowadays.

She takes a deep breath and then sits up from her bed.

Would I still be teaching at the university, or would I have started that business?

Victoria thinks back to the earlier days, when she'd just gotten married. She and David's first years of marriage were tough. David was still in medical school, and the girls were born shortly after their wedding. Like any other student, David worked his way up in the hospital, which resulted in long hours and inconsistent work shifts for many years. This left Victoria with the girls almost 24/7. It was difficult for her to be a stay-at-home mom with baby twins. Not only did she endure sleepless nights and constant feedings, but the judgment about her mental illness was also difficult to endure. Especially from her mother-in-law, who always enjoyed coming over to their house unannounced. She'd watch Victoria from the sides of her eyes, as if doubting her abilities to be a mother. As if begging to tell how she really felt about Victoria being a mother to her first grandchildren.

Even though Victoria got on medication immediately after her schizophrenia diagnosis at the age of 23, most people treated her differently. She expected this because of the stigma, especially during that time, but not the discrimination she faced. It mostly came from the family, mostly on David's side of the family. There were so many examples. Surveillance cameras were installed in the house, which David claimed were for security purposes only. He and his mother also routinely asked Victoria if she had taken her medication.

As an anesthesiologist, David didn't study mental illness much. Yet, he chose not to learn more about Victoria's diagnosis when it came even though apparently mental illness ran in his side of the family. He always explained that mental illness ruined his parent's relationship, leaving him without a father figure for most of his life.

For years, Victoria wondered if David would still have proposed to her if she'd been diagnosed sooner. Probably not.

Resentment slowly built up inside of Victoria. It only amplified when the girls were born as Victoria became the main caretaker while her husband got to escape to the hospital daily. It worsened when her parents, Leanne and Ronald, died. If they would've been alive, Victoria knew they would have supported her through the trial. They would've taken her in. They would've said something to the police.

The discrimination from in-laws was only amplified as the girls grew older and up until the night of the murder. Not only did they turn on Victoria during the trial, but so did the news stations and journalists. They framed her in such an evil light that even Satan would have been impressed.

Even though Victoria has full access to the Internet, she refuses to go online; she'd be too tempted to find and read the stories, watch the documentaries, and listen to the commentary about what others thought about what happened that night.

I hardly remember that night, so how can anyone say they know what happened?

And now Victoria was alone, and still feels alone.

I need to try to make the best of things now. Nothing can be undone, and I have to move forward.

Shimmying out of the covers, Victoria grabs her robe and heads out the bedroom door. She's looking forward to sitting out on the porch this morning. As she closes the door behind her, Victoria notices down the hall that David's office door is open. Usually, it's shut when he leaves for work but today it's wide open.

Victoria walks down the hall and sitting at his computer, David stares intensely at the screen. When he hears Victoria, he looks up emotionless. Eventually, he gives her a wave. She doesn't return it.

What's he doing here? Why isn't he at work?

David looks like he wants to say more, but no words leave his mouth. He focuses on the computer again.

Victoria shakes her head and walks down from the second floor to the kitchen on the first floor. The sound of the garage door opening echoes throughout the house—right on time. This is when Mia usually leaves for her morning Pilates class. It must be her turn to carpool with one of her workout friends. It's also the time when Victoria ventures out of her bedroom for breakfast and eventually out to the back porch.

She leans against the kitchen counter as she waits for her coffee to brew so she can take it with her and sit in silence. Watching the coffee drip into the mug from the machine, Victoria hears footsteps thumping on the stairs. Then, David enters the kitchen.

Sharply, she turns towards him, waiting for him to say something.

David remains silent for a beat before speaking. "The investigator is coming over today."

The investigator?

Victoria's heart drops to her stomach.

"That explains why you're still here and not at the hospital. Why are you telling me this now?"

"Kate didn't yesterday?" he asks, visibly confused.

"No."

"Oh."

Of course. She feels her face start to become warm. "It's getting a little old, being the last one to know things around her," Victoria mutters.

David doesn't say anything.

Victoria sighs, turning back to the coffee maker. "Are they actually coming here to tell us everything?"

"I'm assuming."

"And what time are they going to be here?"

David pauses. "It's actually just one guy, not a 'they.' And soon."

"Soon is too vague. When?"

"I'm not entirely sure. He'll be here when he can to give updates," David says. "I thought you'd be more excited."

Victoria's heart drops to her stomach.

Excited? Did he really just say 'excited'?

She freezes as his comment and it continues to stings. She turns towards David, staring into his brown eyes. Looking back at her there's nothing but emptiness and unfamiliarness in his eyes.

You really are not the man I once married. He is nowhere to be found. Victoria grabs her coffee mug and pushes past David.

"If I had to guess I think he'll be here at eleven," he calls after her.

She continues walking, not turning around to look at him. Victoria lifts her hand above her head to give him a thumbs-up.

* * *

EVERY DAY FITNESS– MINNEAPOLIS, MINNESOTA

ME

Blood.

I curse under my breath and push up from the ground. When I'm on my feet, I look down to see a line of blood trailing down my leg from scraping my leg on the treadmill.

You have got to be kidding me.

Quickly, my hand reaches down to cup the blood. I accidentally smear it on my skin like a child, looking like I've dunked my finger in paint. Damn it. Reality slaps me in the face, and I instantly look around, feeling panic fester inside me.

Did anyone see that?

"You alright, hon?" a random voice asks.

Yep. People saw that.

There are many pairs of eyes on me, but it's a heavy-set woman who spoke and now stares at me, her eyes full of concern. My heart races faster as I feel my cheeks flush a deep crimson color.

I smile an 'I'll be okay' type of smile, waving a hand in her direction. "I'm fine, thanks. Just a little clumsy." Before I can respond again—let alone think—Brandon is already beside me. The sight of him causes me to jump.

"Ah! I mean, sorry. You scared me."

Again, like a child, I try to hide my blood-smeared hand. It feels as if I'm going to get in trouble.

Brandon notices, of course. "Whoa, I guess I shouldn't have told you to jog," he teases. "I saw what happened when I was heading back over. Are you okay?"

This is mortifying. "With nothing more than a bruised ego," I chuckle.

Brandon tries not to smile. "What happened?"

"I guess I was a little too motivated. I started jogging and forgot to let go of the button. Maybe I should blame you for this."

He laughs and grabs a paper towel near the dispenser. He presses it against my leg to wipe the blood, which causes me to jump slightly.

I want to back away, but I don't. Instead, he helps me.

"Are you sure you're not in any pain?" he asks.

"I'm not, promise."

"Okay, good."

"I guess that was worth the great first impression," I say, laughing.

Brandon chuckles, shaking his head. "Definitely one I won't forget." He returns my smile, holding my gaze for longer than I expect.

Chapter 11

The warm Summer morning greets Victoria as she opens the back porch door. As she steps outside, she is awestruck by the view. Hundreds—if not thousands—of gigantic trees are in front of her. It's an explosion of bright green, a shade of green only really found in the summertime in Alaska.

Every morning, Victoria comes here to relax. To soften and recharge.

Yet, this time is different now. Her neck is tense, and a headache is lingering. Her mind is racing, thinking about what the investigator is going to tell them today. Will he answer all of the questions she has? Will he finally explain how exactly she was able to immediately be released from the hospital? Will she finally be able to fill in the dots on what happened that night with new information?

Victoria closes the porch door and turns and sits down on the patio furniture with a racing mind. She stretches out her legs, and once she's comfortable, takes a sip of her coffee and then closes her eyes.

In a trance, Victoria listens to the sounds around her to try and relax. The birds are chirping. A distant neighbor is mowing their lawn. Near the side garden, a windchime echoes. It's all calm, everything she needs at this moment. Up until the sliding door opens again.

"Geeze, I could've sworn you were Hayley."

Victoria opens her eyes, turning her head. There stands Kate. Not sure how to respond to Kate's comment, Victoria only observes her. Kate's remark stings, yet also strangely flatters Victoria. It's an unusual paradox, and one she's probably going to experience often now that she's living with David and Mia, and everyone can see the resemblance between Victoria and Hayley. Slight resentment and hurt wash over Victoria as she focuses on Kate. *Why didn't you believe me?*

A big smile explodes on Kate's face as she looks down at Victoria. Kate's dressed in a short jean jacket and black capri pants. Her blonde hair is pulled back into a low ponytail, and simple gold earrings hang from her earlobes. Dark bags hang underneath Kate's eyes. Are those recent? Victoria hasn't noticed them until now. Maybe Kate's daughter Natalie has been keeping her up at night again. Or maybe more realistically it's the stress of her knowing the truth is finally out.

"What are you doing here?" Victoria asks.

"Well, good morning to you, too," Kate teases, taking a seat next to Victoria. She looks at the mug. "I see one of us is drinking coffee this morning. After I dropped Natalie off at daycare, the line at Starbucks was too long."

Victoria continues to stare at Kate, unsure of what her sister will say next. *Let's just cut to the chase.* Victoria clears her throat. "I'm guessing you're here because of the investigator?"

Kate nods, but her eyebrows turn inward in confusion. "Well, I come here every day to see you, don't I? I'm just here early because, yes, I guess he's finally coming to the house. You remembered?"

"Remember what?" Victoria asks sarcastically. "David told me this morning. Nobody told me he was coming."

"Oh. Well, yes. He is. It's finally happening today."

Victoria nods. *It seems like you chose not to tell me.*

The unacknowledgement from Kate triggers Victoria, causing her blood to boil. Kate appears as if she's about to say something, but then stops herself when she notices Victoria's expression. Silence lingers between them. The tension could be cut with a knife.

Eventually, Kate forms the words. They're words Victoria does not expect. "So how are you doing with everything?"

Victoria is stiff. *How am I doing? This is the first time you've asked me this since I've been at David's.*

Victoria clears her throat. "How do you think I'm doing?"

Kate looks down as if regretting asking the question. "Probably nervous."

Victoria raises her eyebrows. *Nervous? Yes, I am but I feel so many more things, as well.* Victoria doesn't say anything.

Kate nods supportively even though Victoria doesn't answer. "That's okay if you are. I mean I don't blame you."

Aren't you nervous? Nervous to learn more details about how you screwed up by not believing me? While Victoria doesn't remember everything that happened the night of the murder, she knows she didn't do what they said she did. *Don't you realize how much Mom and Dad would be so disappointed in you for not fighting for my side? For keeping my letters from Hayley after I spent years trying to have a relationship with her.*

Victoria looks away, and her mind continues to race with thoughts. She thinks back to when she was charged with murder of her daughter, Emma. When they had found Victoria in Chugach State Park with Hayley roaming around, Victoria had regretfully admitted to shooting Emma with a gun. But this wasn't true. It wasn't really admitting. It was an explanation lost in translation between her and the police officers. Victoria knew what she said wasn't true but the way that the police had asked her what happened was confusing. Overwhelming. Sneaky.

So much happened that night and Victoria's memory was almost nonexistent due to the trauma and the head injuries she experienced. During her trial, Victoria's family turned on her after the police had said she initially confessed to the crime, refusing to believe her side of the story and instead went along with the police, including blaming what happened on her schizophrenia. And, of course, it was easier for the police and court system to run with this narrative than believe Victoria. In a matter of minutes, Victoria's life and reputation was set on fire; burned at the stake just like the so-called witches in the Salem witch trials.

Raised from ashes like a phoenix was not justice but instead a murder charge and a division in her family.

That's when Victoria became mute. She experienced so much heartbreak and trauma all at once, her body shut down. For almost two years, Victoria didn't speak to anyone and instead lived in her mind. While she heard words around her, Victoria's body forced herself to shut down during the trial, closing her off from the world and communication.

Slowly, the truth got further and further away and Victoria couldn't help but start to believe all of the terrible things they said she'd done to Emma and Hayley. Victoria ignored what she remembered and instead, internalized the words and believed silence was better.

For years during her murder trial, Victoria remembers reading all of the headlines as she passed televisions and newspapers. "Woman started fire that killed daughter; body not discovered"; "Fleeting stability for a woman charged with killing her daughter"; and "She killed her daughter; Can we forgive her?"

When you're told something so many times that you're the one who did it, you start to believe it. You start to question yourself, your sanity, and what you believe is true. That's what happened to Victoria.

Even after fragments of the truth would pop in and out of her mind while at the hospital, she didn't say anything to anyone. Why? Guilt and grief for losing Emma still consumed her. Besides, there was no way to confirm her thoughts were true.

Until now.

Now, at this moment, Victoria looks back at Kate. Her sister smiles, telling the latest story about Natalie as if oblivious to Victoria's emotional state. As she speaks, Victoria focuses sternly on Kate, her stare becoming cold as her emotions start to run wild.

Don't say it. Don't say it. Don't say it. But she says it. The words she's been dying to say finally escape.

Victoria interrupts, asking, "Why didn't you believe me, Kate?"

Silence.

Kate freezes. Her blue eyes widen. "W-what?"

"You know what I'm talking about," Victoria whispers angrily.

Kate shakes her head. "Victoria…I—"

"Why? Why didn't you?" *Keep asking her. Get her to give you an answer.*

"We've talked about this before."

"When? Ten years ago? No, we haven't," Victoria says sternly. "You let me rot away in the hospital. You're my *sister*. You didn't believe me when you were the one person who should've. At bare minimum I deserve to know why."

Kate pauses, looking away as tears fill her eyes. It takes her a few minutes to answer. "I just couldn't, Victoria. I'm sorry. I don't know what else to say."

The words sting. "That's it? You just couldn't? What do you think Mom and Dad would think? What do you think they would say to you, keeping my letters away from Hayley and keeping her away from me?"

Kate whispers, immediately lowering her gaze. "Please don't say it like that, Victoria. I tried my best, and you know how sorry I am. All of this is so complicated. Like what I said at the hospital, I kept the letters away because David and I thought that was what's best at the time. If I could do it over again–"

"But you can't. You can't do it over again."

It's at this moment when Victoria decides that the reality of the situation isn't what hurts the most. Instead, it's the non-acknowledgment from her family, specifically her sister. Not once has Kate owned up to anything. Her lack of any accountability is astonishing. The absence of any empathy is deafening.

Tears fall from Victoria's eyes. While she's proud that she was able to confront her sister, the pain resurfaces again. Victoria blinks the tears away, feeling more alone with her sister even though she's sitting next to her.

Nobody believed me, including the person who was supposed to be there the most for me.

Victoria nods and stands up, heading back inside the house.

Alone.

Chapter 12

THE TED STEVENS ANCHORAGE INTERNATIONAL AIRPORT– ANCHORAGE, ALASKA

HIM

"Enjoy your flight," the flight check-in agent says, smiling a smile that's too bright for this 7 a.m. flight.

He nods, grabbing back his one-way ticket from her hand and then giving her a kind smile. It's a few weeks later and things are finally progressing.

For the flight to Minnesota, his carry-on is a small duffle bag. With a coffee cup in one hand and the duffle bag in his other, it's finally time to see Hayley. His friend flew there a few weeks ago and now it was his turn to see how everything was unfolding with Hayley.

He feels monstrous as he walks through the echoing terminal—a feeling he doesn't like. But he needs to feel this way in order to get things done.

At the end of the terminal, he waits in line to board. He sets his carry-on down, taking a sip of black coffee.

Everything's coming together perfectly, almost too perfectly as planned. *You need to go through with this. There's no point not to now. You've done this before and you can do it again.*

He breathes in deeply, folding his printed ticket. Then, he maneuvers it into his jacket pocket next to the photograph. Slowly, he traces the perimeter of the photograph, feeling a wave of sadness rush through him again, thinking about his wife.

Then, the man reminds himself just how much of the plan is left. There's a lot. *I'm going to see her again. She's going to face me, after all of this time. Hayley's going to look exactly like her.*

His two friends have been immensely helpful as they should. The man has already helped both of them execute their revenge plans flawlessly. Now it was his turn.

As he creeps closer in line and towards the plane, he whispers to himself, "Soon, it'll be all over."

* * *

MY ART STUDIO– MINNEAPOLIS, MINNESOTA

ME

Weeks go by and it's a Monday evening, and I should be finishing up my freelance project. Instead, I'm at my desk mapping out a plan for how to take my health more seriously. On one side of the paper, I've written down everything that's working well for me. Jotted down are things like working out with Brandon, walking up flights of stairs, and making sure I'm taking my early afternoon walks before I grab lunch. On the other side of the paper, I'm writing down what I need to improve on, like my diet, water intake, stress levels, and overall sedentary lifestyle.

I look up from my desk and at the canvas in the corner of the studio as a distraction. I'm not sure if I'm in love with my work or if I hate it. I decide I hate it, at least for now. It's too familiar, and I've been looking at it for too long tonight. Oh, the life of an artist.

I need to get back and work on it as I'm already behind again on the deadline. But I am excited to finish it and meet with my client to finally give it to him. I don't know much about this client besides that his name is Mike and that he's planning on picking up the canvas.

Another thing I know is that he should have the canvas by now, and I only have myself to blame for the delay. Procrastination is my weakness, and considering the strange events that have been going on, it's only gotten worse. I can barely keep myself focused for more than a half-hour at a time. However, maybe the more I take care of myself, like working out with Brandon and staying on a routine, the more I'll start to feel like I have some control.

Opening my laptop, I quickly email Mike an update on the canvas, explaining that he'll be able to pick it up on Friday as we agreed even though this is a few days past our agreed deadline. Slowly, try to think of what excuse I should use to explain my lack of communication but I chose to disregard it.

And then, as I sit in thought, something *thumps* behind me. The sound echoes through the studio and every nerve in my body freezes.

What the hell was that?

I turn in my seat, observing the space behind me. Nothing's on the ground. Nothing looks out of place. Then, I turn and notice the mirror.

"You're fine," I tell myself as my eyes focus on the mirror. "That was nothing."

Suddenly, I stop in place, understanding that I just spoke, but it wasn't the sound of my voice. It was the voice of a little girl.

That wasn't *my* voice.

I stand up. My chair falls to the ground. Sweat pools on my forehead as I back up towards the windows. Do I speak again to see if that was my voice or was that someone else?

The *thump* returns, but this time, it comes from a different direction.

Then, I hear a soft knock at the door. Is it Beks again? Maybe she's probably hearing this, too. Maybe this isn't just me.

I race towards the door, looking through the eyehole. I expect to see Beks on the other end, but I don't. My mouth drops open. Standing on the other side of the door is not Beks. Instead, there's a little girl with long dark hair in two messy braids, and she's wearing jean shorts and a white top with a puppy printed on it.

It's Emma, just the way I remember her as my seven-year-old sister. She's looking up at the eyehole and wearing the same outfit she wore in the picture Kate hung in her house for years.

Every hair on my body stands straight up. Usually feelings of fondness appear when I think of Emma, but that's gone. Instead, fear replaces them and my throat closes, as I'm unable to breathe in air.

No, this isn't real.

I step back, placing my hands on the side of my head. This isn't real. This isn't real.

But what if it is?

In one quick motion, I grab the door knob and swing open the door.

She's gone. Emma is no longer in the hall, as if vanished into the air. I step partially into the hall, noticing the empty hallway on both sides of me. Sweat falls from my temple and along the sides of my face. I'm able to breathe again.

"What is happening to me?"

It's now when I'm reminded how I'd see the Phantom, not Emma and Victoria, when I'd have hallucinations as a kid. Why haven't I seen him yet? I've spent so much time thinking about Emma and Victoria recently. Unsurprisingly, the Phantom is a recurring figure right out of a horror movie. Its body is lanky, legless, and floating looking very similar to a dementor in the Harry Potter series. It's faceless, and wears a black, ripped, hooded cloak covering its body. What's most noticeable is the color of its bony hands, which resembles that of a gray rotting body and is stained with patches of blood. It's everything I don't like remembering or thinking about.

Growing up, my art therapist was the only professional who could get me to talk about the Phantom. I'd draw pictures of it during our sessions, explaining to her that it appeared inside and outside of my dreams. Eventually, though, the Phantom stopped showing up, and disappeared altogether for many years.

Instead of seeing the Phantom, I'm seeing hallucinations of both Victoria and Emma. Why? No matter the reason, I need to get out of here.

Quickly, I close the door and race through the studio. First, I grab my purse from the desk, and then I unplug the hanging lights, grabbing the keys from the hanging Alaska decor. This time, I remember to lock the door and bolt down the hallway.

My head is spinning as I race down the stairs, thinking about Emma, reminding myself that this is the first time that I've seen– imagined– her ever since the night of the murder. Fear and curiosity dance inside of me as I exit the studio complex and head towards my vehicle, parked across the street.

Why haven't I ever seen Emma before until now?

When I reach my vehicle, I unlock it and maneuver inside. The door is closed and my world is quiet again.

Breathe.

Exhaling deeply, I lean against the headrest and close my eyes as they fill with tears. Why did I see Emma? First it was Victoria and now it's Emma?

Instead of thinking more about my sister, all I can think about now is Victoria.

With what's happening, it feels like I'm becoming her. Is this how Victoria felt when her symptoms started? Was Victoria scared just as much as me? The last thing I want to do is become like Victoria. I don't want to end up like her.

"No!" I yell. "I'm not becoming like her."

I don't have schizophrenia. I refuse to believe I have what Victoria has. I'd never do what she did to Emma.

My body starts to shake, and I focus on getting myself to calm down. It takes a few minutes, but I eventually get myself to relax enough to drive so I can go home.

I'll call a doctor tomorrow. I'll make an appointment to get checked out, and everything will be okay.

Taking a deep breath, I look down at my phone, realizing I have nobody I want to call. I feel more alone than I ever have before, and that's saying something. Sure, I've passed my hardest moments alone while everyone else has convinced themselves I'll be okay. But this time, I'm not okay. Maybe I've never been okay.

I look out the window at the complex in front of me. My throat becomes tight. What if I see something again? What if something worse happens and I'm not able to compose myself in public? Then what do I do?

Before I allow my mind to continue to ruminate, I put my vehicle in drive.

Once I'm home, I can sleep this night off and then decide what to do in the morning. I'll call a doctor. That seems like the best decision but who knows how I'll feel in the morning? A big part of me doesn't want to know what the doctor will say.

Slowly, I drive off, starting to feel a little bit better. As I turn on a blinker, a pair of headlights turn on behind me. I glance up in the rearview mirror, noticing a black van trailing behind my vehicle. I don't think much of it and focus back on the road. It isn't until miles later that I notice the black van hasn't turned since I started driving. It's still behind me.

My throat becomes tight again. Is this something I should be worried about or am I just so overwhelmed and overstimulated? Sure, there's not a lot of people out driving because it's so late in the evening, but it doesn't mean he's following me.

But the black van continues to follow behind me and does for many miles.

Is this real? Or am I imagining this?

I look in the rearview mirror again, squinting. My heart beats aggressively against my chest wall, and feelings overwhelm me.

Do I need to try and escape? But what if this isn't real and someone isn't following me?

Tears fall from my eyes and down my cheeks. I look back into the rearview mirror, trying to observe anything about the vehicle. The only thing I can tell is that it's a black van. I can't make out the license plate number or anything unique about it. Eventually, I turn off the interstate and drive down a random street to see if I can lose the black van. It only continues to follow me.

Don't panic. It'll only make things worse. Maybe I should call the police? Again, what if this isn't real, though? What if I'm imagining and then what?

Taking another random left, I keep my eyes focused on the road. Fear takes over the wheel, not me, and I'm flying down the road at thirty miles over the speed limit as I push down on my Impala's accelerator. I look in the rearview mirror to see the black van still following behind.

I have to let someone know, even if this isn't real. Just let it be the police. What if something terrible happens and nobody will know what happened to me? It's not worth the risk.

Grabbing my cell phone with a shaky hand, I type 9 and then 1, but I stop myself before finishing the number sequence.

This may not be real, though, and what if my sanity is questioned if I call? What if they don't believe me? *Again.*

I'm instantly triggered and memories from the night of the murder start to plummet into my mind. Like a light sprinkle before a rainstorm, tears fall down from my eyes as I'm reminded of what happened so many years ago.

Quickly, I look up again and stare at the black van. Taking a deep breath, I set my cell phone back down and never finish typing the last number in 911.

Chapter 13

DAVID AND MIA ROSSI'S HOUSE–ANCHORAGE, ALASKA

VICTORIA

"Victoria," a voice says. "Victoria!"

While she hears her name, Victoria doesn't respond. Staring blankly at the floor, she only sees the vacuum marks on the carpet. Victoria memorizes the shape and traces them in her mind.

Sitting on one side of the living room are Victoria, David, Mia, Kate, and Eric, Kate's husband. On the other side is the lead investigator, Paul, and a psychologist, Dr. Sullivan, who Victoria assumes is here to keep a close eye on her.

It's only minutes since Paul broke the news and said the dreaded words that caused Victoria to disassociate.

'The night Emma was presumed dead.'

Victoria no longer feels in charge of her body. His words triggered an avalanche of emotions and loosened the memories from that night in her mind.

'The night Emma was presumed dead.'
'The night Emma was presumed dead.'
'The night Emma was presumed dead.'
Again, Victoria feels voiceless. Powerless.

The voices in the background are faint until she hears David snap at her again, "Victoria!"

She jumps in place, glancing at her ex-husband. Her heart beats aggressively against her chest, reminding Victoria of the hanging clock from the night of the murder. She stares at David, seeing that his eyes are filled with tears.

Woah. I haven't seen him tear up since... that night. Victoria opens her mouth to speak, but nothing comes out. It reminds her of all of the times at the hospital. Even though she feels eyes on her, the fragmented memories coming into Victoria's mind are of more importance. In her mind, she sees a time when Hayley and Emma were babies lying peacefully together in their crib, looking like two kittens pressed up against one another. Next, she's visiting her parents at their Malibu home with David when they were just in college and meeting each other for the very first time. Victoria's dark curly hair was past her waist and David wasn't wearing glasses. But suddenly, a memory from that night pops into her mind. It's one that she's never remembered before.

In this new memory she sees what looks to be a man wearing a black ski mask. His brown eyes flamed with fury. Glass was shattered all over the kitchen and living room like hazardous puzzle pieces. Two kitchen chairs are missing from the table. The fire's flame engulfed the kitchen in a matter of what felt like seconds. Then, she sees one of the three men walk towards Emma and Hayley.

Victoria jumps to her feet, almost tipping over from the rush of blood flow leaving her brain. She wants to say something, but her head is spinning too much. It won't stop, as if she's stuck on a merry-go-round from hell.

Did I really just remember that? How is this coming to me now? Why didn't I remember this sooner?

Victoria hears someone ask if she's okay, but she doesn't respond. She sits back down as she tries to focus on the memories again, which have now vanished.

Kate whispers to her sister, "You can do this."

A touch brushes against her but Victoria hardly notices it. She thinks back to their earlier conversation on the porch. Heat overwhelms her cheeks as she remembers that Kate never gave a reason to why she never believed Victoria.

David returns to the conversation, asking, "What's the evidence?"

The word shakes Victoria back to reality, distracting her from the furry she feels for her family. Silence fills the room.

Paul clears his throat. "It's a video recording from the night. There's video footage of a man shooting Emma with a gun—someone who isn't Victoria. He's wearing a black ski mask."

'He's wearing a black ski mask.' The truth is set free and it's finally louder than the blatant ignorance Victoria feels family has been embodying for almost fifteen years.

His words replay over and over in Victoria's spinning mind as if she's still on the merry-go-round from hell. *They finally know the truth.*

He said it. Somebody finally said the truth, somebody else who is not Victoria.

Victoria looks at David who's now staring at her, finally giving her *the look,* the one she thought she wouldn't see again. He was staring so intently at her, Victoria could've swore that he was memorizing her face. His brown eyes are full of tears, his face quivers, and he never looks away from her.

He sees me. He really sees me at this moment.

Eventually, David shakes his head, turning back to Paul. "It shows that?"

Victoria watches her ex-husband, unraveling more and more emotion as the seconds pass.

Paul hesitates but then nods.

Mia reaches for David, but he barely moves with her touch. Again, he looks back at Victoria and can't take his eyes off of her. The seconds turn into minutes and the air appears to feel like razor blades moving through him as he breathes.

They all finally know that Victoria didn't kill Emma.

Victoria turns towards Paul, breaking eye contact with David, and whispers, "There were three of them, right? Three men with ski masks?"

Paul nods. "Yes. How did you know that?"

Kate looks solemnly at Victoria, but Victoria keeps her focus on Paul.

Victoria clears her throat. "I'm starting to remember more. It's coming back–"

Eric, Kate's husband, clears his throat. "So did this man take Emma?" Eric asks. "They never found her body, so does this video tape show where they took her?"

Silence fills the room until David turns and nearly screams, "Eric, her remains were found at Chugach Park. We searched for years."

Victoria is taken back from the loudness in David's voice. Seconds later, she remembers the hours after the murder and waking up in Chugach State Park, not recalling how she had gotten there. Only Hayley was by her side when she awakened in the woods. Emma was nowhere to be seen.

Paul clears his throat. "The footage stops after Emma was shot, so we don't know if they took her or not. We're assuming they did…Victoria and Hayley were found at Chugach, but they were alive and conscious as you can probably recall. We're assuming the fire must've been started shortly after the filming ended. There's a lot of details missing, which is what we're still trying to find out."

And just like that, Victoria remembers more of the lost details from that night. The movie of that night plays on the screen in her mind. The three men were standing in the little blue house's entryway, faces covered by black ski masks. They must've come through the glass sliding door. Victoria remembers being in the kitchen, and seeing the men as she was unloading the dishwasher.

When she saw them, Victoria ran away, trying to find the girls, but one of the men grabbed Victoria. Screams exploded throughout their home, with Victoria yelling the names of her daughters. Next came the sounds of chunks of glass on the floor, screams of terror from the girls, and echoes of chaos heard only in movies.

The pain came shortly after that. Victoria remembers the torture that the men put her through. Bruises, cuts, marks were everywhere across her body. For years, the police convinced everyone, including herself, that she was the one who did it to herself. But how could she have done what the men did? None of it was self-inflicted, yet that was what was reported.

Victoria was thrown across the kitchen, dragged across the floor with broken glass, and hit in the ribs if she didn't move fast enough. And she remembers it all. The physical pain was excruciating but it was nothing compared to the mental and emotional pain.

All Victoria wanted was for Hayley and Emma to be okay. For them to make it out safely. But they didn't. Only one of them did.

Now, in this memory, one of the men grabs two kitchen chairs and pulls them into the living room. He maneuvers the girls onto the chairs and quickly ties rope around their bodies.

Victoria finally remembers what comes next, as well. Shotgun sounds. She refuses to let in anymore of the memories implode in her mind, replacing them with her own sounds of sobbing. Kate reaches for her, but Victoria pushes her away.

How am I just remembering this all? Why did they do this to us? Why didn't anyone believe me? Not one person believed me.

Something snaps inside of Victoria. Suddenly, she stands up and looks around the living room at Paul, Dr. Sullivan, and her family.

Victoria focuses on Paul. Her words are barely a whisper. "I need you to say it."

His words are gentle. "Say what?"

Kate tries to reach for Victoria, but Victoria pushes her sister away.

They need to hear it. I need to hear it. "What everyone in this room is now thinking."

Pauls nods, and then clears his throat. "Victoria…you were wrongly accused. You didn't kill your daughter."

Victoria exhales sharply, her shoulders finally dropping down. The truth breaks like glass as all eyes are on her.

Chapter 14

DRIVING THROUGH MINNEAPOLIS, MINNESOTA

ME

As I look back at my rearview window, the black van is gone—as if it evaporated into the air.

"What the hell?" I cry, driving down another road. Tears overwhelm my eyes and I can hardly see where I'm going.

Where did it go? It was just behind me. There's no way it could've turned without me noticing it.

I continue to drive, focusing on controlling my breath so I don't crash my vehicle. My hand shakes as I set down my cell phone.

What is happening to me?

I gulp, looking at the clock and remembering the time difference between Minnesota and Alaska. A tightness overwhelms my chest, as I think about Kate, but I turn off onto another road, driving into a residential area. I take a deep breath and lean my head against the headrest, feeling the tears start to swell in my eyes.

What's happening to me?

The black van doesn't return, surprisingly. Once my breaths are even and my tears stop, I start driving again.

"What if that was real?" I whisper to myself, confused.

Just get home. Call the doctor tomorrow, and they'll see what's going on. I'll have an answer soon. Hopefully. I need to do something about this before it gets worse. It feels as if I'm getting to the point that I don't know what's real and what isn't. What's in my head and what's in reality. It's all a blur–like trying to see far in the distance as heavy rain pours down on your windshield.

Ten minutes pass and I recognize I'm driving through an old part of Downtown Minneapolis. Nothing looks familiar, especially in the dark, but I keep driving.

My eyes bounce back and forth between the rearview mirror and the road ahead. What if the van comes back? Would it be best to go to the police station to play it safe? Does it really matter if they question sanity or if they don't believe me? No. It doesn't. At least then I'll still be safe if that was real.

Before I can think about typing the number sequence on my phone, the image of Victoria forms in memory, appearing like a ghost. Strangely, this time it's different, as I'm not scared to see her in my mind. She looks young, like how I remember from when I was a child. Her dark hair is pulled back into a high bun with a few strands hanging near the sides of her face. She's wearing overalls stained with red and white paint splatters. While talking to me, she's hustling back and forth between her art room and the kitchen. Her voice is warm. Deep. Her eyes are soft and the color matches mine.

Then, she's in the kitchen, unloading the dishwasher. Victoria looks at me and smiles, asking me a question. In my mind, I don't answer her. Instead, screams engulf the space between us. The memory always stops there.

Tears return and slide down my cheeks.

She's the one who took my sister away from me. I always need to remember this.

"Why did you do this to us?" I scream, gripping the steering wheel. "Why?!"

In my mind, Victoria frowns at me, and then her entire body turns into glass. As if right on command. She shatters into a million tiny pieces, landing on the kitchen and living room like dangerous confetti.

Snap out of it!

And I do. I come back to reality. But before I can collect or calm myself down, I unexpectedly see a black figure on the road.

What?!

The headlights from my vehicle shine like two yellow laser beams upon the figure. I hit the brakes. It takes a few seconds, but my vehicle comes to a stop. My mouth drops open as my eyes remain focused ahead.

Light brown hair. Large stature. Tan skin.

"You have got to be shitting me."

It's Brandon Hess.

In front of me stands Brandon. He's emotionless and standing on top of train tracks that divide the downtown street. One of his arms is slightly outstretched in front of him as his eyes stare straight ahead towards one of the train track's directions.

This can't be real. Am I also imagining this?

Then, Brandon moves. He's walking on the tracks and as I watch, a faint light in the distance in the direction he's walking. The sound of a train whistle goes off. My heart drops to my stomach.

Oh my God. This is real. This is happening.

Quickly, I push down on the car horn. The horn blares, but Brandon remains emotionless. I continue to honk, but he doesn't look my way. He hardly flinches. Instead, he keeps walking with his hand outstretched towards the approaching light.

What if this isn't real, though? What if I'm imagining this? Could I be hallucinating Brandon?

"But what if I'm not?" I whisper.

The train whistles again and the crossing lights come to life only yards away, turning Brandon bright red. Adrenaline rushes through me like the climax of a scary movie. I put my vehicle in park and jump out of the car.

Now I run. The train whistle is much louder as I race from my vehicle towards Brandon. The bright light in the distance only gets brighter, which is now much closer than before and no longer faint. It's loud. Deafening.

"Brandon! MOVE!"

He's still not moving. WHY IS HE NOT MOVING?!

I maneuver myself under the crossing light's lever and jump over the first set of tracks to grab Brandon.

The smell of alcohol hits my nostrils as I tug at him. This is real. This is happening.

"Brandon, come on. Move!"

We start to move together until his foot catches a track. Brandon loses his balance, falling to his knees on the tracks. My heart drops to my stomach.

"Get up!"

My head turns towards the light coming towards us. Quickly, I pull Brandon up and push us off the tracks. Seconds later, the train whooshes past. My hair is flung behind my shoulders and the bottom half of my shirt flies up. The cool Summer air tickles my skin menacingly.

I stare at the train, disorientated, realizing what could've happened. The truth stares at me, feeling it like a knife pressed to my throat.

Looking back at Brandon, I see he's on his knees again, dry heaving. I reach down and grab his chin, lifting his head up so that his eyes can meet mine.

"Brandon, what the hell? We could've died! Were you trying to kill yourself?!"

There's no familiarity in his eyes. No sign that he even recognizes me.

"What are you doing out here? How did you get here?"

I smell the alcohol again and drop his head from my hand.

How is he so drunk that he doesn't recognize me? Many more questions fill my mind, but instead of focusing on them, I'm reminded of the black van. Reminded of what happened in the studio. Reminded of too many things at this moment.

Quickly, I examine the space around us. No cars are present. There's not a soul in sight, which is surprising. It's just the two of us.

I turn towards Brandon again and squat down. I gently touch his face, motioning him to look at me. "Brandon?"

His eyes start to close slowly.

No!

"Don't you dare close your eyes." I shake him. "Brandon, hey, look at me!" Brandon starts to dry heave again. "Brandon. It's me. Hayley. Hayley Crowe."

Quickly, I reach down and look through Brandon's pants pockets for a cell phone to see if anyone has tried reaching out to him. There's nothing. No wallet, keys, or cell phone.

Looking up from the pavement, he finally finds my eyes. He stares at me blankly again, but a word escapes from his mouth. "Spencer."

"Spencer?"

Who's Spencer?

Instead of focusing on the name he just called me, I instead think back to the black van from earlier, and then of Emma standing in the hallway, staring up at me at the eyehole. Now, I am here. In this moment with Brandon as a train nearly killed us.

Did all of this happen tonight or only some of it?

Taking a deep breath, I whisper, "This is gonna be a long night."

Chapter 15

DRIVING THROUGH MINNEAPOLIS, MINNESOTA

HIM

His flight landed hours ago and now he is driving through Minneapolis, Minnesota. The streets are quiet for a Tuesday evening, which surprises him because of how large and populated the city is. Only moments ago is when he had followed Hayley in his rented vehicle, causing her to seemingly panic in her white impala–driving crazy down the road and trying to lose him.

Of course, this is all a part of the plan. He wanted to follow her to see where she was living. He recognized that maybe he'd need that information at some point. Plus, he was just curious at this point. Of course many months ago, his friend had flown to Minnesota and was able to find out where her art studio was located. From there, his friend kept track of her comings and goings throughout the day and night, and found a free moment to place the hidden camera inside her studio. Now he could keep an eye on her through the app on his phone.

However, in a perfect world, he would be able to do all of this himself. Except that wasn't reality. Sure, things would go a lot faster, but he needed the help. Not only did his friends understand why he was doing this, but they were his family at this point. They agreed they'd die together if needed, trying to help one another get the revenge they deserved—no matter how many rounds of revenge they desired.

Plus, he had a lot of responsibility at work and inside the walls of one of the cabins. He couldn't necessarily drop everything like his friends because of his work and personal commitments. He needed to keep working as a park ranger, especially since they needed to keep the two cabins in Chugach State Park included in their plan. If not, their plan wouldn't be executed successfully. Just like the quote 'With great power comes great responsibility,' The man knew the sacrifices he needed to make.

It's only days away until *the day*.

Taking a deep breath, he continues to drive. "It's all coming together."

* * *

MY APARTMENT–MINNEAPOLIS, MINNESOTA

ME

The clock reads two in the morning when we arrive at my apartment complex. Without many options, Brandon comes home with me. I wasn't going to leave him in the middle of the street drunk. From the driver's seat, I look at Brandon, sleeping in the passenger's seat. Is he even going to remember any of this in the morning? Am *I* going to remember any of this?

Thankfully, my roommates have gone to bed and aren't in the living room when I help shuffle Brandon inside my apartment. The TV and the kitchen lights are off. The dishwasher runs quietly in the background. I turn on a light and breathlessly guide Brandon into the living room. We make it to the floral couch, where I lower him down gently.

He settles back with a plump.

I position his body for sleep. Grabbing a blanket from the other couch, I lay it over Brandon. Then, I look down at him with one hand resting on my forehead.

"What's happening to me?" I whisper to myself.

What the hell did I do in my past life to deserve all of this tonight?

As I ignore my words and thoughts, I reach for his shoes and take them off. I try not to think about Brandon waking up tonight. Would he leave if he recognized he wasn't at a familiar place, or just go back to sleep?

Once his shoes are on the ground, I stand up and look down at Brandon again. His eyes are closed, and his mouth hangs open. He's obviously not wearing gym attire tonight—just a white shirt and black cargo pants cover his body. His hair is messy, and his skin is a golden tan. It's strange seeing him outside his normal gym attire.

I take a deep breath and then exhale sharply.

Turning off the light, I head to my bedroom. As I pull the covers over my body, my brain plays and replays everything that happened tonight, all of the scenes fighting for my attention. I guess the positive is that Brandon serves as a good distraction from spiraling out of control. I'll worry about everything tomorrow once he's gone.

Before falling asleep, I send my roommates a heads up text message that Brandon is over here so they don't freak out in the morning if they see him. That's the last thing that needed to happen.

Eventually, I fall asleep to the sound of Brandon snoring in the living room, only to be reawakened mere hours later by the sunlight peeking in through my curtains. It's around eight in the morning.

Before reaching for my cell phone or changing clothes, I hurry out of my bedroom and into the living room and hear Brandon's soft snores. Tiptoeing into the living room, I see him.

Well, this is going to be an interesting morning.

Before I move again, Brandon sits up abruptly as if immediately sensing me. His face is emotionless, and his eyes look tired. It takes a few seconds for him to adjust to the light coming from the windows, but he looks at me when they do. He stares, confused, and then looks around the living room in a slight panic. I watch as a realization of where he's at pops into his mind.

"Oh my God. Hayley?"

There's the awkwardness I've been waiting for.

"Um. Hi, Brandon."

Before I say anything else, Brandon shakes his head as if trying to shake away this moment. He looks at me again. "Hayley?"

"Hi. Um, I'm not really sure how to start this."

He pushes his hair back, then turns to face me. "What am I doing here? Is this your place?" he asks.

"Yes, it is."

"What happened? I'm confused."

I take a deep breath, thinking about last night. "Well, we saw each other last night. Do you remember anything?"

His face starts flushing red. Is he remembering what happened or why is he getting so red? "Not much. I went out last night...to Uptown...but I don't remember anything after that. Were you out, too?"

I shrug. "Not exactly."

"Then, how did I get here?"

We stare at each other, tension fluttering between us.

Do I lie? Do I tell him what happened last night? It's at that moment when I think about all the times that people—mostly strangers—made me feel bad about what happened to me and my family that night. While I know I shouldn't associate myself with this moment, I can't help it. I don't want Brandon to feel embarrassed. Ashamed. Just like I continuously have to feel those emotions as a kid and into adulthood. Plus, if I tell him the truth, will our relationship change? Will he not feel comfortable with me anymore? Will *I* not feel comfortable anymore?

"What?" Brandon asks. "It looks like you're scheming something together in your mind."

If you're going to lie, you better be convincing. I disregard his response, trying to focus on what I'm going to say. "I found you last night. Something almost happened..."

Is he going to believe me?

"What do you mean?"

My eyes squint. "Are you sure you don't remember anything from last night?"

"No," he says. "What happened?"

I sigh. "Brandon...so, I'm not sure how to start this any other way. But a train almost hit you. Yes, an actual train. I found you standing on train tracks near Downtown when I was coming home from my studio last night."

His head tilts slightly. "You're joking, right?"

Why would he think I'm joking? "No."

"Train tracks?" A slight chuckle escapes from his mouth.

"Yep, train tracks."

He pauses, looking away. "What the hell. Well, I'm not really sure what to say, Hayley. Other than wow and that I'm sorry. This is embarrassing."

The word causes a ping to spike through my body. See. I knew he'd feel embarrassed. Do I go on? Do I add in the Spencer part? I mean, who even is Spencer?

"You don't need to be embarrassed," I say, shaking my head. "I just wanted to make sure you're okay."

"I'm fine. I guess last night just got a little out of hand." Brandon clears his throat. "So, where does this leave us?"

"Huh?"

"I'm assuming you probably don't feel the most comfortable with me right now."

I shrug. "I'm fine," I answer honestly.

He shakes his head. "If you want, we can see about switching—"

Why won't he just drop it? I don't want him to stop being my trainer. "Brandon, it's fine. I promise." I say and then laugh. "Besides. We're even. You saw me fall and now I've seen you–"

"Almost get hit by a train."

I laugh, telling myself that we're going to be just fine. There were more important things to worry about than this.

Before I can say anything else, he says, "I owe you big time, Hayley."

Taking a deep breath, I nod and think back to everything that happened last night: hearing the thump in my studio, Emma standing in the hallway, the black van following me, and Brandon and I almost getting killed by a train. Out of all of that what was real? The only thing that seemed real was what happened with Brandon.

Eventually, I find his eyes again and nod. "I guess you do then."

Chapter 16

DAVID AND MIA ROSSI'S HOUSE–ANCHORAGE, ALASKA

VICTORIA

Today was the day that Victoria has dreamt about for years: the day that her family would possibly know the truth. Part of her never thought she'd get to experience it. But now, she is living, breathing, and finally experiencing it—yet it hasn't gone how she envisioned it would.

She expected to feel free, relieved, and joyous. But she's not. Even though Victoria's happy that her family knows the truth, there's still an emptiness inside her lingering. Just like her, they're all in pain. Sure, Victoria feels she's more justified to feel the pain, but everybody else in her family is also experiencing hurt, confusion, and regret.

It's been hours since Victoria discovered the truth about the evidence. Paul and the psychologist are gone, and the house is quiet. She lies on top of the covers of her bed, her eyes trailing from the ceiling to the gold light fixture.

Victoria thinks back to the night of the murder, remembering how she never saw a video camera in their home. Then again, how could Victoria remember being filmed when she hardly remembered what happened that night? The new memories coming into her mind are helpful but she can't recall everything. Yet.

Victoria remains lost in thought until there's a knock on the door. "Can I come in?" Kate asks on the other side of the door.

What is she still doing here? With that, Kate walks into the bedroom then, no longer wearing her gold earrings, and with her hair in a messy bun. The bags underneath her eyes are even darker—if that's even possible.

Victoria sits up and then sits crossed-legged on the bed. "Hi. What are you still doing here?"

Kate wanders in, keeping her eyes on the floor. "I wanted to talk to you. How are you?"

"How do you think I am?" Victoria asks gently. Instead of feeling frustration with her sister, Victoria chooses to be kind.

Kate exhales deeply. Her head drops forward so that her blonde hair covers her face. She doesn't look back up at Victoria. "Not good?"

Victoria nods, but doesn't say anything else.

Then, Kate whispers, "Victoria?" She looks up and tears are swimming in her bright blue eyes.

She's actually crying? "Yes?"

Kate's now looking at Victoria in a way she's never seen before. It's a look full of sadness, desperation, and guilt—as if all mixed together into a heartbreaking concoction. Instead of seeing the mid thirty-year-old before her, Victoria sees teenage Kate, who was the scared little girl who stepped up and helped raise Hayley during a time when she really needed someone. Victoria sees the young woman who came to the hospital to visit Victoria, over and over again, even though she was convinced and led to believe Victoria killed Emma.

"I-I can't believe I didn't believe you," Kate whispers.

Even though Kate's words are faint, the meaning is loud. They're what Victoria has been waiting to hear for years. Yet, they feel so different than what Victoria expected. The emptiness still lingers.

Then, Kate starts spewing out of her thoughts, all at once. Breathless, she says, "It's just not fair. Why did this have to happen to *us*? Our family? You didn't do it. Y-you tried to tell me for many years in different ways, but I never believed you! I never stopped to ask you if you remembered anything more and what happened. I just pushed everything to the side."

Wow, she's taking accountability? She's actually admitting to all of this?

Victoria looks away, feeling tears fill her eyes.

Kate continues, "I didn't believe you…. I-I don't know why. You're my sister and I didn't. All I did was blame everything on you, on your schizophrenia."

The tears now fall from Victoria's eyes like raindrops on a windshield.

"I should've said something, question it," Kate says. "But, I was so scared. I didn't know what to do. Mom and Dad weren't around and I was scared that I was losing you, too."

The world stops, then. It feels as if Victoria's heart pauses, but it doesn't. She takes a moment to really sit with Kate's perspective, imagining the difficulty she must've faced.

Suddenly, Kate starts whimpering, covering her face and breaking down in front of Victoria. It's a side of her sister that she's never seen before.

Kate says through her tears, "Victoria, I am so sorry. I know I don't deserve your forgiveness. But please, please know how sorry

I am! If I could take it all back, I would. I promise I would in a heartbeat but I know I can't."

There they are, the words. Victoria's finally hearing so much of what she's always wanted to hear. But so much of it hurts her more than she expected it to.

As Kate continues to sob, Victoria's mind goes elsewhere as the feeling of emptiness continues to linger more. She thinks back to when the two of them were younger. Since Victoria is twelve years older than Kate, their age gap made Victoria a mother figure to Kate more so than a sister. Growing up, Victoria remembers helping their mother change Kate's diapers, playing with Kate after school, and taking her on walks when the weather was nice.

However, when Victoria was sentenced to the North Star Behavioral Hospital, it was like their roles were reversed, especially after Victoria's sentencing. Kate was the only family who consistently came to visit Victoria, while everyone else ignored her. Even though Victoria and Kate still didn't really have a relationship, Kate's effort was at least still there. Regardless, she's the one who stuck by her side. She tried her best.

Now, Victoria reaches for her sister, watching as Kate continues to break in front of her, one word at a time.

"Kate, stop…I understand," Victoria whispers, gently patting her back. "I do."

Kate shakes her head. "How? How can you understand? Nobody believed you, Victoria! I mean, for God's sake, I'm your sister and I didn't believe you. Just like the rest of the world, I believed you murdered your daughter!"

The familiar words sting, but also bring healing. Sure, they're the exact words Victoria always wished she would hear but now she wants them to stop. They're no longer what she wants to hear.

Victoria whispers, "You didn't know. I shouldn't have blamed you for so long. Even when you kept my letters from Hayley, you did that because you thought that's what was best. I shouldn't fault you for that."

Victoria hears her nickname and comes back to reality. Kate says, "I-I just don't know what to think, Vic. I feel so ashamed. So confused. I-I—"

She shakes her head, reaching for Kate. "Don't. Don't feel that way, please."

"But I do. I-I just—"

"Kate, I forgive you."

Kate's eyes widen from Victoria's words, and tears fall from her eyes. "You can't."

Victoria nods. "Yes, I can."

"No—how can you?! I'm in the wrong. We all are to you. I don't deserve that."

Victoria shakes her head, hugging her sister. "It's not about deserving it or not. It's about trying to understand. I see things from your perspective now. I do. You were just a kid, Kate. Mom wasn't around, and you were by yourself. You didn't know what to do. For years, I punished you but I don't blame you anymore. I never should have in the first place."

"But that doesn't excuse that I didn't believe you, Vic," Kate says, pulling away from Victoria.

"But what happened to you helps explain it," Victoria says. "Remember how intense…how conniving the trial was? Or the media? Yes, it's hard to admit this, but how could you not be convinced that I did it? I should've admitted sooner that they're the ones who did this ultimately, paint an evil picture of me. So I don't blame you. I really don't."

From the very beginning, Victoria's mental illness was weaponized against her. Never had Victoria been dangerous or violent before or after her diagnosis, and the media and the trial said she was. The night of the murder was a feeding frenzy for journalists. But there was a real family behind their ink. A real family who desperately needed privacy and compassion, but didn't receive either and instead got exploited.

"Explaining can't undo anything, though."

"No, it can't. But I want to be free, Kate. I just want to be free from this." Victoria continues, "I want to make the best of the years I have left now. So many have already been taken from me. No, that doesn't mean I'm going to forget what happened. At this point, I just want to move on."

Kate nods her head. "Okay, I get that. So where do you think we go from here?"

"Let's start by getting Hayley here."

Chapter 17

MY ART STUDIO–MINNEAPOLIS, MINNESOTA

ME

It's a couple of days later and I still haven't called the doctor yet. Even though my fingers have typed the number out many times on my cell phone, I never hit *call*. Sure, I want answers. I *need* answers. But a part of me is still paralyzed by fear. Paralyzed in knowing the truth. It's like my heart needs more time to process what my body already knows to be true—that something is happening to me.

Do I really want to know what they'll say? There's freedom in some ignorance.

Surprisingly, what's keeping me in good spirits is Brandon. In the past few days, Brandon has been the person I see the most consistently. The energy between us is also noticeably different— for the better.

After Tuesday night when I found him Downtown, I assumed our interactions would change for the worse, even though he said they wouldn't. But I was wrong. Pleasantly wrong.

While I still have many questions surrounding that night, including who Spencer is, it has somehow strangely brought us closer. Instead of tiptoeing around conversations, we're now open with one another. In a way, it's like we're both hanging onto this little secret that nobody else knows.

At my early morning session on Thursday, Brandon's wearing all black again, making his green eyes pop. When we finish, Brandon turns toward me as we sit on the mat stretching. His face flushes a light pink before he speaks, reminding me of the night he stayed over at my apartment.

"Hey, Hayley?"

"Yah?" I ask, looking up at him from stretching.

His voice is quiet, too quiet, as if hoping no one around us will hear. "I know this may not be the most appropriate since I'm your trainer—"

"I think the rules for what's appropriate or not appropriate don't really count for us anymore," I tease.

Brandon smiles. "Okay." He clears his throat. "The client after you canceled, and I have an extra window of time. What are you doing after this?"

Sweat forms on my forehead. "Oh, cool. I just have to work at some point today."

"If you're free, I'd like to take you out for breakfast."

Is this appropriate? He's not going to get into trouble if he does, is he? "Sure, let's do it. As long as you don't mind me looking like a hot mess," I laugh.

"That's the furthest thing from what you look like," he says. "Plus, I still owe you one."

Now my cheeks turn pink.

We finish stretching and are ready to leave. Brandon opens the door for me as we exit the building together. The restaurant is much closer than I thought it would be, only a few blocks from the gym. Brandon and I walk side by side and then cross the street. Inside the restaurant, the hostess brings us to a booth in the back. She offers us coffee, but I ask for tea. We settle in and examine the menus.

As Brandon looks through his menu, I look at him. I'm reminded of how handsome he is. His green eyes are piercing, and his muscles protrude from his tank top. I gaze back down at my menu before he catches me looking at him.

Soon, we fall into conversation. It starts with work, but then we discuss our personal lives until our waitress drops off my tea and Brandon's coffee.

As the waitress leaves, Brandon asks me, "Not much of a coffee drinker?"

I shrug. "Nope, not a fan of a drink that tastes like dirt."

"Dirt?" Brandon laughs. "It does not."

"I don't lie."

He laughs, but then his tone changes as he asks, "So, you seemed a bit distracted this morning."

"Oh?" I need to play dumb.

"What's going on?" he asks, taking a sip of his coffee.

I gulp.

He noticed? How?

I shrug again. "Just a lot going on with work. I'm working on this really intensive project, and it's been keeping me up. It's due tomorrow actually."

He nods, but I can tell he doesn't believe me. "So, what are you thinking about?"

I wish I could answer honestly. I'm thinking about how Brandon almost got killed by a train. I'm thinking about my dead sister standing in the hallway, unsure if what I'm seeing is real or not. I'm thinking about the black van that nearly drove me off the road and disappeared into the night. I'm thinking about how I'm terrified that I'm turning into my mother.

I say none of this and instead: "What?"

"As in thinking about getting?" Brandon nods towards my menu. "What sounds good to you?"

Oh. The menu. That's what he means.

My eyes widen. "Oh, yes. Any recommendations? I'm guessing you've been here."

"Eggs Benedict, for sure. It's a classic here."

I go along with the conversation and smirk. "Will you scowl at me if I don't get something healthy?"

Brandon laughs. "No. Besides, everything in moderation, right?"

"That's what they say."

The waitress comes back and we order. Once she leaves, I consider letting Brandon in. Maybe if I open up about what's been going on, he can also tell me about Spencer. That feels like too much of a risk? I don't want to scare him off.

"So, I have a confession to make," Brandon says.

"Well, I'm not a priest, but go ahead."

Brandon chuckles but then continues. "Yes, I know you're not a priest, but you are an artist. I googled you the other day."

My heart drops like it does anytime someone tells me that they've searched me online. While most artists would be humbled, I'm usually not. At least not at the moment. Even though I've changed my name, part of me is still fearful of what someone has found online when they've searched for me.

"Oh, yeah?" I ask, taking a sip of my tea. My hand starts to shake, so I set the cup down.

"You never told me you're a *famous* artist," Brandon says.

My shoulders drop and I chuckle, "Why would I tell you that? I'm not famous."

Brandon shakes his head, his light green eyes becoming brighter. "Well, for starters, there's a *New York Times* article about you. You have a waitlist for clients. Those don't count you as famous?"

My chest becomes warm. "I suppose… Well, thanks. I feel bad now. I never Googled you," I add sarcastically.

He laughs and then winks. "You're forgiven. I like to know what I'm getting myself into."

"Sure you do," I tease, then remind myself to switch conversations. "So, tell me more about you, Brandon. Haven't we exhausted all of our small talk and general topics yet?"

"Oh, so that's how you consider our conversations, as small talk?"

I laugh. "No, you know what I mean."

"Well, what do you want to know?"

If I told him the truth, what I really would want to know is why he was on those train tracks? Why was he drinking heavily on a Tuesday night? Was he there to potentially kill himself? Who is Spencer? But I don't ask him any of those questions.

"Hmm, what do you think Tina thinks of this?" I ask, referring to the receptionist.

"So, you do know her name."

"I do. I'm observant every once in a while."

He shrugs, looking away momentarily. "I told her that we're close."

"Close? That seems vague."

Brandon raises his eyebrows. "What do you think *this* is?"

My cheeks flush pink into red this time. "You tell me."

Brandon laughs, a little too loud. "We're really going to go back and forth like this, huh?"

"I guess we can keep it a mystery," I say.

He nods, taking another sip of his coffee. "Deal."

Chapter 18

DAVID AND MIA ROSSI'S HOUSE– ANCHORAGE, ALASKA

VICTORIA

Victoria is already sitting on the back porch, melting and enjoying the early summer morning. Dew lays on the grass from the night before and the sing-song birds chirp peacefully in the background.

Unfortunately, she didn't sleep well last night after her conversation with Kate. Sure, the conversation with her sister was immensely healing. Never did Victoria think she'd be able to step into her sister's shoes and forgive her genuinely. However, Victoria feels as if she's coming down from an emotional high after realizing that her family finally knows the truth. That *she* knows the truth. Plus, it'll only be amplified again after she watches the video tape.

I'm starting to remember what happened that night and it's a lot. There's a heaviness and a scariness in remembering. But Victoria chooses to believe it'll be the catalyst for her healing—no matter how much she still isn't ready to feel what's been festering inside of her for so long.

Now, though, questions ping-pong in her mind. *Do I really want to watch the tape? Am I a failure as a mother—again—if I don't watch it? Are they going to be suspicious if I don't want it?*

Even though the tape apparently proves her innocence, what if the police change their minds? What if Victoria has to return to the hospital for some reason? What if she never gets a chance to see Hayley? *It feels as if everyone is watching me and how I'll react. It's debilitating as it's like constantly walking on eggshells.*

Victoria closes her eyes, focusing on her breathing. *I need to calm down.*

But she doesn't calm down. Instead, her brain does the opposite. Victoria imagines scenarios like the media stations exposing their family's story before Hayley finds out and Hayley never talking to Victoria again, even though she knows the truth. Victoria knows it's only a matter of time before journalists start their frenzy, just like they had so many years ago.

What will they say about us now? About me? How much time do we have left before our world is turned upside down?

As Victoria remains lost in thought, she looks up, observing two singing birds flying above her. She thinks of Hayley and Emma then and finally relaxes.

* * *

MY ART STUDIO–MINNEAPOLIS, MINNESOTA

ME

"Shit," I whisper under my breath, trying to panic clean up my art studio. Beads of sweat cover my forehead.

It's Friday afternoon and my client, Mike, is on his way to pick up his canvas. The beautiful painting that I've spent, what feels like years, is finally done. It's complete, covered in shades of blues, whites, and golds and now blacks that abstractly creates a chariot and horses in an explosive sky. In a way, it looks similar to the painting, the Chariot of Apollo, by Odilon Redon. However, it's so much darker, more radiant and immersive–exactly what my client requested from me but with my own twist.

As I finish shuffling some papers on my black desk, my cell phone rings. "Hello?"

There's a pause on the line. "Hi, is this Hayley? It's Mike. I'm here to pick up my canvas."

Oh good, he's here. "Hey, Mike, yes it is. Are you here? I'll come down and get you."

Quickly, I grab my keys from the wooden Alaska decor. Before locking the door, I stare at the doorknob, reminding myself that I am locking the door. I put the key in the knob and turn it, watching as it's now locked.

Once I get downstairs, I see a man with a very large stature. He stands over six feet tall and has deep set wrinkles on his forehead with whiskers above his lip. Dark jeans cover his legs and a plaid long-sleeve shirt covers his arms.

Immediately, I feel intimidated but push through my feelings. This is my client and I need to make him feel welcomed. Opening the door, I immediately greet him. "Hi, are you Mike?"

"Yes, I am," he smiles.

"Oh, great. It's so nice to finally meet you. Come on in."

His smile is large and his laugh is cheery. His voice is a lot higher than I expected. "It's so nice to meet you in person, no longer just on email."

My body softens. In a way, he feels more like a grandfather than my client. I didn't expect him to be this old. Then again, my clients are never what I expected when I met them. Everyone has such a different background, story, and essence–always reminding me how art brings everyone together, no matter who they are.

While I know it's not the safest to have my clients come up to my art studio alone, I've never had any issues. In fact, it's kind of refreshing to have people in my art studio besides myself, considering everything strange that has happened in my studio.

As I unlock my studio, I can sense Mike is watching my movements. I try not to read into it. When the door is open, Mike immediately sees the canvas. A gasp and then soft chuckle escapes his lips. "Hayley, this is beautiful. It's even better in person than the photos you sent."

Tears fill his eyes and I freeze in place. Many clients have cried when I present them with their work, but this feels different. It's as if every muscle in Mike's body relaxes and he's a sponge, soaking up every moment of observation and staring in awe at my work in front of him. Mike moves closer to the canvas, reaching a hand forward.

"This is exactly what I wanted." His voice is quiet, his look is mesmerized. Softly, he touches the canvas as if it's a newborn baby.

Warmth engulfs me. Creating art, and in this case painting, is the most therapeutic and passionate thing I spend my time on. Sitting on the easel in front of us is the canvas, which now metaphorically sings a song that both Mike and I can hear. It's no longer just me.

Gracefully, I thank Mike and give him time to take the canvas all in. A few minutes later, he turns around. The tears are gone from his eyes and his face is more serious. "Thank you so much."

Mike looks above me, towards the ceiling. The gesture is strange, unexpectant. Before I can turn around and see what he's looking at, Mike thanks me again.

Now, a pit forms in my stomach. There's something about the change of his emotions that makes me feel on edge. I try to ignore the feeling. As I walk towards my desk to hand him his invoice, the corner of my eye catches him looking up at the ceiling again. Trying to stay professional, I ignore him.

It's not much longer when Mike heads out of my studio with the now packaged-up canvas. I offer to help him bring it down to his vehicle, but Mike insists he can manage it on his own. With the large canvas in his hands, he thanks me again before walking out the front door.

"This really is spectacular, Hayley! I can't thank you enough. You have no idea how much this means to me," Mike says before closing the door behind him.

"Absolutely! Please take care and thank you again."

Mike nods, closing the door behind him. Patiently, I wait a few seconds before locking the door behind him. As I'm about to pull away from the door, I decide to look through the eyehole.

There, Mike stands in front of the door, looking towards the door. My heart drops to my stomach and the hairs on my arms stand up. What is he doing? A few seconds pass and then a few minutes pass. Eventually, Mike walks away from my door and the pit in my stomach only gets more painful.

I pull away from the door, reminding myself that I'm secure, safe, and that the door is locked. He can't get back in even if he wanted to. Maybe he's just a weird man?

Slowly, I head to my black desk, shifting through paperwork and trying to distract myself from our strange, awkward exchange. At least this is done and I can move onto my next client.

A few minutes later, my cell phone dings and there's a message from Lillie, who asks when I'll be home. Tonight, we're celebrating me finally completing this painting, which feels very special. I'm so thankful to have my group of friends who genuinely support and celebrate me.

I respond to her and then begin packing up as it's the late afternoon. As I turn towards the windows, my attention is caught by movement outside the window and near the street. Outside a black van drives down the street.

My stomach drops as I move closer to the window.

There are a million black vans in Minneapolis. I'm being paranoid if I really think that black van is the one from the other night. Honestly, there's nothing for me to worry about. I'm probably just on edge because of my weird interaction with Mike.

My eyes follow the black van as it drives away and disappears into the rush hour traffic. The pit in my stomach disappears and my shoulders finally relax.

Chapter 19

MY APARTMENT– MINNEAPOLIS, MINNESOTA

ME

It's later in the evening on Friday night. Catherine, Lillie, and I are grabbing dinner at a restaurant called, Spoon and Stable in the North Loop in Minneapolis. It's a cozy, rustic-chic restaurant with a delicious french-inspired menu.

The night was wonderful. Carefree. Exactly what I needed– especially after today with my strange interaction with Mike and everything that has happened. It's moments like these that I don't take for granted: laughing with my friends, clearing my mind as we talk about endless topics, and eating good food that I don't have to cook.

Hours later and once we're back home for the evening, my cell phone rings as I'm about to sit down on my bed. Absent-mindedly, I pull it out of my pocket, almost dropping it after reading the name on the screen.

Brandon Hess?

Staring at the screen in confusion, I tap on the answer button and bring my cell phone up to my ear.

"Hello?"

"Hey, Hayley. It's Brandon," his deep voice echoes into the line.

"Hi, is everything alright?"

He pauses. "Oh, yeah. Say, I wanted to see if you're busy tonight."

Oh. I guess he's not calling to cancel our session.

I clear my throat. "Like, right now?"

"Yes, like now."

I stand up from my bed. "Oh, no, not particularly.... I just got done grabbing dinner with my roommates. I'm back at my apartment now."

"So, you're free then."

I pause, my head tilting to the side slightly. "Yes?"

"Are you in the mood to be spontaneous?"

Spontaneous? "What do you mean?" I laugh. "Spontaneous like going somewhere, or spontaneous like me helping you hide a body?"

Brandon chuckles. "Not the last part. Let me surprise you. Can I come pick you up?"

"Yes."

Fifteen minutes later, Brandon lets me know he's arrived at my apartment complex and I head downstairs. As I walk through the kitchen to the front door, Catherine calls from the couch, "Where you going?"

"I'll be back!" I call out, closing the front door behind me.

Where am I going? I don't know.

Brandon's black pickup is parked across the street. My throat is tight. He waves from the driver's seat, and I wave back. Crossing the street, I head towards him and then make my way inside.

My nostrils wave in his cologne as I take a seat. Brandon's wearing khaki shorts and a black t-shirt. The top of his brown hair is damp from what was probably a shower. His light eyes stare into mine, making me hold my breath.

"So, we're being spontaneous, huh?" I ask.

Brandon laughs. "That, we are. You'll see." He observes me up and down, making my cheeks blush. "You look really nice tonight."

The gesture is innocent, but the movement of his eyes catches me off-guard. Good thing I didn't change my outfit.

"Thanks," I say, putting on my seatbelt. "So no hints?"

"Naw, that would be too easy."

"Lame."

For the next ten minutes, we fall into conversation. It's easy to talk to him, like breathing or even painting. However, each time Brandon looks at me for too long, my body becomes fidgety and warm. The space between us feels different this time, and I really like it.

We drive out of Minneapolis, and before I know it, we're in Stillwater, a city in Minnesota that sits near Wisconsin. Brandon parks on a street when we're downtown.

"Stillwater, huh? That's the surprise."

"You said you've never been here the other day," Brandon says. "So, I thought we'd go and check it out together."

My cheeks flush pink and my heart softens. "Great memory. I'm impressed."

Wow, he remembered. I only mentioned that once to him, too. "It's a beautiful night. What better night to explore the town than now."

We exit the pickup and then venture through the streets of Stillwater together. It's a charming town—something out of a Hallmark movie or romance novel. Lillie and Catherine talk about Stillwater all the time, but I never got around to visiting it myself.

Stores and restaurants of every kind line the busy streets, and sparkling lights cover the light posts. We explore, popping in and out of shops. About an hour later, we make our way down to the waterfront of the St. Croix River, which divides Minnesota and Wisconsin. Immediately, we see dozens—if not hundreds—of people flocked near a loading dock.

On the river is a large white yacht.

"Look, a party," I say, motioning towards the yacht.

"It looks more like a wedding. Should we go see?" Brandon asks.

I shake my head and laugh. "What? No."

"But aren't we being spontaneous tonight?" Brandon asks cheekily.

I scoff, playfully hitting his arm. "We're *not* going to be wedding crashers?"

"You don't want to be Owen Wilson to my Vince Vaughn?"

"Who says you get to be Vince Vaughn?" I tease.

"Come on," he says, grabbing my hand and heading towards the yacht.

"Brandon, no!" I snap. "We can't. What if we're caught?"

"And what are they going to do? If it really ends that bad, we'll jump ship. You know how to swim, right?"

I laugh. "This is feeling very Titanic-like to me. You're acting like Jack when he won that ticket."

"If I'm Jack, you can be Rose."

"You realize Rose leaves Jack for dead, right?"

Brandon laughs louder than I've ever heard him laugh before. He also continues to guide me closer to the yacht. "I'll take the chance."

"You're insane, you know that?"

"Only with you I am," he winks.

Chapter 20

THE MAJESTIC STAR ON THE ST. CROIX RIVER–
STILLWATER, MINNESOTA

ME

As if we're two characters out of a story, Brandon and I hop onto the yacht. Nobody really notices us. We fit in, and not a soul bats a suspicious eye. While I'm filled with nerves —scared someone is going to ask how we know the bride and groom—Brandon keeps me calm.

The yacht is massive, almost overwhelming. It has four levels. The first is mostly closed off, so I assume it's mostly for the staff. The second level holds the dining hall, where dozens of tables and buffet stations are present, including snack and bar stations. The third level features a dance floor and DJ. Lastly, the fourth level is the smallest—almost too small to be considered a level. It consists of only supplies for the staff.

Brandon and I grab drinks from the bartender and food from the snack bar, which is sprinkled with plenty of hors d'oeuvres and cupcakes. Staff replenish it consistently because of the number of guests.

When the formal meal starts, Brandon grabs my hand and pulls me away. We find a staircase and make our way to the top of the yacht—away from the crowd and staff.

At the very top of the fourth level, we find a private corner.

"I can't believe we're doing this!" I say, laughing and taking a seat.

Brandon plops down next to me and looks out at the river. "Sometimes you gotta live a little, Hayley."

I shake my head. My shoulder touches his, making my heart flutter and my breath come short. Mesmerized by the surroundings, I look out at the river, admiring its beauty. The water is dark, but the yacht's light makes sections bright.

Laughter and music from the dinner can be heard below our feet. For a few minutes, we sit in silence. While no words are heard, my thoughts are bombarding my mind. The curiosity inside of me is killing me. Is now really a good time to ask him about Spencer? Will it kill the mood? When else am I going to get a chance to talk about this? Maybe the alcohol will loosen him up.

As Brandon takes a sip of his drink, I turn towards him and take a deep breath. "Hey, can I ask you something?"

"Of course."

I gulp, pausing before speaking. "You know what happened earlier this week? Can we talk about that?"

"Sure, what about exactly?"

I pause again. "So you really don't remember what happened?"

Brandon shrugs. "Besides almost getting hit by a train? No."

I nod, feeling the words right on my tongue. "Okay, well, I didn't tell you this because I wasn't sure how to bring it up, but I left out one detail."

"What's that?"

I take a deep breath. "You said something to me. I'm not sure what it means, though."

"Oh God, what was it?"

I half-smile and then look at me curiously. "You called me 'Spencer.' Or, you said 'Spencer.' Who is that?"

Brandon's eyes widen at the name, and he looks back at the river.

I wait patiently for him to respond, forcing myself to not ask anything else and give him time to collect his thoughts.

Brandon clears his throat. "I really said that, huh?"

I nod. "Who is he?"

"Spencer was my best friend," Brandon says. "He died of alcohol poisoning five years ago. It's really strange that I said his name."

My heart drops to my stomach. "Oh my God. I'm sorry, Brandon."

"I must've been thinking a lot about him. It was his birthday... and also the anniversary of the night he passed away."

I look out at the river, unsure what to say next.

Brandon turns to me. "It's fucked up, what happened. He died of alcohol poisoning, and yet I went out and got plastered this week. I'm not sure if you knew this, but it's been five years since I drank alcohol. Unfortunately, I broke that streak the night you found me."

"Wait, what? I thought you're drinking alcohol now? What's in your drink, then?" I ask, motioning towards the cup in his hands.

"Water."

"Oh? I thought it was a *tequila* water."

Brandon chuckles, but he doesn't say anything else.

"Are you okay?" I ask, reaching for his hand. He lets me touch him.

"Yes," he says. "But most of the time, I still carry the guilt."

"Do you want to talk about it?"

Brandon shrugs. "Not really. There's not much to talk about besides saying that I was there that night when it happened. That's why I feel guilty."

I nod, waiting for him to continue.

"We were in college and at some random house party. It was one of the first weekends back, and Spencer...went too hard. I should've said something to him, but I didn't."

"You were also drinking, right?" I ask. "How could you have known how bad he was?"

"True, but in my mind there's no excuse," Brandon says. "We were supposed to look out for each other. I saw him throwing up, which he had never done before."

I massage the top of Brandon's hand.

Brandon continues. "Sometimes, I look back and wish a cop would've seen us. Instead, we went back to our dorm, Spencer fell asleep, and he never woke up."

Shaking my head, I say, "Brandon, I am so sorry."

He looks at me then, giving me a small smile. "Thanks. It's something I haven't shared with many people. I appreciate you letting me talk about it."

My heart warms as I watch the light in his face come back. It's amazing how easy he's able to open up, and how he doesn't shy away from the details.

"Can I ask *you* something?" Brandon says in a teasing voice, interrupting my thoughts.

I nod.

"What did *you* think when you saw me that night?"

Well, I felt like I was hallucinating everything. But that's probably not the best answer to give him right now.

"I was confused. Scared. Part of me thought you were trying to kill yourself."

"Really?"

"Yes. Well, it's hard not to think that when a man is standing on train tracks and a train is coming towards him."

Brandon nods. "Fair. I promise you that wasn't the case, though. I still have no idea how I got there. I think about it often, trying to remember."

I nod. "It's okay. I'm just glad you're okay."

"It just blows my mind, thinking what could've happened if you weren't there. You're kind of like my hero, swooping in and saving the day. Our roles have reversed. Too bad I can't be like that for you. You beat me to it."

I nod, wanting to tell him that in a way, he has been my hero. Somebody who has distracted me from all of the chaos I've been experiencing and all of the confusion I've been feeling. But it's too soon. Nobody has felt like a hero to me before, and I don't want to risk getting emotional with him.

"Well, switch them back! Traditional roles are more of my thing."

Brandon laughs but then gets serious. "So how about *me* asking you if I can kiss you counts, right?"

My heart flutters at his words and my head nods without me recognizing it.

His lips touch mine, feeling as if I'm melting into what feels like the St. Croix River.

Chapter 21

THE MAJESTIC STAR ON THE ST. CROIX RIVER–
STILLWATER, MINNESOTA

ME

After our first kiss, Brandon and I explore the yacht. Dozens of children and tipsy adults flood the dance floor, and the music gets louder. Once we've finished looking around, we grab dessert from the dessert bar and head back up to our spot at the top. All the while, I feel more and more relaxed, protected.

We fall back into conversation, but this time, we ask one another lightning round questions.

"What's the biggest lie you've ever told?" I ask, taking a bite of my marble cake.

Brandon pauses, appearing deep in thought. "I backed my dad's car into a pole when I was in high school. I told him someone hit it, and he believed me."

"What? Couldn't he tell by the damage?" I ask, talking with bites of cake still in my mouth.

Brandon laughs. "My dad's a city boy, Hails. He can't even change a tire, which wasn't the greatest example. But my mom knew right away. She called me out on my bullshit, but never told my dad."

"Your mom sounds great."

"She is. I had to basically learn everything handy on my own. Your turn to answer."

I set the plate of cake on my lap. "Hmm. Well, I can't compete with that, but mine's pretty innocent. I used to tell my family I had summer classes in order to avoid coming home from college."

"To Alaska, right?"

Something drops in my stomach when he says 'Alaska,' and I immediately want to change subjects. "Yep."

Brandon's eyebrows turn inward. "Why didn't you want to go home?"

I pause, feeling my face become warm. "We're not really close. Okay, it's your turn."

Brandon doesn't push for more details. Instead, it looks like he's focusing on figuring out what question to ask. "What's the best compliment you've received?"

I half-smile. "That I'm resilient."

Brandon looks at me dubiously. "Really? I would've guessed your eyes. Why do you think they said resilient?"

I gulp and then tease, "Maybe I'll tell you the story one day."

"Well, we have time now."

I smile, brushing off his comment and changing the subject to focus on him. "I want to know yours."

Brandon nods, observing my nonverbal communication—and probably deciding not to push it. His face lights up. "That I'm intelligent. Your turn."

"Hmm. What's your zodiac sign?"

Brandon laughs. "I have no idea."

"Well, when's your birthday?"

"April 2nd."

"Ah, you're an Aires."

Brandon laughs. "Is that good or bad?"

"Depends on who you ask."

"I'm going to go with good then. Well, what's yours?"

"Gemini."

Brandon nods. "Ah, you're a twin, then."

My stomach drops and my face tightens. Immediately, the tone of my voice changes. "What?"

Brandon's eyebrows turn inward. "Aren't Geminis known as the twins? Or am I thinking of a different sign?"

Oh. That's what he meant. The irony is almost hilarious. "Oh, right. Yes. They are known as that," I say, taking another bite of my cake as a distraction. "Okay, it's your turn."

Brandon pauses. "Why aren't you close with your family?"

I stop chewing, looking back at the river. Beads of sweat fall down my neck. The last thing I want to do now is meet his eye contact.

"You didn't think I was gonna let you off that easily?" Brandon asks, elbowing me softly. "You've been avoiding a lot of questions tonight."

A laugh escapes my mouth even though I wish it were a scream. "It's a long story."

Should I tell him the truth?

"I told you, we have time. If you're not comfortable, though, I get it, and—"

"Just a lot of family drama," I interrupt, smiling. "Maybe I'll tell you one day, but for now, it's just too much to get into."

"I get it, I get it," Brandon says. "We don't have to talk about it. I'm guessing that's why you moved to the Midwest?"

And yet, here we are still talking about it.

I nod. "Yep. Before my grandparents passed away, my family and I would visit them in Minnesota and California. They had a summer house on Lake Minnetonka and lived in Malibu during the winters. I always saw myself going to the U of M, so it was a no-brainer when I graduated high school."

"I'm sorry to hear that they passed away. Were they your mom's parents or your dad's?"

"My mom's."

Brandon looks at me more seriously. "Do you miss her?"

"Who?"

"Your mom," he says. "It sounds like you do."

My cheeks flame into a soft pink color and my jaw tightens. I blink slowly, looking up at him. It sounds like I do? How?

I don't think about Victoria but the words slip out of my mouth before I realize it. "You know, yes. Yes, I do. I think so."

Wow, did I really say that? That I miss her? Why? Is that how I really feel?

Brandon nods. "I get it. Leaving home, no matter how much family drama there is, can be tough."

I nod, unsure what to say next.

Brandon takes a deep breath. "I think I've asked enough follow-up questions. How about your turn," he suggests.

I smile, choosing to finally lighten up the mood. "What are your real thoughts on my squat form?"

Brandon laughs, leaning closer to me. "My real thoughts?"

"Yes! That's why I'm asking," I tease.

He clears his throat. "Well, I think you're doing great. We're just ...going to keep working on it."

"Yikes," I say, laughing and pushing at his shoulder. "Maybe I need to hire a new trainer if I'm still not very good at it."

"No, you don't," Brandon laughs. "Okay, I have one more question."

"Okay?"

He stares at me seriously, and then asks softly. "Can I kiss you?"

I smile, shaking my head and basking in the protection I feel with him. "Yes, and you don't need to keep asking me."

Brandon laughs. "Yes, ma'am." He presses his lips onto mine and I forget about the world.

Chapter 22

Today's the day.

Victoria remains quiet the entire drive to the police station. She doesn't speak. It's as if all of the words she's been ready to say are stuck in her throat—held captive by fear, apprehension, and frustration.

Then again, it isn't only Victoria who's quiet. Everyone in the vehicle is silent. David, Mia, Kate, and Michael. The radio isn't on, and the only thing anyone hears is the sound of cars driving on the road.

Victoria gulps, trying not to lose her breath. *It's going to be okay. You can get through this. Just like you have so far.*

She knows everyone is thinking about her, thinking about what's going to be on the videotape. As much as it's hard to admit it, Victoria doesn't feel ready to watch it. At all. Yet, she's here: sitting in the car that is driving them to the police station to watch it. It's a bittersweet acceptance: Her family will soon have access to the terrible truth of what really happened, and she isn't sure how she feels about it anymore.

Victoria's jaw trembles as she looks out the car window. Ten minutes later, they pull into the police station and, as their vehicle parks, tension bounces off everybody in the car like pool table balls hitting each other during a game. Everyone continues to remain silent, step out of the vehicle, and then walk towards the police station. Victoria's heart starts to race and her head is dizzy as she focuses on the police station.

David's finally going to see what happened. Everyone is going to see what really happened.

As if sensing her uneasiness, Kate comes up near Victoria and reaches for her sister's hand, lacing their fingers together. While the gesture is small, it's everything Victoria needs at this moment. Slowly, Victoria locks eyes with Kate and forces a smile.

Victoria mouths, 'thank you' and then they walk together.

Entering the police station, their family is directed to the back of the building by someone who knew they were coming. Each step Victoria walks reminds her more and more of the times that she was forced to be at the police station, so many years ago.

As they walk down the hall, they see Paul, the investigator. He's wearing a tan suit with a striped red and blue tie. Bags hang underneath his eyes—just like Kate's—but his smile is bright as he sees them. Around the corner, then comes the psychologist, Dr. Sullivan, who looks nervous as she tries to fake a smile. Almost immediately, her attention is on Victoria.

They're going to watch me. Observe to see how I react. This can't be some kind of test, can it?

Breaking the silence like a hammer to glass, David asks Paul about the videotape. Victoria hears their words, but doesn't comprehend their conversation. The reality of their situation starts amplifying, creating panic and fear in Victoria.

Is this actually happening?

What felt like only seconds later is when they're directed towards the very back room.

Am I really going to watch this? Will I get accused of something if I don't watch? What if what they're saying on the tape isn't there? What if it's something else?

Victoria's head starts to spin as thoughts keep penetrating her mind. Again, Kate seems to sense her sister's uneasiness and tries to get Victoria's attention through eye contact. Victoria doesn't meet her gaze and keeps looking forward, focusing on the open door.

I can do this. I have to watch this tape or else they're going to suspect me of something again. I need to see what's actually on the tape, as well.

Paul signals them to take a seat near a large table as they walk into the room. As Victoria nears the door, she sees a laptop resting on the table, assuming the videotape footage is on it.

Her heart beats faster.

Kate's hand rests behind Victoria's back, but the touch feels nonexistent. Victoria whimpers, backing away from the door as she keeps her eyes on the laptop.

Everyone turns towards Victoria, watching as she begins to fall apart. She looks around the room frantically, looking back and forth between Paul, the laptop, and the hallway. Thick tears slip from her eyes and down her cheeks.

I can't relive this again.

Words finally slip out of Victoria's mouth. "I-I can't do this."

I don't need to know everything in order to understand what happened that night.

Paul nods his head. "That's fine, Victoria. You don't have to—"

Before Paul says anything else, Victoria turns and runs down the hallway. As she flees from the room, more memories of that night pop into her mind. But this time, they're different.

What's happening?

As if a veil on top of the memory has finally been lifted, Victoria remembers more of what happened that night now. The three men with the black ski masks came through the patio door in the guest room. The door must've been unlocked because Victoria had cleaned the glass door earlier that day, inside and outside. Similar to Kate and most of the women in her family, Victoria often forgot to lock doors. It was a habit their mother had also had when she'd been alive.

Guilt consumes Victoria, causing her head to spin even faster as she thinks about the glass door. Abruptly, Victoria takes a seat on the bench inside of the police station.

Why am I just remembering all of this now? When will Hayley finally get here so I can see her? I just want to start over with everyone.

Victoria closes her eyes, leaning her head against the wall. In the background, she hears officers chatting, phones ringing, and a clock ticking. Victoria focuses on the sound of the ticking.

Suddenly, a scream echoes down the hall. It's one that belongs to Kate.

Victoria's head drops forward and tears fall from her eyes, realizing the tape has started.

Chapter 23

The warm night slips into an even later evening. The yacht stays on the water until 2:00 a.m., and we sneak off by herding together with the groups of drunk wedding guests. Holding hands, Brandon and I walk back to the vehicle. Instead of driving off right away, though, we sit in his pickup and continue talking for another hour and a half about everything and anything.

Eventually, Brandon drives us back to Minneapolis, heading towards Uptown and then my apartment complex. As he drives, his hand holds mine. I melt into his touch, feeling calm, safe, and centered—things I've never felt before, especially altogether. If I could bottle up this feeling and save it forever, I would.

Shaking my head, shocked at how I told Brandon about my family. Honestly, when was the last time I even alluded to anything about my family to anyone? Lillie and Catherine, my closest friends, don't even know anything about my past.

"Thanks for tonight," I say softly, turning towards Brandon.

He half-smiles, still looking at the road in front of him. "Thank you for coming out."

I laugh. "You know, tonight was my favorite kind of spontaneity."

"Good. We'll do more of this, then," he says, kissing the top of my hand and then parking near my apartment complex. Brandon turns towards me, smiling again. "I hope you get some good sleep tonight."

Then, Brandon reaches to kiss me then. He pauses before his lips touch mine as if contemplating whether he should ask permission or not. Instead of saying anything or waiting for him, I lean in and press my lips to his. The feelings of calmness, safety, centeredness return.

Eventually, we pull away and Brandon says my name.

"Yah?"

He looks at me curiously. "What are your thoughts on switching trainers?"

I wasn't expecting that.

My eyebrows raise. "Oh? Why?"

He shrugs. "I want to see where this goes."

"What's this?"

He smirks. "You and me."

"I do too. Do we need to do that, though?"

Brandon chuckles. "Good. I mean, I think it's for the best if we do. I'll work with Tina on Sunday to see who we'll place you with next. It's best if we either remain completely professional, or not."

A laugh escapes my mouth. "Did you know I originally requested to work with a woman?"

His eyebrows turned inwards. "What? No, I didn't."

I nod. "Yep. But I was too scared to request someone different. I mean, how could I when I saw I was with you."

Brandon laughs. "Well, it was meant to be, then."

I like the sound of that. "I guess so," I say and then reach for the door handle. "Thanks again for tonight."

"I'll see you soon, okay?"

"Okay." I smile.

We say a final goodbye to each other and wave before I walk towards my apartment complex. Brandon waits to drive off until I get inside the building.

Still smiling, I wave goodbye once I'm inside and then head in the direction of my unit.

Tonight really was a dream.

My eyelids are heavy, and start to close as I walk. Unfortunately, the feelings of calmness, safety, centeredness start to fade and eventually disappear.

As I'm about to round the corner, I see a figure down the hall, stopping me in my tracks.

No. Not again. This isn't happening.

The figure standing down the hall is one that belongs to Emma. As if experiencing a déjà vu on acid, Emma looks exactly like what she did when I saw her through the eyehole of the door at my art studio. Her dark hair is in two messy braids and she's wearing jean shorts and a white top with a puppy printed on it. Emma is looking up at the eyehole, seemingly emotionless, and then she turns to look at me.

Slowly, Emma looks back and forth between the eyehole and me.

My blood is ice cold and I'm unable to move as my eyes refuse to leave her.

I take a deep breath, feeling my lungs struggle to inflate and work as I remain focused on Emma.

This isn't real. I know this isn't real.

Part of me wants it to be real, though. That's my sister. I'm seeing her, but I know I'm actually not. It's hauntingly comforting but simultaneously terrifying.

Shaking, I force myself forward and place one foot in front of the other and walk. As I get closer to Emma, an eerie sensation conjures up behind me. For many seconds, the feeling lingers behind me.

The beats of my heart now feel painful against my chest as I walk closer and closer to Emma. As I'm only ten feet away from her, everything goes black, as if the apartment complex loses power.

I freeze, seeing Emma's silhouette in the dark.

She whispers. "Hayley?"

My heart drops to my stomach.

Suddenly, the light in the hallway returns. But instead of seeing Emma, she's gone. I turn around frantically, observing the space all around me. I'm alone in the hallway with nothing out of the ordinary.

Quickly, I race into my apartment. Once the door is closed and locked, I turn around and slide down the door, my legs and arms shaking–just like I had done in my studio.

Tears slide down my cheeks as my hands grab my hair in frustration.

Chapter 24

DAVID AND MIA ROSSI'S HOUSE – ANCHORAGE, ALASKA

VICTORIA

Everyone watched the videotape except Victoria. As to be expected, it showed the gruesome details of what happened that night of the murder, causing an uproar of reactions from the back room as Victoria listened from afar on the bench down the hallway.

I'm not going to relive it. I can't, and they can't ask me to do that.

After twenty minutes passes, Victoria decides that she'll never watch the tape. At least not willingly. She will if she has to for some reason.

When the videotape finished playing, Victoria was still sitting on the bench listening to the cries coming from afar—forgoing the opportunity to join in on her family's pain and grief in the back room.

They finally know what happened now. They saw it.

More memories come seeping into Victoria's mind, like an avalanche breaking free. She leans her head against the wall, thinking about Emma and Hayley and how large their eyes were when the men tied them to the kitchen chairs. Then, a new, painful memory: Victoria had to choose between saving either Emma or Hayley. She learns in that moment that this was a memory that had tried to come alive in Victoria's mind many times in the past. But somehow she managed to push it down each time it would surface.

Victoria could spare only one of her daughters' lives. That's what the men in the ski masks had said that night. After what felt like an hour of torture, Victoria finally said a name. She chose to save Emma. And then what did the men in the ski masks do? They shot Emma instead —resulting in Hayley hearing Emma's name being picked by her own mother.

Why am I remembering this now?

In this memory now, Victoria recalls how the tallest man in the ski mask laughed, yelling at her that Hayley would always know she'd not been chosen.

How did the man know who was Hayley and who was Emma? Victoria reminds herself that most of her family members had a difficult time telling the girls apart, let alone strangers wouldn't be able to.

Does Hayley remember this? Does she remember me picking Emma?

Then, the door down the hallway opens. Kate comes running towards Victoria, focusing her eyes on her. Victoria stands up from the bench, and immediately, Kate wraps her arms around her sister. Within seconds, Kate sobs hysterically, holding Victoria tightly.

"I am so sorry, Victoria!" Kate cries, shaking in Victoria's arms. "I am so sorry, I never believed you."

It's in that moment when Victoria's reality finally feels real, causing an abrupt acceptance. Her mind, body, and soul can finally relish that her family finally knows what happened that night.

Before Victoria can react, her attention is captured by David, walking down the hallway. She looks towards him, whose eyes are looking straight at the ground.

He can't even look at me. Is he going to say anything?

Kate's cries echo throughout the police station and she whimpers, "They made you pick one. Why did they do that? I can't believe they put you through all of that!"

Hearing Kate's words causes Victoria to become dizzy. *It shows everything. It shows my memories.*

Finally, Victoria sees it. David finally gives Victoria the look. It's the look full of empathy and understanding that Victoria's been waiting for. At this moment, it's like David is actually seeing Victoria. No words between them were necessary but David finally says, "I'm sorry, Victoria."

Chapter 25

MY APARTMENT– MINNEAPOLIS, MINNESOTA

ME

It's days later, and I refuse to leave my apartment, barely leaving my bedroom. I tell Catherine and Lillie that I'm not feeling well, and they leave me alone for the most part. Each time I walk into the kitchen and look at the front door, I think of Emma— remembering how she stood outside, staring up at the eyehole. Just like at the studio.

More than ever, I want to call someone to tell them what's going on, but confusion and fear have a tighter grasp on me. They pin me down as if we're fighting, and I can't get up.

It's not until Thursday rolls around when I force myself to leave the apartment. I have a workout session scheduled with my new trainer and Catherine wants to celebrate her birthday later with

Lillie and I. I've already canceled two of my workout sessions, so I have to go in today.

I drive to the gym with the radio off and in a trance. As much as I don't want to think about Emma, I do. Until this Summer, Emma and Victoria have never been in any of my hallucinations, even in the ones I had when I was a kid. If I am hallucinating, I usually hear loud voices—like a bunch of people talking over one another—see bright flashes of white light, or glimpses of the notorious figure that's haunted my dreams for years, the Phantom. The hallucinations never lasted more than a few seconds, and I'm usually able to block them out if I really want to. Now, these hallucinations have morphed into something unimaginable and refuse to leave my mind, like unwanted guests.

Why is this happening? Why is it getting worse?

For years, I trained myself not to think about them, especially Emma. Again, what was the point of remembering my sister when nothing about our past was ever going to change? Our twin telepathy is dead. She's never coming back, and things will never be different.

Once I park and head inside, Brandon's near the front and greets me with a warm but slightly confused smile. My stomach drops when I see him. He knows I've canceled two of my sessions, and I haven't returned his text messages.

Strangely, I don't feel comforted when I see him. Instead, I feel more anxiety since near him is a woman who I think is named Shannon, who is in fact my new trainer. The bottle of these feelings of calmness, safety, and centeredness has shattered. Once again, I feel as if I'm on my own.

I can sense Brandon watching me but I don't see his eye contact. If I do, I know I'll start crying.

Shannon introduces herself and before I know it, we start our session. She does a great job of distracting my body, but not my mind. As I workout, I have to actively push away my thoughts about Emma, sometimes even stopping in the middle of a set to remind myself that I can't mentally break down in front of everyone here.

Naturally, I caught Brandon watching me a few times during my session. He looked over with concern but, of course, didn't say anything.

When my session ends, and Shannon moves on to her next client, Brandon finds me. His eyebrows raise. "What's up?"

"What?"

"You're acting strange," Brandon says. "You also haven't texted me back. What's up?"

Guilt washes over me. I take a deep breath, looking away from him. Should I finally tell him what's going on? Should he be the person who knows what's going on, or will that scare him away?

"Just...a lot's been happening recently."

"Like what?"

I look around at the space between us. My voice is soft as I look back up at him. "I don't really want to get into it now."

"It sounds serious."

That's because it is, Brandon. "It is."

Tears start forming in my eyes and Brandon immediately notices this.

"Okay, are you free later? How about tonight?"

I shake my head, starting to feel dizzy. "No. I can't. Catherine, Lillie, and I are going downtown for Catherine's birthday. Maybe tomorrow?"

"Yes, that works." Brandon looks at me seriously. "Are you sure you don't want to just tell me now, Hails? Or I can talk for longer in about two hours."

"No, it's okay. I need to get to work anyway. We'll talk more tomorrow. I gotta go."

Before Brandon can say anything else, I quickly turn and walk out of the gym, not looking back and exiting the building alone. The tears finally slide down my face as I head to my vehicle.

Chapter 26

It's later that evening and Lille's voice drowns out my thoughts. "You guys ready? I'm about to order an Uber." She's standing in the kitchen, leaning against the kitchen island with her cell phone in her hands.

"In like five minutes!" Catherine calls, holding up a container of eyelash glue from the bathroom. "My eyelashes still aren't on."

I'm in the bathroom with Catherine, fake laughing as I watch her bring the tweezers and eyelashes up towards her eye. Even though I'm laughing with her, my mind is still racing and I feel empty. I want tonight to be the perfect distraction, but it doesn't feel like it. Emma is still on my mind.

"So, what's new with you and loverboy?" Catherine asks, wafting a hand near her eye to help the glue dry.

She's wearing a silver mini dress that compliments her jet-black hair and pale skin beautifully. Her eyes and lips are decorated with striking colors—making nothing about her ordinary.

"We're, ya know, enjoying our time together."

"So, that's what you want to call it?"

I fake laugh. "We're taking it day by day."

"Such a cliche. Getting with your trainer." Catherine chuckles.

"Says the woman who was with her coworker last year. Now that's the ultimate cliche."

"Hey now, that was one Summer," Catherine says sarcastically. "Technically only for two months which is less time than you and Brandon."

Lillie pops into the bathroom, reminding us the Uber is on its way and we need to hurry up or else we'll be charged the fee. As I walk into my bedroom to grab my purse, my cell phone rings loudly. Grabbing it from my nightstand, I glimpse at the name that pops up on the screen.

Kate.

Sweat forms on my forehead as I lower the phone down.

Maybe I should pick it up. This could be a sign to tell her what's going on. But what will she say? What if she's scared I'm turning into Victoria? Will she tell David?

"It's here! Let's go!" Lillie calls again, opening the apartment door.

Reluctantly, I press the end button. Catherine peeks her head in the doorway, eyelashes on. "Ready to go?"

I sigh before turning towards her but she doesn't see it. "Yep. Ready."

"Who was that?" Her eyebrows raise.

"Nobody," I smile.

Catherine sighs dramatically. "So secretive."

Play-pushing her out of the way, I leave my bedroom. A few minutes later, we exit the apartment complex and meet up with our Uber driver. Driving towards Downtown Minneapolis, Catherine and Lillie chat with the driver the entire ride, hardly noticing my silence.

As we arrive Downtown, I store away my thoughts about Kate and try to enjoy the evening as best as I can. The next few hours are a distraction, but probably not the best considering all of the alcohol involved. We hop from bar to bar, celebrating Catherine's birthday, dancing, and swiping our debit cards for cocktails. Naturally, Catherine's socialite personality helps us easily get into most of the bars. Even though it's a weekday, the streets are very busy.

It isn't until the end of the night when we naturally find ourselves at a grungier nightclub. Once we get inside, we wait in line near the bar until Catherine asks. "What do you guys want?"

My eyebrows raise. "It's your birthday. You shouldn't the one who should be buying drinks."

Catherine shakes her head. "Lillie bought the Uber and you helped me get ready. Fair trade. Vodka soda for you, and whiskey sour for Lillie?"

I laugh. "You know me too well."

With that, Catherine sneakily budges her way up to the bar.

As I'm about to say something to Lillie, a tall man comes up from behind us. He taps Lillie on the shoulder, and when she sees him, her face immediately lights up. Lillie gives him a familiar hug before turning back towards me. "Hayley, this is my friend Mark from high school."

I smile, introducing myself. Then, Lillie and Mark start chatting, catching up with one another. Before I realize what's happening, another man approaches us. His words slur as he says to me, "You have the most beautiful eyes."

I smile, feeling more awkward than appreciative. "Thank you."

"What's that on your neck?" he asks.

I realize he's referring to my scars and it triggers me. Before the man can make more conversation with me, I turn towards Lillie and grab her arm softly. "Lill, I'll be right back. I'm gonna use the bathroom."

Lillie nods, still listening to her friend talk. "Okay. Sounds good. Do you want me to come with you?"

"No, it's okay. I'll be gone for like only a few minutes."

Sneaking away, I push past groups of people and head to the back of the bar. From a distance, I see the restrooms, including the long line for the women's restroom.

As I'm about to get in line, a group of women come up a flight of stairs from the lower level. One of them stumbles slightly, but then makes eye contact with me as she sees me in line. As she passes me, she whispers, "There's more stalls downstairs."

Looking at the long line again, I decide I'll do just that. "Thank you," I say to the woman who gives me a thumbs up.

I walk down the flight of stairs to the lower-level. Once I'm at the bottom, I see one unisex bathroom and an opened storage closet. One woman is in line, and she smiles at me as I stand behind her.

As I wait in line, Brandon pops into my mind. I think about him, distracting myself from thinking about Victoria or Emma. When it's my turn to use the bathroom, I head inside and lock the door behind me. I don't look into the mirror as I pass it.

Sitting down on the toilet, I think about what it may feel like if I tell Brandon what's been going on with me. Would I feel relieved? Embarrassed? Obligated to tell him more about my past so he has context? What am I going to end up telling him tomorrow?

Before I can unzip my pants, a high-pitched sound fills space around me. Immediately, I jump and cover my ears from the piercing sound.

The sound continues to overwhelm me, causing me to freeze in place. And then, suddenly, it stops all at once. My head turns slightly, and I see movement in the corner of my eye. My heart drops to my stomach. And whatever it is, it moves again.

I turn again, but this time to face whatever had just moved. But nothing is there and nothing out of place.

Quickly, I exit the bathroom, seeing nobody else waiting in line. I'm alone. Again.

As I'm about to walk up the stairs, a sound comes from the storage closet, sounding as if something is being pushed around on the floor.

Then, it's replaced by the high-pitched. My hands cover my ears again, my eyes close, and I freeze in place.

What is happening to me?

Seconds pass, and when I open my eyes, dozens of cocktail mixtures, rags, and paper towels surround me. It takes a second to realize where I am: I'm in the storage closet with the door shut and the lights on.

Then I see it, floating in the corner is the lanky, legless figure of the Phantom.

The lights turn off.

Chapter 27

COWBOY JACK'S – DOWNTOWN MINNEAPOLIS, MINNESOTA

ME

My eyes flutter open and I'm lying on the floor in the storage room. I'm not sure how much time has passed but the lights are on again. It takes a few seconds, and the memories of what happened resurface.

I sit up from the floor, pushing my body up and against the wall. Breathing in and out, I look around the room, searching for the Phantom. There's no trace of a floating, faceless, body anywhere in the room.

A single tear falls from my eye and down my cheek. Slowly, I count in my head how many times something strange has happened to me, and I lose track.

Whispering, I ask, "What is happening to me?"

While the high-pitched sound is gone, another voice is heard. My head turns sharply towards the direction of the sound.

Sitting beside me is Emma. Dressed the exact way as before, she looks up at me innocently. Surprisingly, she says, "Are we going to be okay, Hayley?"

Immediately, I forget all about the Phantom. I scramble away from her on the adjacent wall, staring at Emma in fear as she continues to look at me.

Those are the words. The words that Emma had just said to me are the words she asked me the night she died. I remember them finally.

"Go away!" I scream, covering my ears.

Quickly, I look away, sheiling my ears and pushing against the wall. When I open my eyes, Emma is gone and standing in the doorway is a woman. Keys dangle from her short pockets and she looks at me with concern.

Silence bounces between us. We make eye contact but I don't speak. I can't speak.

As if all at once, flashbacks and fragments from my childhood fill my mind. The woman in front of me disappears from my vision. First, I see my younger self in the temporary house that David, Kate, and I stayed in after the night of the murder, which was weeks later after I physically healed from the fire–leaving me burn marks on my neck. We are all silent around a dinner table.

The next memory is of David and I, sitting together on a couch and he's begging me to speak to him, to say something to anyone. But I remain silent, disassociating from him and the world around me.

Then, another memory comes, this one is of me staring at the walls in a psychologists' office, memorizing all of the lines and curves around the room instead of answering her questions.

All of these memories, they're all the times I didn't speak to anyone. Instead, I kept the words in my body. As if I was storing everything inside.

Finally, I come back to reality when the woman touches me. Instantly, I jump, looking at her with wide eyes.

She asks me if I'm okay again, explaining that she's one of the bartenders. Meeting her eye contact, I convince myself she's real and not a hallucination. "I-I need to leave," I whisper.

"Leave? What happened?"

I don't answer her. Instead, I scramble to my feet and rush past the woman. Racing up the stairs, my breaths are short. Once I reach the top, I maneuver through the crowds of people in the bar.

Emma's question echoes in my brain. "Are we going to be okay, Hayley?" It repeats over and over. My heart pounds, feeling as if it's going to stop, but I keep walking. I keep pushing past dancing bodies.

Suddenly, someone grabs my shoulder. I gasp, freezing in place, but it's only Catherine.

Her eyes are full of concern as she watches my expression. "There you are! Where the hell did you go?"

"I'll be right back," I say in a trance, pushing away from her touch and continue to walk.

"What? Where are you going?" Catherine asks.

Catherine yells something after me, but I don't hear it. All I can think about is that I'm turning into Victoria. My worst fear is finally here: I'm turning into my mother.

I rush out of the bar and exhale sharply when I'm outside as if there was no oxygen in the bar. Groups of drunk people maneuver past me as my body remains in place until I'm able to gather myself.

With tears in my eyes, I slowly pull out my phone, dial a number, and bring it to my ear. The line comes alive. "Hello?" Brandon answers.

His voice immediately calms me, but it's not enough. I pause before words finally escape my mouth. "Brandon, can you please come get me?"

"Wait, what? Where are you?"

My head is dizzy as I answer him and send my location. Brandon says he'll be here soon but it still feels like it's not enough.

"Please hurry."

Thankfully, Brandon does hurry and my friends haven't come to find me. My phone is filled with text messages, and I reassure my friends that I'm safe and heading to Brandon's place.

In about fifteen minutes, his black pickup pulls up in front of the bar. I walk towards it and open the door. Immediately, I climb in and avoid his eye contact momentarily.

Brandon asks. "Hayley, what's wrong?"

I look up at him, feeling as if I'm seven years old again being bombarded by questions from David, Kate, and multiple therapists. Then, he sees the tears in my eyes.

"Did something happen?" he asks

I shiver from his words as I sit back further in the seat. It's as if my body is remembering all the times when I was in a psychologist's office, being forced to communicate what I hardly remembered what happened that night. My heart pounds against my chest, feeling as if it's going to explode.

Brandon tries again. "What's going on? Is this about what you mentioned at the gym earlier?"

His words cause my ears to perk up. I force words to come out of me this time. "Yes."

"Okay, then what is it?"

I don't answer, trying to push away my memories. In my mind, I see the psychologist look at me disappointed, frustrated that I'm not speaking to her.

"Okay. Well, should I take you home, then?"

When the words leave Brandon's mouth, I picture my apartment complex, imagining seven-year-old Emma standing in the hallway and looking between me and the eyehole on the door. Then, I envision her sitting near me on the ground in the storage closet, asking, 'Hayley, are we going to be okay?'

I can't go back to my apartment. I don't want to risk seeing her again. Quickly, my head shakes back and forth and I spit my words out. "I can't go home."

"Why?"

My throat gets tight. "I'll explain everything tomorrow. Just please don't make me go home."

Brandon nods. "I won't. Do you want to stay with me then?"

"Yes, please."

Chapter 28

BRANDON'S APARTMENT –
DOWNTOWN MINNEAPOLIS, MINNESOTA

ME

The next morning comes quickly. Last night, I fell asleep in Brandon's bed, listening to him snoring from the couch. This situation that I'm now in reminds me of when Brandon stayed over at my place after I found him on the train tracks. Now, we're in completely different circumstances compared to that night.

I'm awake now, groggy, and thinking about too many things at once as my eyes adjust to the sunlight beaming in. His room is as I expected, messy and unorganized.

As I pull the comforter closer to my chest, I hear movement from the living room. Brandon comes into his bedroom, looking at me curiously when he realizes as I'm up.

"Oh, good morning. I was just coming to see if you were up."

I smile softly, feeling warmth return to my cheeks. "Morning."

"If I knew you were coming over, I would've cleaned up more," he says, half-smiling and leaning against the doorframe.

I laugh. "Don't worry about it. What time do you work today?"

"3 p.m, so I have a few hours." Slowly, he walks towards his bed and sits down at the end, rubbing the top part of my leg under the comforter. "So what's going on?"

I exhale sharply as my mind races. "A lot of things."

"Let's start with, are you okay?"

Nodding, I say, "Right now, I am."

"What about last night, though?"

"No."

"You wanna talk about what happened?"

Slowly, I sit up in his bed and turn away from his eye contact. It's as if all of the events from last night are floating around in my mind, waiting to be dealt with. I'm reminded of the high-pitched sound, the Phantom, and the seven-year-old version of Emma from last night.

So much happened to me, yet, I haven't fully processed any of it. I look back at Brandon, and his facial expression is gentle and full of concern.

Sighing, I remind myself that I have to choose to trust him. I must choose to trust Brandon even if I regret it later. I need someone, and specifically I need someone like Brandon to be here for me.

Tears fill my eyes and the words fall out of my mouth. "I-I'm really scared."

"Why?" he asks, rubbing my leg again.

Exhaling sharply, I say, "There's a lot..a lot going on with me. I don't even know where to begin."

"Try."

I nod, looking away again. My head drops slightly and my voice cracks as I continue, "I'm really nervous to tell you this, but somebody needs to know. I haven't told anyone this but something is happening to me."

Brandon waits for me to continue and I do.

"There's so much. I know you don't know this but a lot has happened to me, to my family, when I was younger. So much stuff that I had to change my name."

"Really?"

"Yes, my name used to be Hailee Rossi and now it's Hayley Crowe. Some bad things happened to my family when I was younger and I'm starting to see them again."

"See them again? What do you mean?"

I gulp, looking away from Brandon's eye contact again. "This is really hard for me to talk about but I'm starting to hallucinate those memories."

"Hallucinate as in seeing things?"

"Yes, things that aren't there. Sounds that aren't real."

Brandon interrupts. "You don't need to explain yourself. Even if you are, that's fine."

"But I'm not."

Brandon nods. "Okay. I'm sorry this is happening. What are the memories of?"

Do I tell him they're of my dead sister? Or do I tell him they're of my mom who's locked away for the murder of my twin sister? Or maybe I tell him they're of the creature that's haunted me in my nightmares since I was a kid?

"They're really dark." Tears escape my eyes, falling down my cheeks but I hardly notice. "I'm really scared, Brandon. I-I don't know what to do."

Brandon moves from the end of the bed to be closer to me. Near my side he says, "Hey, hey, hey, it's okay. Don't be upset."

"It's hard not to be. It's only been getting worse and worse, and it's really scaring me."

"Does your family know what's been going on? I know you said already that you're not close with them."

My heart drops to my stomach. "No. They don't know."

"But this has been happening since you were a kid, right?"

"Yes, it has. But you know this, my relationship with my family is really complicated."

"Because of what happened between you all?"

I nod. "Yes."

"Have you thought about going to a doctor?"

My head spins. "I want to but I'm scared. I don't want to see another doctor. I've been seeing them all of my life. What if they tell me I'm just like my mother?"

"What do you mean by that?"

"My mom, she has…"

I don't say the word. I don't say schizophrenia.

Brandon doesn't keep pushing, instead, he says, "Do you want to call someone now? I can be here for you when you do. Who can you call?"

I nod. "I could call my aunt? It's early, though. 8 am in Alaska."

"It doesn't hurt to try. I'll be here while you make it."

Finally, a sliver of courage enters me. "Thank you, but can I do it alone? I have something I'd like you to do when I call her, though. It'll give you the context you need."

Brandon's eyebrows raise. "Oh? Sure. What's that?"

Taking a deep breath, I say. "I want you to type in the name into Google, my real name. 'Hailee Rossi.'"

Brandon nods. "Okay, I can do that. What am I going to find?"

I exhale sharply. "What really happened to me."

Chapter 29

DAVID AND MIA ROSSI'S HOUSE– ANCHORAGE, ALASKA

VICTORIA

As Victoria sits on the back porch in the early morning, she's lost in thought and looking at the gigantic trees. Like clockwork, Kate's at the house and is opening the sliding glass door. "Hey, morning."

"Morning," Victoria says.

"This has become quite the little pattern, huh?" Kate says. "Sitting out here in the mornings."

"It has," Victoria says, returning her sister a small smile. She then takes a sip of her coffee.

Kate half-smiles, taking a seat. "I'm here a bit early since I couldn't sleep after yesterday. I wanted to check on you. How are you doing?"

Victoria's nods, gripping her coffee tighter as she remembers. "The feelings come in waves…Part of me feels like a terrible mother for not watching the tape. Then another part of me feels relieved that I didn't."

"That's understandable, Vic. You shouldn't feel like that at all, though."

"Easier said than done, ya know? Did you know that I've been remembering what happened?"

"As in what happened that night?"

"Yes, the memories are finally coming back. Part of me feels like I don't need to see the tape."

"Wow, really. That's great. I mean, I think that's probably a good thing. Or maybe it's not."

"I think it's good. I need to tell Paul about them, but I'm nervous he'll accuse me of withholding them."

Kate's eyebrows turn inward. "Why would he do that? Especially because your innocence is proven."

"I'm still scared," Victoria admits. "I feel as if I have to walk on eggshells." *It feels great to finally let the truth out.*

As Kate is about to respond, her cell phone goes off. Her mouth hangs open as she stares at the device in her hand. "What?"

"What's wrong?" Victoria asks.

Kate looks up at Victoria. "It's Hayley."

Hayley? My Hayley?

Victoria's stomach drops. *Is it really her?*

"She's actually calling *me*," Kate says. "She never does. Ugh, should I answer it?"

"Of course!" Victoria says, moving closer to Kate. "Why wouldn't you?"

"Okay, okay. I just wanted to check." Quickly, Kate answers her cell phone. "Hello?"

Victoria holds her breath as she watches Kate, observing her facial expressions. Setting down her coffee and with sweaty palms,

Victoria positions herself closer to Kate. Then, Victoria motions for Kate, mouthing 'can I hear her voice?'

Kate nods, hitting the speaker button on the cell phone.

"Are you alone?" a deep voice asks.

That's Hayley?

As if punched in the stomach, Victoria bends forward slightly from the sound of her daughter's voice. Tears form in her eyes but they don't slide down her cheeks. Hayley's voice is lower than Victoria expected, not sounding like anything she imagined. In Victoria's mind, she sees her little girl with long dark hair in two messy braids who has a high-pitched voice.

"Yes, why?" Kate says.

"Promise me you won't say anything to anyone else yet?" Hayley asks.

Kate and Victoria make eye contact at Hayley's request. *What's going on?*

"I promise. What's going on?" Kate says.

Hayley takes a breath in and exhales sharply before answering. "Kate...I don't know how to sugar coat this so I'm just going to say it. I think I have schizophrenia."

Hayley's words take Victoria by surprise– it's as if someone punched her in the stomach and robbed all of the oxygen in her lungs. *Schizophrenia? Like me?*

Victoria shakes her head. *I can't believe this is the first thing I'm hearing my daughter say.*

Kate looks paler than she's looked for weeks. "W-what makes you think that?"

Hayley pauses on the other end. "I've been having hallucinations for months, and it's only getting worse."

Months? She's been experiencing this for months? And Kate's just hearing about this now?

Kate pauses, shaking her head. "Where are you right now?"

"At home."

Kate clears her throat. "I think you should come home. To Alaska. Take a break from Minnesota. We can talk more about this and get you to be around family. Can you come home?"

Victoria shoots a look at Kate, smiling a thankful smile. *Kate's finally making steps to get Hayley home.*

Kate continues. "I really think it's for the best. You'll feel so much more comfortable being around us than being there in Minnesota by yourself."

Hayley sighs. "I'm not sure. I'm scared."

Victoria's chest tightens at Hayley's words, and her head drops in shame and empathy. *So was I.*

"I need you to, Hayley," Kate says. "We can get you into your family doctor. She knows your medical record from the inside out. She'll know what to do. Besides… your dad and I also need you here."

"Why?"

Kate pauses, making eye contact with Victoria again. "Something's happened."

"What happened?"

Kate clears her throat. "It's kind of a long story. Once you can get here, I can explain more."

"What? You're confusing me, Kate," Hayley says, her tone harsher.

"It's something your dad and I need to sit down with you and explain."

Victoria's heart starts to race even faster. *What if this conversation pushes Hayley away, and what if she won't come home now? Maybe I should tell Kate to stop pushing her so much.*

"Why can't you just tell me now? I'm already going through a lot. I don't think I need *this* to also stress out about."

Victoria rests her head in her hands in frustration. *She sounds stubborn. What if Hayley doesn't come here now? She's scared and focused on what's going on with her, not what Kate is insinuating.*

"We just need you here. That's all I can say, Hayley."

Victoria shoots Kate another look but this time it's in dissatisfaction. Kate nods but doesn't say anything.

Silence holds the line until more seconds pass, but Hayley eventually says. "Okay, fine."

Victoria's shoulders drop and the tension in her jaw immediately melts away. *She's coming. Hayley is really coming to Alaska, and I finally get to see her.*

Kate raises a fist in the air, but keeps quiet. Her eyes light up and she smiles largely at Victoria. For many seconds, they meet eye contact and feel connected on a deep level, the most since Victoria was released from the hospital.

"Great, I'll book you a ticket today and email you the confirmation information. What day works best for you this week?"

"After Friday."

"Perfect."

And just like that, there is finally a plan, and it's happening. It's been almost fifteen years since Victoria has seen, held, or looked at her daughter. Now, the time is finally coming. *Soon she will be here with me.*

Chapter 30

BRANDON'S APARTMENT–
DOWNTOWN MINNEAPOLIS, MINNESOTA

BRANDON

As Hayley is on the phone, Brandon closes the bedroom door and walks to the living room. He sits down and opens his laptop, typing in Hayley's name in the search bar. Her real name. H-a-i-l-e-e R-o-s-s-i

Brandon hits the 'enter' key and hundreds—if not thousands—of results populate on his screen. In the matter of seconds, the truth of who Hayley is hits him at once, all on a screen.

"What?"

Brandon realizes he already knows of Hayley. Her real name is associated with the Rossi murder case. It was the murder case Brandon heard about when he was in elementary school. While no pictures of Hayley show up immediately, pictures of Victoria do.

"Jesus," Brandon says, rubbing the top of his head. "They look identical."

Brandon observes, seeing how Victoria and Hayley are carbon copies of one another. With the same hair color, and similar body types and facial structures, the adult version of Hayley and Victoria look mostly identical besides their skin tone. Most distinctly, they both have the same beautiful light blue eyes.

He reads article after article, his eyes skimming headlines like 'Mother found guilty of murdering twin daughter during schizophrenic break' and 'Schizophrenia at its very depths drove mother to kill twin daughter'—they all tell the same story with a similar narrative, but include no emotion or empathy.

Then, he gets to the videos. Dozens of videos of news clips appear in his search, all of which have millions of views. Plus, there are hundreds of videos of content creators covering the Rossi case, all of which have thousands of subscriber comments and discussions underneath each video.

As he reads through the comments, Brandon realizes that the opinions are split on what happened that night. Some are vile, others are empathetic. All of them don't know the truth.

'Mother is innocent. She may have admitted to it, but I don't believe it's true.'

'She definitely did it. Her fingerprints were on the gun. She admitted it!'

'The gun was planted there. She was framed for sure.'

'She had a psychotic break. How can you guys not see it?'

'I think it's the husband. It's always the husband.'

'She's innocent. If she was guilty, how did they end up all the way in the woods when her car was still at the house? It doesn't add up.'

So many opinions, so many assumptions.

And just like that, Brandon learns what apparently happened on the night of October 17th. In Anchorage, Alaska, a fire started in David and Victoria Rossi's small blue house, burning almost everything to the ground. It was reported that David was working at the hospital that night, as he was still in his doctoral residency, and Victoria and Hayley—Hailee—were found hours later by deputy officials, wandering in Chugach State Park in Alaska.

Hailee's twin sister Emma wasn't with them. She was never found alive even after multiple search parties went out. The police discovered some of her remains, a few of her fingers, along with a gun. But that was enough to get Victoria charged for murder.

Apparently, when Victoria and Hailee were found in the state park, neither of them spoke to anyone. Not to the police, David, Kate, or each other. Instead, they were mute. The only sound Hailee made were screams when Victoria came too close to her. Everyone noticed how scared Hailee was of her mother, causing the police to keep them separated as much as possible.

Victoria's only words were, "I shot her," which she said to her husband, David. A police officer witnessed the interaction and, almost immediately, Victoria was brought into the police station. These three simple words would haunt her as the defense team tried to retract them during the trial.

In the end, the words counted as Victoria's confession and she was deemed as mentally incompetent by a judge, meaning she was not criminally responsible for Emma's murder on the grounds of insanity. Locked away, she was to be hospitalized for psychiatric care and treatment—sentenced for over twenty years.

Their story ends there, apparently.

Coming back to reality, Brandon eventually comes across a picture of the surviving dark-haired, blue-eyed, seven-year-old girl.

Hayley.

He stares at the image of Hayley that pops up in the video, noticing how small, scared, and vulnerable she looks. Her bright blue eyes are filled with tears.

Shaking his head, Brandon exhales sharply. *How could her Mother do something like that? Does Hayley really think she has schizophrenia like Victoria? Why hasn't she told anyone about this?*

"That's why she's scared," Brandon whispers. "She's scared she'll be like Victoria."

Finally, it makes sense to Brandon why Hayley doesn't want to go back to Alaska and why she changed her name legally. She's tried to start over, to get away from her past.

Brandon sets down the laptop in awe and closes his eyes. As he tries to process all the information, the image of seven-year-old Hayley stays in his mind: the one of the small, scared, and vulnerable girl who never asked for any of this to happen.

Chapter 31

BRANDON'S APARTMENT– DOWNTOWN MINNEAPOLIS, MINNESOTA

ME

I exhale sharply, ending the phone call with Kate. The call didn't go as I had hoped it would go. Instead, now I have more questions. Why does she want me home? Why can't her and David just tell me what's going on over the phone? My mind races, and it won't stop. I sit with my thoughts for over ten minutes, processing everything as my mind feels like the roadrunner Looney Tunes cartoon, running down the highway at full speed.

What am I supposed to do now? Did I really just agree to go back to Alaska? I can't go back. I promised myself I would never return home, but this feels like an exception.

Shaking my head, I swing my legs over the bed and stand up. My legs are wobbly and tight, and I grab onto the wall as I walk slowly into the living room.

Did Brandon search my name up? What's he going to think when I tell him how the phone call went?

From the couch, Brandon looks up at me. The laptop on his lap is closed, and his eyes are full of concern. "Hey. How'd it go?"

At first, his words don't cause me to react. Instead, I slowly nod my head, and a smile escapes. However, tears soon fill my eyes and slide down my cheeks as the roadrunner in my mind returns and bombards it of overwhelm.

"Hey, hey, hey," Brandon says, "it's okay." He motions for me to sit by him on the couch. "Come here."

Don't cry. Brandon doesn't need to see me cry. Through my tears, I say, "I don't even know what just happened."

"What do you mean?"

I shake my head. "I-I told my aunt, but...the conversation changed."

"How?"

"Like, she convinced me to come back home. Apparently something's happened back in Alaska, but she didn't say what. I'm really confused, but I feel like I do need to go back."

Brandon stands up, grabs my hand, but then embraces me gently, wrapping his arms around my body.

For the first time in a long time, I let myself cry without feeling guilty. I feel all of the emotions, the ones I've told myself are terrible. Now, at this moment, I don't care. I need someone like Brandon who's safe and secure to hold me and be there for me.

As he embraces me, I remind myself that I'm going to be okay even though it doesn't feel like it. Regardless of what happens. I'm resilient, remember?

Eventually, I pull away from Brandon and look up at him, smiling slightly with my cheeks stained with tears.

"Do you feel better?" Brandon asks, brushing a strand of hair out of my face.

"I'm not sure."

He nods. "It's okay," he says. "A lot has happened."

I shake my head. "I'm just surprised she wasn't more concerned. I've been seeing–experiencing– things for months, and she doesn't even care."

"I'm sure she cares."

"No, she doesn't. Well, it doesn't seem like she does."

Brandon motions for us to sit down and he says, "How about you tell me more about it, then?"

I half-smile and nod. "Did you look me up online?"

"Yes."

He knows about me. He knows my story now. "It's awful, isn't it?" I clear my throat and look away. "I've started seeing and hearing things… regularly. Probably only for a few months now, but it hasn't always been like this. To give you some context, I've had hallucinations before. They're not something new but I also never talk about them with anyone. Essentially, I see things that aren't there sometimes or hear things that just don't exist. However, it's only gotten worse these past couple of months. I've seen my mom and sister, who I've never seen before. And that's really starting to scare me."

"Your mom and sister? Isn't your sister dead?"

His words sting, causing my jaw to tremble. "Yes."

Brandon nods. "You know, I remember hearing about your story when I was a kid."

"Really?"

"Yep, I learned about it through my friends. I also remember my parents talking about it a few times." Brandon pauses before he adds, "I'm so sorry you had to go through that, Hayley."

Tears begin to swell in my eyes. "So, you know my mom has schizophrenia, then? That she—"

"Yes. I know what she did."

He knows Victoria killed Emma. Brandon also knows I'm seeing things, just like how Victoria saw things.

"Do you want to talk about what happened that night?" Brandon asks.

I gulp and shrug my shoulders. "I hardly remember anything to be honest. I like to say I remember nothing to make it easier."

"Really? Nothing from that night?"

I nod. "I mean, actually…I've started to remember more. But my brain shuts them down, and I don't get much information."

"Why do you think it does that?"

"Because it probably doesn't want to relive everything again. *I* don't want to relive everything again. It's not fair. I've lived through it once, and I don't need or want to again."

Brandon reaches for my hand, and my body relaxes to his touch.

"It's just really scary," I say softly. "I feel out of control. My mind feels out of control."

"I don't want you to be scared," Brandon says. "You're not like her. You're going to be okay."

His words cause me to melt. My biggest insecurity brought to light and there is no judgment from Brandon. "I just really don't want to turn into my mom."

"Hayley, you're nothing like her," Brandon says, holding my eye contact. "Just because you're seeing things doesn't mean you're turning into her. You're you, not Victoria."

Fear overtakes me and my mind starts racing again. "But you don't know that. What if things get worse? What if I change? I'm pretty sure hers got worse throughout the years."

"You're strong, Hayley. After learning about everything you've gone through, I think you're the strongest person I've ever met. I'll be here for you as you deal with this. But I don't want you to think that way about yourself. You have to give yourself more credit."

Warmth enters my body again. His words soothe my anxiety, and I don't take it for granted.

"Really?"

"Yes."

I take a deep breath, shaking my head. "What do you think I should do? Do you think it's okay for me to go back to Alaska?"

"What do *you* want to do?" Brandon asks.

I shrug. "I don't know. I promised myself I'd never go home, but things feel different now. I feel like I should go back home."

Brandon nods. "Then you should listen to that intuition of yours."

"But what if it's not my intuition and it's my trauma?"

Brandon shrugs. "Well, the best part of this is that you can always fly back. You can see how it goes, and come back immediately if it's too hard. It may be nice to be home. You can talk to your doctor, get the answers, and see what your aunt needs to talk to you about."

"You're right."

Brandon clears his throat. "And if you need me, I can come with you."

My head tilts from the surprise of his words. What? He's really offering to come to Alaska with me?

"What? Like, fly with me?" I shake my head. "Brandon, I can't ask you to do that."

"Why not?"

"Are you serious?" I ask, shaking my head.

"Yep, I've never been to Alaska, you know? Nor have I ever seen a moose."

I chuckle, looking down towards the bed with pink cheeks. "Well, I'm speechless. Thank you so much." Just Brandon's offer in itself gives me the strength I need. "How about this? How about I go there for a few days and you join? I think I am going to need you, which is hard to admit but I'm glad I'm admitting it. I want at least some time alone with my family, but then I'd love for you to come for support."

Brandon nods. "Absolutely. You mean a lot to me, Hayley. You need someone to support you, someone who's going to be on your side. I can be that for you."

Tears fill my eyes again from his words, and I reach out to hug Brandon. Melting in his embrace, the world and my mind finally feels quiet.

Maybe I can do this after all.

Chapter 32

DAVID AND MIA ROSSI'S HOUSE– ANCHORAGE, ALASKA

VICTORIA

Victoria loses her breath, but finds it quickly. She stares at Kate as the phone call with Hayley ends. Immediately, Kate turns towards Victoria and sees the tears in her eyes.

"She's coming. Hayley is really coming!" Victoria gasps.

Kate nods, looking as if she's in a satisfied trance. "Yes, I can't believe it. She's finally coming." She pauses, her eyes beaming. "Was that the first time you've heard Hayley's voice?"

Victoria nods. "Yes. Since she was seven."

Kate's eyes widen, and she exhales sharply. "Wow, I can't believe it. H-how do you feel?"

Ecstatic. Nervous. Free. So many emotions. "I feel relieved. Part of me thinks it's too good to be true, as in, do I really get to see her so soon?" Victoria says. "Plus, I'm not sure what to say about her thinking she has schizophrenia."

Kate nods, pushing her blonde hair away from her face. "Me either. I wasn't expecting that at all. But hey, let's just focus on getting her here. We can deal with that once we catch Hayley up on what's going on…and of course, you two seeing each other. To me, that's the biggest priority."

Victoria nods, smiling and thankful for Kate's words. "Yes, I think that's a great plan. Should we order her ticket now?" Victoria says. "Before she changes her mind."

Kate's eyes brighten. "Yes, good idea and good point!" She pulls out her cell phone from her pocket and searches for flights.

Victoria leans back in her chair, taking a deep breath. She thinks about the photograph she's kept with her for so many years–that's laying upright on her nightstand. It's the photograph that captures one of Victoria's favorite memories: when Hayley and Emma were just two years old and wearing matching pink one-piece swimsuits and holding onto each other tightly, smiling into the camera.

Her little girl is not so little anymore. So much time between the photograph and now has passed.

Before Victoria can say another word, thick tears fall from her eyes. Then, she says. "It's actually happening. We'll finally have a chance to see each other, to start over."

Kate looks up from her phone, immediately seeing Victoria's tears. "Hey, don't cry," Kate says softly, reaching for Victoria's hands. "Yes, you will! It's so exciting. I want you to be happy, no tears."

"I am happy," Victoria says, and then laughs as more tears fall. "I really am. They're happy tears. This is all that I've ever wanted, and it's finally happening."

* * *

MY APARTMENT– UPTOWN MINNEAPOLIS, MINNESOTA

ME

It's an hour before Brandon's shift and he drives me home to my apartment complex. We quietly chat during the drive, but I'm mostly quiet. My mind refuses to stop racing, but at the same time, I'm thoughtless. How is that possible? I don't know how but it's happening.

Brandon holds onto my leg all the way to my apartment, which helps me to relax. Now parked in front of the complex, I turn towards Brandon and thank him again, even though I must've thanked him a dozen times already.

Brandon looks at me understandingly, seemingly noticing the hesitation in my voice. "I'm here for you, remember? Let me know what you need."

I nod. "I will. Thank you."

Gently, he kisses me, and again, I melt into his embrace. Eventually, I pull away from his touch and smile up at Brandon. "I really appreciate you. You know that, right?"

His smile turns upward. "You better."

Brandon kisses the top of my hand before I motion towards the car door. His gesture is small, but it's everything I need at that moment.

I wave a final goodbye and head towards the apartment complex. Taking a deep breath, I open the door and step inside. It's difficult not to think about Emma. I keep myself distracted by thinking about Brandon.

Since moving to Minnesota, I've come across many amazing people, including phenomenal mentors in my university program, to whom I could've opened up if I wanted. But I never did. It felt too risky. But with Brandon, it's easy. I've never met anyone like him before, someone who can make me feel so safe, calm, and secure at any moment.

There hasn't been one time that I mentioned my hallucinations or past to anyone. Not Catherine. Not Lille. Nobody. It's been easier that way. When all I've ever done in life is run away from what's happened to me and my family, it's nearly impossible to trust anyone. For years, I felt exploited by the media and police, and didn't want to give anyone else the power to make me feel that way again.

While I know I need to be my own hero and my own healer, Brandon feels like a close second. He somehow makes it easier for me to feel like I can embrace the hard things in my life, including my past.

Now, I walk inside the apartment that's filled with chatter. Catherine is standing near the sink in a sports bra, shorts, and glasses. She's filling up the water dispenser as Lillie sits across from her on a barstool.

Instantly, they look at me. In a sing-song voice, Catherine says, "Well, well, well. Look what the cat dragged in."

Don't think about what happened last night. Don't think about Emma or anything.

I fake chuckle and take off my shoes. "Well, good morning."

Catherine places the water dispenser back in the fridge and keeps an eye on me. "So, you stayed at Brandon's last night, hugh? I thought I was gonna have to fill out a missing person's profile since you didn't answer your phone."

I laugh again. "I texted you, remember? He was in the area and it was just easier to go with him."

"Surreeee," Catherine says, rolling her eyes sarcastically.

Thankfully, Catherine and Lillie don't ask for too many more details. I deflect from the conversation, and we talk about the fun details of the previous night—from Catherine and Lillie's point of view, of course. Not mine.

As they take turns telling their stories, I continue to throw in fake giggles and follow-up questions so nothing looks suspicious. Yet, as the conversation continues, I don't say anything else. Part of me wants to contribute, but part of me also wants to scream. The words—wrapped up like a confession—are on the tip of my tongue. But it feels as if I'm constrained, as if I'm tied up and my mouth is covered.

Trapped. Trapped in my body. Trapped with my own thoughts.

Eventually, the conversation halts and I'm able to sneak away to the bathroom. Washing the night off seems like a great first step. I close the door behind me and strip off my clothes—avoiding looking in the mirror like I always do. Then, as I'm about to pull back the shower curtain, my phone lights up. I look down at the screen. An email notification is there. The subject line reads 'FWD: Your trip confirmation (MSP – ANO).'

ANO: The Ted Stevens Anchorage International Airport.

I sigh, realizing I'm officially going to Alaska.

Chapter 33

When Wednesday finally comes, anxiety boils in me as if I'm a teapot ready to burst. For years, I promised myself that I would never return home to Alaska, and here I am. Doing just that.

The flight from Minneapolis to Anchorage is around six hours, and I'm sitting in the aisle on the plane. I doze in and out of sleep, blinking myself awake when my eyes have gone closed for too long. What keeps me from falling asleep fully isn't my anxiety, but what seems like my intuition. It's like it's whisper-screaming at me, trying to tell me that something isn't right. That something is happening.

Or is this just my fear of going to Alaska rather than my intuition? I'm not sure.

I jump in my seat when the intercom wakes me. My eyes flutter open all the way, and the person next to me also wakes up.

Over the intercom, the pilot says, "Hi, folks, we are now descending into Anchorage. We're about 30 minutes from the gate—"

I don't hear the rest. Instead, my mind finally goes quiet, and I turn towards the airplane window. The land is on fire with beauty from the Fall. Knife-tip mountains cover the landscape, and hardwood trees are decorated with the oranges and yellows of aspens. Cars on the interstate look like toys and out of place since nature is the star of the show.

Nothing is ugly. Nothing is average. That's Alaska, a tourist hotspot filled with beautiful scenery that never gets old.

As I continue to look out the window, I realize that I feel like a tourist more than a person returning to the place she grew up. I guess that's not the worst thing.

What feels like only moments later, the plane lands. While I wait with the rest of the passengers to get off the plane, guilt washes over me. Am I betraying myself for coming back to Alaska? Am I weak for coming back here?

When it gets closer to my turn to exit the plane, I stand up from my seat, ignoring my thoughts. With my carry-on luggage in hand, I stroll down the aisle and off the plane.

A burst of familiarity hits me as I step into the airport. Goosebumps cover my arms, but I keep walking.

The Ted Stevens Anchorage International Airport is the type of airport that's big enough to feel busy, but not so big that it's overwhelming. It's also filled with art that commemorates the history of Alaska, including depictions of a variety of wildlife, Alaska Native handicraft, and artwork displays. The airport always reminds me of my childhood. As a kid, Emma and I would make David take us to see the polar bear exhibit before going to our gate.

Sweat forms on my forehead as nostalgia overwhelms me. I pass the familiar eating spots like the McDonalds where I'd get biscuits as a kid when traveling to see my grandparents in California. Then comes the Norton Sound Seafood House, where we'd eat often if we got to the airport early.

I exit the terminal and head to the pick-up station. Walking outside, I immediately see Kate, and my heart drops to my stomach. She's dressed in a black denim jacket and cargo pants. Kate's blonde hair is pulled back into a low ponytail, and simple gold earrings hang from her earlobes. She's thinner, a lot thinner than what I remember, and she looks as if she hasn't slept in weeks. Neither Natalie nor Michael are with her.

Instead of nervousness, excitement fills me when I see her which is a strange feeling.

When I'm near enough, I hug Kate. Again, it's hard not to notice the dark circles around her eyes. The touch shakes me completely awake.

"Hayley, it's so good to see you," Kate says, almost looking as if she's going to cry. "Thank you so much for coming. It's been so long!"

Then, she pulls me into a hug again, holding me to her for a few minutes. Tears form in my eyes but I ignore them.

"How are you?" she asks.

I exhale, looking away momentarily. "I'm not sure."

Kate pulls away, looking down at me gently. "We're going to get everything figured out, okay?"

"Wait, Kate," I say, my throat thick with mucus. "What's actually going on?"

Kate's face drops. "I can't say just yet."

My eyebrows furrow. "Why not? You said that you and... David...need to sit down with me to tell me."

"And we will. Just not yet."

"You're scaring me," I say. "Why can't you just tell me now? I'm already going through a lot right now and I don't want to have to wait to have this conversation with you guys."

"We have to get out of the way," she says, deflecting and motioning towards the other vehicles behind hers. "I promise we'll talk about it soon."

I exhale, feeling as if we're in a game of charades. Quickly, I throw my luggage in the back of the vehicle and climb into the passenger's seat.

Kate drives away and out of the airport. We're both quiet. The radio isn't even playing in the background. Instead, the only sound is the vehicle driving against the pavement.

I look out the window, feeling frustration boil. It feels as if secrets are being kept from me.

Eventually, Kate speaks. "How was your flight?"

I don't answer her question. "Why can't you tell me now, Kate?"

She keeps her eyes on the road. "It's complicated." Tears swell in her eyes, and my heart drops to my stomach.

"Kate, what's wrong? It's making you cry?"

She keeps her eyes forward at the road. Kate hardly blinks even though tears begin to slide down her cheeks. "Let's please wait until we get home to talk about this."

"You're scaring me," I say again, and my voice cracks. "Can't we just talk about it now, please? I came all the way here."

Her voice is barely a whisper. "Soon. I promise. We're almost there anyway."

Silence fills the car again, neither of us speak. I decide to not keep pressing, and look out the window and wait until we're at the house.

For twenty minutes, Kate drives through and then out of Anchorage. The radio now plays lightly in the background as a distraction. We drive towards the city's outskirts, which I don't remember well. Eventually, though, I see it: David's new home. Kate sent pictures last year, but I don't remember if I ever took the time to actually look at them.

It's beautiful.

The house is the exact opposite of the one I grew up in. It's ginormous, geometrical, and white with black accents; it looks to be right out of an architectural magazine. The number of windows seems endless, and the greenery and plants around the perimeter are manicured professionally. The space around the home even looks to be on fire with beauty from the oranges and yellows of aspens and hardwood trees.

Kate pulls into the driveway, which is long and zigzags up to the house. Multiple vehicles are parked near the garage, which is strange.

Kate puts the vehicle in park and pauses before speaking. "Hayley, thank you again for coming." The tears in her eyes have dried, and a gentle smile is on her face. "You ready to go inside? We can finally talk now."

I nod, but don't say anything. As I look back at the house, I see David standing in the doorway.

His face is cold and expressionless, exactly how I remember him.

Chapter 34

DAVID AND MIA ROSSI'S HOUSE– ANCHORAGE, ALASKA

VICTORIA

Finally. They're here.

Victoria observes from the second-floor bedroom window, holding the curtain open enough to see but without being seen. Her heart races and sweat pools on her forehead as she sees Kate's vehicle pull into the driveway.

"This is it," Victoria whispers. "Hayley's in here."

Time stops as her eyes follow the vehicle driving on the zigzag driveway. *Will Hayley want to see me today? Did Kate mention anything to her yet? How is Hayley going to react?*

Victoria's mind is racing but everything around her feels still. It's as if all of the atoms in the world have frozen in place. She's almost too scared to blink, because what if she misses Hayley?

Victoria squints, trying to see Hayley through the windshield as the vehicle gets closer, but she doesn't see anything. The windshield is too dark and far away to see any details. However, as the vehicle gets closer and parks, the outline of someone in the front seat is visible.

It's her.

Slowly, Victoria pulls the curtains back a little bit more. *Why aren't they getting out yet?*

A few more minutes pass but eventually, the vehicle doors open. Finally, Victoria sees Hayley for the first time in almost fifteen years.

* * *

DAVID AND MIA ROSSI'S HOUSE– ANCHORAGE, ALASKA

ME

I'm taken back. David standing in the doorway doesn't look like the David I remember when I left for college. Sure, his face is cold and expressionless, exactly how I remember him. But physically, he looks different. There's grayness in his dark hair, deep lines on his forehead, and a sadness in his eyes.

Eventually, he waves at me. Then, Kate hops out of the vehicle, grabbing my luggage before I can and, together, we walk towards the house. When we get close enough, David greets the both of us.

"Hi, Dad," I say.

Standing stoically, David reaches out to give me a hug. The touch is awkward, as he's never been a hugger, but I embrace him anyway—trying not to let myself be undone right there and then with my emotions.

He pulls away seconds later and asks, "How was your flight?"

"Long, but I'm here."

Mia stands in the doorway, greeting me and is the next one to give me a hug. Soon, we're all just standing in the entryway, awkwardly waiting for someone to make the next move.

I clear my throat. "So, what's going on?"

David's eyes widen slightly, and he meets Kate's gaze. She doesn't react and instead says, "Let's go inside. We can talk."

Finally.

David shuffles us all inside the house, and I'm awestruck by its beauty. I take off my shoes slowly, mesmerized by the sight around me. It isn't until Kate drops my luggage by the staircase when I snap out of it.

It's finally time to learn what's going on.

Mia excuses herself politely, heading upstairs, while Kate guides me into the all-white, modern kitchen. Seated at the giant glass table in the breakfast nook are a man and a woman, neither of whom I recognize.

Who are these people and why are they here? Is this an intervention? Didn't David and Kate do this to Victoria once?

I stop in my tracks and pull away from Kate's touch. "What's going on?"

"Take a seat first," Kate whispers.

Then, Kate pulls back a kitchen chair from the table and motions me to sit. David walks into view and leans his body against the sink. His arms are crossed, and he doesn't make eye contact with me.

I want to speak again, but my head is spinning too much for me to focus on my words. Reluctantly, I take a seat next to Kate.

This must be bad.

"Hi, Hayley," the man says from across the table. "My name is Paul Sullivan, and this is Dr. Leanne Johnson."

Doctor?

I side-eye Kate. She really told David already about my schizophrenia? He just had to bring in another doctor to the house to deal with this?

"So, that's what this is about, huh?" I ask Kate.

Kate's eyebrows turn inward. "What?"

"About what I told you on the phone. About me potentially having schizophrenia. You brought them here because of that."

"What?' David asks. "You think you have schizophrenia?"

The surprising in David's voice catches me off guard. Wait, he doesn't know? What is this about, then?

Kate looks at David nervously, but then turns back to me. "No, it's not about that. We can talk about that in a bit."

"What's this about, then?"

David clears his throat. "Let me just cut to the chase. Hayley, you're here because…we thought it was best to tell you this news in person. Something like this isn't…appropriate…over the phone."

"Okay?"

My heart starts to race.

David continues, "Before you say anything, we need you to listen to everything first. There's a lot of information that needs to be covered. We have Paul and Leanne here for support and to help us communicate if need be."

I look at the two new faces across from me. Strangely, their eyes don't meet mine. They're focused on David still.

"Yes," Kate says, grabbing my hand gently, "we need you to have an open mind and listen to everything first."

Her soft touch causes goosebumps to cover my arms. I take a deep breath, reminding myself to be brave. To prepare for the worst, but expect the best.

I nod.

David clears his throat. "I'm just going to get right to it. Hayley…our murder case has been reopened."

It takes me a few seconds, but then the meaning hits me. My mouth drops open. Our case has been reopened?

David continues, "New evidence has recently been brought forward and—" He pauses, and tears swell in his eyes.

My heart drops to my stomach, realizing the last time I saw him cry was at Emma's funeral. And that's when I hear the words that could break me.

David continues, "This is going to be hard to hear, but your mother was wrongly accused of Emma's murder."

Chapter 35

DAVID AND MIA ROSSI'S HOUSE– ANCHORAGE, ALASKA

ME

This is real. This is really happening.

I hear my name being called, but I don't move. Over and over I remind myself that what's happening in front of me is real. David is real. Kate is real. Paul and Leanne are real. This news is real.

David's words echo in my mind, over and over again: 'Your mother was wrongly accused of Emma's murder.'

It's at this moment when I don't know what to think, let alone say, to the concerned and broken faces around me. I remain a statue—frozen in place, unsure if I'm still in my body or not.

Sure, the words around me are inaudible. Only my thoughts come through.

"Hayley, are you okay? Hayley?" Kate says.

I hear Kate's voice, but it's as if I'm a third-party entity, out of my body and in another room. Each time she speaks, she sounds quieter, and I retreat further into my mind.

My chest is tight, and I hold my breath.

Victoria's innocent? He's saying she's innocent. So Victoria didn't do it?

Multiple emotions hit me all at once. Disbelief, sadness, grief, confusion—all battling it out for the spotlight in my mind. She never did it? Victoria didn't kill Emma like they said. The story that was told to me—and the one I told myself—isn't true.

Then, the image of Victoria pops into my mind. She smiles a gentle, relieved smile.

"NO!" I scream. The sound echoes throughout the house, causing everyone to jump and stop talking.

"Hayley!" Kate reaches for me slowly. "It's okay."

"No, it's not! What's happening?" I ask breathlessly, pushing away her touch. "This can't be true. It can't!"

Desperately, I try to think through everything about the night of the murder. Even though I don't want to, I do. However, the details don't come up. All I remember is that it was a cold night when Victoria and I ran through the woods and that she was desperate to find a way out. I was so young, only seven years old and was terrified as we ran like animals in the dark. I'd look up at Victoria with tears in my eyes, crying and asking where Emma was.

And then, the most painful thought slips into my mind: I didn't believe Victoria, nobody did.

I come back to reality. My thoughts disappear, but my head is still spinning. "No, no, no. This isn't happening. You're really telling me she didn't do it?"

I hear Paul begin to speak, but I don't comprehend his words. Instead, my thoughts do all of the talking.

Victoria never did it. She never killed Emma, and I didn't believe her.

Victoria's face pops into my mind and guilt washes over me. I think back to all the times I cursed her name under my breath and spoke ill about her. How I was embarrassed to be compared to Victoria each time a family member said how much we looked alike. I think about how much shame I felt for being artistically talented, all because I knew my mother also had the same gift. Most importantly, I remember how rarely I questioned what actually happened that night.

What if I'd gone to a traditional therapist more often and tried to talk about that night? Would I have remembered what happened that night? Would I have come to the conclusion that she was innocent all along? What if I could've been the one to help her?

This proves that I hated Victoria for no reason.

That's when I hear Paul's words more clearly and can make out what he's saying, "In other words, the trial against your mother has been represented as an injustice. David and Kate wanted me to mention this, but they decided that it was best if you didn't see Victoria—"

My ears instantly perk up when I hear her name again.

Coldly, I stare at Paul. "What did you say?"

He looks at me regrettably and then glances over to David, as if asking for permission to repeat himself. Paul clears his throat and repeats, "The trial—"

"I got that," I say. "What do you mean by that last part?"

Paul pauses again. "Your family decided it was best if you didn't see Victoria—"

They didn't let me see Victoria? For years, they told me Victoria didn't want to see *me*. Hence why I didn't get any phone calls, letters, or messages.

I look at Kate and David in disgust. "Is this true? You both told me she didn't want to see me."

They're both quiet, which gives me my answer.

"You lied, you lied to me!"

My head is dizzy as the image of Victoria makes a home in my mind. My heart breaks as I think of her. Heartbreak consumes me as I realize I'll spend another lifetime getting over this. Like a deity, the truth had always been there lurking—refusing to leave—and now we could all finally see it.

I can't help it and a scream escapes from my mouth, "YOU MADE ME HATE HER! How could you? She was my mom and she didn't do it! Why would you keep me from her and lie to my face about it?" The words feel like poison as I spit them out but I don't care.

"Hayley—" David protests.

I think of Victoria fondly now, which I've never done. Sure, it doesn't mask the pain. It only distracts me momentarily until the anger returns again.

"How could you?" I yell. "I needed her!"

"We thought it was best if you didn't see her," David starts. "You were so young, Hayley and—"

Tears fall down my cheeks as I interrupt David. "Let's call it what it is. A lie. You told me that she didn't want to see me."

David yells, "I thought she killed Emma, Hayley! Any father would've done what I did. How could we...I...just let Victorita see you after everything that happened? I wasn't going to let her—"

"It doesn't matter!" I yelled back. "It should've been *my* choice to see her. For years, you let me believe that she hated me. Maybe if I would've seen her, this would've been figured out sooner. But now we're here."

The truth hurts: Victoria never did it, and I didn't believe her. For years, she rotted away in the hospital for nothing.

Kate shakes her head. "Hayley, you don't know what it was like to see Victoria in the state she was in and—"

Something snaps in me and the words slip out of my mouth, "But I needed my mom. I needed *her*, Kate. Not you, as much as you wanted to pretend to be my mom."

As soon as I say my words, I regret them. Pain visibly overtakes Kate. This is probably the first time I've watched myself break someone's heart.

"Kate, I'm sorry," I say, looking down. "I didn't mean it."

She nods, looking away, so I don't see the tears in her eyes. I want to say something again to Kate but David whispers, "We tried our best."

His words sting and I can't focus. Instead, I do what I do best and I run. Without hesitation, my feet move me. I grab Kate's keys from the kitchen island and run towards the front door.

"Don't follow me!" I scream behind me.

"Where are you going?" David yells.

"Just don't follow me! I'll be back. I need some space."

Outside, the fresh air feels nice on my skin but I hardly notice it. I feel as if I'm on fire, a familiar feeling. I race towards the vehicle and jump inside. Every cell in my body wants to drive to the hospital to see Victoria, but I can't yet.

What would I say? How would I go about that?

Instead, I drive to the only place I know to go, where the little blue house used to be. It's the place where I became an only child.

Chapter 36

DAVID AND MIA ROSSI'S HOUSE– ANCHORAGE, ALASKA

VICTORIA

Hayley finally knows the truth.

Victoria is still upstairs, briefly hearing the conversation from the kitchen but remaining out of the way. Earlier, she'd agreed to stay in her room during their conversation. It was easier that way. However, Victoria broke that promise. She hovered in the hallway on the second floor. Victoria couldn't make herself stay in her room when her daughter was finally in the house.

Victoria needed to hear Hayley's voice—not over the phone like before, but in real life. Unfortunately, she could only hear muffled sounds, at least until the screams started. *What is going on?*

Eventually, she hears footsteps from downstairs and then the front door slams. *Who just left?* Victoria races to her bedroom window, seeing Hayley. She watches anxiously from the window as her daughter drives away in Kate's vehicle—aching for her daughter to return.

Where is she going? Why isn't anyone following her to get her? She isn't going back to Minnesota, is she?

Without thinking, Victoria races down the stairs and into the kitchen, where she sees David, Kate, Paul, and Leanne.

David jumps at seeing Victoria. "Victoria, what are you doing down here? I thought you were going to stay upstairs and—" David begins.

"Where is she?" Victoria interrupts and asks breathlessly. "Where's Hayley going?"

David looks away as if in shame. "I don't know but she said she'll be back. She said she needs space."

Victoria looks back and forth between Kate and David. "Why aren't you following her? Go and get her! What if she goes back to Minnesota?"

"She's not going to leave," David says calmly. "She said she'll be back. At this point, we just need to trust her word."

"How do you know that?" Victoria asks, and then stares at David. "She could just be saying that. Please follow her. Make sure she's okay."

David nods. "Okay." He storms off into the garage, closing the door behind him.

Around the kitchen corner comes Mia, who stares at Victoria and Kate nervously.

"What's going on? I heard screaming," Mia says. Her brown eyes are filled with franticness.

"Hayley left," Victoria says.

"She's coming back though," Kate says reassuringly. "The news was a lot for her to take in."

Mia's lips purse, but she nods. "Where'd she go?"

"We don't know. She just took my car," Kate says.

"She took your car?" Mia says in disbelief.

Everyone is quiet.

Victoria turns towards Paul and Leanne noticing how they're not intruding—presumably giving the family the space. It's a nice change.

"When do you think she'll be back?" Victoria asks.

"I'm not sure," Kate says, looking over at Paul and Leanne. "What do you guys think?"

Leanne clears her throat and sits up straighter in her seat. "I'm assuming she's processing everything right now. A lot's happening, so I don't blame her. I'm sure she doesn't have the tools to cope, so that's why she ran."

Kate sighs, dropping her head in her hands.

"What did you all say?" Victoria asks.

Paul says, "That you were falsely accused and indicted. Oh, and that David made the choice for Hayley not to see you while she was growing up."

She knows some of the details then. As much as Victoria wants to hold her daughter and tell Hayley that nothing else matters besides her, Victoria knows she's hurting. Victoria can imagine Hayley's experiencing a lot of emotions just like Victoria once had—presumably guilt, shame, sadness, and frustration.

Victoria thinks back to nearly fifteen years ago, when David told Victoria in the hospital that he didn't want Hayley to be around her. At first Victoria didn't agree, but eventually she did. As the truth of what happened got further and further away from her, Victoria couldn't help but believe all of the terrible things the news and court system said about her.

Tears fill Victoria's eyes. The weight of remembering everything is exhausting. She clears her throat. "Does she…does she know the details of the tape?"

Paul shakes his head. "No, not yet. She doesn't even know there's a tape. We didn't get that far."

Victoria's throat becomes tight.

Will Hayley still want to see me? Victoria exhales sharply, walking away and going back upstairs.

* * *

PROPERTY OF CHILDHOOD HOME– ANCHORAGE, ALASKA

ME

My mouth hangs open as I look out the driver's seat window. I'm parked on the street near a large red house. It's what replaced our little blue house, my childhood home, after the fire. Rumor has it that tourists still drive by here, whispering under their breath something along the lines of, 'This is where the Rossi murder happened.'

It's all entertainment for them, while it's my reality. Everyone forgets that.

Thick tears fall down my cheeks as I observe the house. My hands are still on the steering wheel even though I have no plans to drive away. Here is where I need to be, no matter how scared I am. As I was driving earlier, I didn't know where else to go besides here. Maybe some memories will come to me if I stick around long enough.

I close my eyes, imagining the blue house. Sadly, nothing was salvageable after the fire except a bible in the living room.

Our lives were destroyed and an inaccurate story of what had happened grew stronger in the media.

For fifteen years, I believed the lie that Victoria killed Emma. And instead of putting my ego aside, I stayed away from her. Sure, both Kate and David told me that Victoria didn't want to see me, which made me believe that she hated me. But that was a lie, as well.

I should've known better. I should've questioned things more.

Yes, there's a heaviness in remembering, but I'm now seeing that there's more hurt, more damage, in not remembering.

I rest my head against the headrest and a memory is finally loosened.

Chapter 37

YEARS AGO IN DR. SUSAN FAUST'S
OFFICE– ANCHORAGE, ALASKA

ME

The memory is inflamed in my mind. Dr. Faust, my talk therapist, tries to give me her warmest smile, but I can tell she's frustrated with me. My-seven-year-old self can sense it as I watch her mouth purse after she repeats herself.

"Hayley, dear, what's on your mind?" Dr. Faust asks me gently.

I look up at her with an emotionless, pale face. But I don't say anything. No words leave my mouth, and I sit in silence. Silence continues to fill the space between us.

Dr. Faust tries again. "Hayley, sweetheart, can you tell me what's on your mind?"

Again, I want my words to be set free, but I can't do it. They won't leave my mouth. Instead, tears fill my eyes and my vision blurs. Now, instead of seeing Dr. Faust, she's replaced with Emma. Her face is emotionless just like mine.

My seven-year-old self gasps loudly when I see her. Emma's identical, piercing blues eyes stare deeply into mine. She looks at me as if she's trying to communicate with me telepathically.

Then, Emma's head aggressively leans backwards and then forward in the chair. She looks down, staring at her chest. A hole is near her heart. Blood spills out, pouring down her body and then filling the entire therapy room up.

Everything goes black.

That was the day I lost my voice—a voice that was hardly there to begin with.

I'm awakened from this memory from the sound of a large thump. My eyes blink open, and I immediately turn. Standing outside the vehicle's door is a man. He looks to be in his mid-forties and is staring at me angrily.

"I'm asking you to leave," he says loudly. "We've had enough tourists this week already."

Quickly, I wave at him nervously and mouth 'I'm sorry.' Shaking the memory away, I drive away, leaving the red house behind me.

I reach for my cell phone, ignoring the dozens of messages and phone calls that have popped up on the home screen. My fingers dial the memorized phone number, and Brandon answers.

"Hayley?" Brandon asks. "Hey, I was hoping you'd call. How was your flight?"

His voice calms me instantly, but it's not enough. Tears flow down my cheeks. "B-Brandon?"

The water coming from my eyes doesn't stop. It's as if I'm trapped in an emotional and inescapable limbo of emotions.

"Hayley? What's wrong?" Brandon asks. "Are you okay?"

My words want to be set free, and I let them. I finally ask for help. "Please. I can't do this."

"What's going on?"

"I need you. Please." My shoulders instantly drop and relax.

Brandon is quiet, but only for a few seconds. "I can be there in a few days. I have to move around a few things for work. Is this the green light for me to come?"

My heart wins this time and not my ego as I don't push Brandon away. "Yes. Please."

"That's all I need to hear," Brandon says. "I'll see you soon."

Chapter 38

DAVID AND MIA ROSSI'S HOUSE– ANCHORAGE, ALASKA

ME

I drive back to David and Mia's house. My shoulders are no longer near my ears but my head aches from crying. As I make my way back to the house, Brandon confirms with me his flight information and we discuss the details–everything like the airport pickup, what to pack, and what to expect. It's a nice distraction until I explain to him what I know so far about Victoria.

Brandon is patient and kind, only asking a few follow up questions. I can tell he doesn't want to upset me even more. When we hang up the phone, questions fill my mind as I drive back to the house. How did our case get reopened? How much longer is Victoria going to have to stay at the hospital? Does she know the truth yet?

Once I'm parked at David and Mia's house, I head back inside. The front door is unlocked and I step inside, bracing myself for the potential consequences of leaving unexpectedly and taking– stealing– Kate's vehicle.

Naturally, the first person I see is Kate. She's peeking around the corner that divides the kitchen and the living room. When our eyes meet, she doesn't grimace or look unhappy. Instead, a soft smile cracks on her face. "You're back. Where were you?"

"I needed to get out," I say, taking my shoes off.

"Understandable." Her soft smile returns. I can tell Kate wants to hug me, to comfort me. But I keep my distance. The trust between us is shattered. She plays a role in keeping me away from Victoria.

Quickly, I walk past her and into the kitchen. Seated at the table are Paul, Leanne, and Mia. Why are they still here? Where is David?

"Where's my dad?" I ask.

The garage door's opening echoes throughout the house.

"He needed to make sure you were okay," Kate answers quietly, walking into the kitchen and looking towards the garage.

I connect the dots and my eyebrows raise. "Oh, so he followed me?"

Kate doesn't answer me. Instead, she sits down at the kitchen table next to Mia. David comes in through the garage door, looking at me sternly.

"Ready to continue our conversation?" he asks.

Hearing his tone reminds me who I got my attitude from. "Yes."

David closes the door behind him and joins the others at the table. He motions for me to do the same.

"I need to see her," I say, sitting near Kate.

David's nods. "You will. You will see her. But first we need to talk to you about some things—some details."

"Okay, what are they?"

Paul clears his throat, then. "Hayley, I'm here to help explain what's going on and answer any questions you have. We know you're experiencing a lot of emotions right now, so I want to acknowledge that."

I bite down on my tongue, not wanting to interrupt.

Paul speaks again. He starts from the beginning, explaining how new evidence was brought forward to the police in an unexpected way. The new house owners had found a video tape in their mailbox one morning. Unfortunately, they—or any of their close neighbors—didn't have any security cameras on their property. If they had, the police would've been able to figure out more easily who left it there. They're currently trying to get street footage from a few blocks down but so far they've been unlucky.

Sweat forms on the back of my neck. "What's on the videotape?"

Paul hesitates before speaking. "It shows what happened that night, specifically your sister killed by a man who was wearing a black ski mask. I'll warn you now. The details are gruesome and… and they will hurt. Are you sure you're comfortable hearing this?"

My heart feels heavy in my chest. "Yes, I want to know," I whisper. "I need to know."

Paul nods. "Three people broke into your home that night, who were wearing black ski masks over their faces. We currently aren't able to identify who they are but we're trying our best. What we do know—because of the tape—is that they tied you and your sister to chairs in your home—"

My body is numb as Paul speaks. It's as if I'm hearing a story that actually doesn't belong to me but rather someone else.

"And then they killed Emma," I say, interrupting. "Why her and not me? Why not both of us? Does the tape explain that?"

Paul looks away from me nervously. "It alludes to it."

"How so?"

"This may be difficult to hear."

Kate caresses my back. Her touch is soft, but the energy inside of her is hard. I can sense I'm not going to like their answer.

"As if any of this is easy. I don't care," I say. "Why did they just kill Emma?"

Paul nods and continues, "The tape shows your mother being forced to pick which of her daughters' lives to spare."

Pick?

"So, you're saying Victoria had to choose between Emma and I? The man made her?"

"Yes."

"And she picked me?"

The room remains quiet and the energy changes. It shifts negatively, feeling heavy which ultimately gives me the answer to my question.

Eventually, Paul speaks. "No. She chose Emma."

My eyebrows turn inward. How didn't I remember this? "She wanted Emma to live?"

"Well, your mother picked Emma. She wanted you both to live but she was forced to choose only one of you."

My mouth drops open as the realization and reality slaps me. This man shot the wrong daughter. Victoria wanted to save Emma, not necessarily me.

"So, it's fair to say that I'm the one who was supposed to die?"

How does this entire conversation keep getting worse and worse? I look around the kitchen again, but nobody says anything.

Paul shakes his head. "Again, your mother didn't want you to die. Hayley, she was tormented. The tape shows how much Victoria was verbally, emotionally, and physically abused when—"

"But the tape also shows her choosing Emma?"

Paul takes his glasses off. "Yes."

I'm breathless because of his words. Like water exploding over a dam, thoughts flood inside my mind. I realize that Victoria had no choice since she was so-called tormented, but why didn't she choose me? Why did she have to even pick between us? What was the point in that, especially since I can't remember any of this? Is Victoria upset that Emma's the one who died and not me?

"I need another minute. Please."

I push away from the table, stand up, and leave the kitchen.

"Don't leave again!" David yells after me.

Instead of heading towards the front door, I quickly turn towards the large set of stairs. At least this house is large enough that I can get away somewhere.

"Hayley, no!" David screams after me. "Don't go up there."

I don't listen to him, and run up the stairs. When I'm at the top, I head towards the first bedroom door, the closest room to me.

Wiggling the doorknob, I realize it's locked.

Chapter 39

DAVID AND MIA ROSSI'S HOUSE– ANCHORAGE, ALASKA

ME

Kate calls from the stairs, "Hayley, come on. Just talk to us."

Again, I wiggle the doorknob but it doesn't budge. Maybe this is my sign to be mature and not run away from my problems. As I look down at Kate from the stairs, I'm reminded of the hurtful words I had said earlier to her. Guilt washes over me.

I sigh, heading back down the stairs. "Fine."

Kate looks at me surprised but doesn't say anything. I walk past her and into the kitchen, taking a seat again at the table.

Clearing my throat, I ask, "So did Victoria want to see me?"

David nods. "Yes."

My heart drops to my stomach and I shake my head.

"Hayley, please try to understand," Kate says quietly. "We—"

"*I* made the decision. Kate, don't blame yourself," David interrupts Kate and then continues. "Again, I ultimately was the one who made it, Hayley. I didn't want you to keep reliving those memories over and over again. Your mother wasn't well for many years. *Many* years. We weren't sure how she was going to—"

Excuses. Yes, part of me understands what David is saying but there's a part of me that doesn't want to accept this lack of accountability or the severity of the situation.

"You had no right to make the decision for me."

"I wanted to protect you," David says.

I shake my head. "I didn't need protection. I needed my mom. I'm never going to get that time back with her."

David nods. "Hayley, I'm sorry. I believed that's what was best for you at the time."

"Bullshit," I say.

David's voice gets louder, then. "Well what was I supposed to do then? You couldn't even look at a picture of Victoria until you were twelve, Hayley. How do you think that made me feel as a parent? That was *my wife*. She was the mother of my kids, and I thought she murdered my daughter for God's sake! I mean, Victoria even told me that night that she shot Emma. She confessed technically! Sure, I know now that isn't what really happened. It makes sense now that Victoria probably said she shot Emma because she had to choose between the two of you. At the time, I didn't want Victoria to destroy you like I thought she destroyed Emma. I'm your *father*. It's my job as a parent to protect you."

Kate cuts in. "Hayley, Victoria was unstable for years. She struggled so much after what happened to Emma. Like you, she didn't say anything for years. Not even to me."

"But why didn't anyone question her?" I asked, confused.

"What do you mean? Of course, they did. They tried. We all tried," Kate says. "We really did. Besides her initial confession, or what seemed to be a confession, she couldn't remember anything beyond a few fragments of memories. And this didn't come out until years later."

"Did you believe her then?" I say, shaking my head.

"That's it. I'm tired of this!" David yells. "Hayley, you have no idea how hard it was. Yes, we could've done better. I get that. But you have no right to judge the decisions we—I— made. Victoria wasn't getting better for years. You didn't get to see that side of her, thankfully. I mean for God's sake she confessed to shooting Emma! I lost a daughter *and* my wife, your mother, in a matter of minutes that night. I wasn't going to lose you, too."

Tears swell in my eyes as I watch my father explode in anger. Leanne gets up from the table, trying to soothe everyone. Nobody listens to her.

David's voice is softer this time. "Plus, all of this wasn't easy for Kate, either. She dropped out of college and moved in to help me with you. Plus, she never stopped visiting Victoria in the hospital. We all had to deal with this in one way or another. Nobody had it easy."

David continues, "I *had* to make this decision for you. When you started to get better, which wasn't until you were in middle school, I decided I wasn't going to let the past torment you anymore by bringing Victoria back into the picture. I wanted to give you a chance of living a normal life. We sacrificed a lot. All of us."

The tears finally fall down my cheeks. Not once have I ever thought of what it must've been like to be in David's shoes or Kate's for that matter. After all of this time, I've only really seen things from my point of view. Why? Because I'm the one who had to live through that night. Maybe David really was just doing his best he could with what he knew? Same with Kate.

I take a deep breath. "Fine, I understand. So when do I get to see her?"

"When do you want to?" David asks.

"I guess as soon as I can."

"How about now?"

"Now? Like go to the hospital now and see her?"

David shakes his head. "Well, no. Victoria's actually here in the house."

My head tilts. "What? I'm confused. So, you're telling me Victoria's no longer in the hospital and she's here?"

David says, "Yes. Are you ready to see her? We can wait if you think—"

No, I can't wait any longer. If she's really here, I need to see her now. "Of course, I want to see her now," I say. "I need to."

"Okay.... I'll go get her."

David gets up from the kitchen chair and turns the corner. Then, he calls what seems to be in the direction towards upstairs, saying, "She wants to see you."

A few seconds pass, and the familiar figure appears around the kitchen corner.

Chapter 40

DAVID AND MIA ROSSI'S HOUSE– ANCHORAGE, ALASKA

ME

She's here—Victoria is really standing in front of me. My mouth drops open, and I instinctively lean back in my chair. This isn't a figment of my imagination; it's not like the times I saw her in the mirror. This is undeniably real, and it's happening right now.

Victoria's lanky figure gracefully advances into the kitchen. Time seems to halt, as if it never existed to begin with. Dressed in dark blue jeans and a white shirt, Victoria exudes simplicity. A delicate gold chain necklace dangles above her heart, and her blue eyes gleam like two saucers.

In this frozen moment, Victoria appears just as I remember— almost identical to me. It's as if I'm standing in front of the mirror in my studio again. Her hair cascades long and beautiful, with the only difference being the gray streaks gracefully woven into her locks. It's not pulled back into a high bun as I recall; instead, a few strands hang loosely near the sides of her face. Victoria's face retains its lean structure, and her high cheekbones add elegance. The faint crow's feet around her eyes serve as a gentle reminder of her age.

For years, I imagined what it'd be like to see my mother again. Never could I have imagined a moment like this. Now, everything around me is spinning, and yet I can't get myself to look away from her. The fear lingers that if I look away, Victoria might vanish, much like the times before.

Victoria's bright blue eyes continue to look into mine, glistening with tears.

"I think it's best if we give them a moment if you're both comfortable with that," Leanne suggests, ushering David, Mia, and Kate out of the kitchen.

Now, standing face to face, it's just Victoria and me.

"Hi, Hayley," she says quietly. Her voice carries a gentleness I hadn't anticipated.

What should I say? How do we go from here? What is she thinking? All I can say is, "Hi."

Victoria moves slowly toward the kitchen table, pulling a chair out from under it, though she hesitates to sit. Instead, her gaze remains fixed on me.

Our eyes meet once more, and within hers, an entire library of untold stories resides—narratives I may never fully comprehend, yet now, perhaps, I'll have the chance to hear them.

Taking a deep breath, Victoria quivers. "Hayley…" Her voice breaks as tears stream down from her piercing blue eyes. "C-can I please hug you?"

My heart aches from her words. I stand up instantly and move towards her. The inner child in me reaches for her, letting her take me into her arms. Minutes pass, and Victoria doesn't let go of me. I don't let go of her—because what if she vanishes again?

Finally, Victoria pulls away, delicately brushing a strand of hair from my face. "Hayley. I am so sorry."

"I know."

Victoria tilts her head, studying me. "I love you so much, baby. Not once did I not think of you. I've always been with you."

Guilt washes over me. I reflect on all the times I silently cursed her, spoke ill of her. I harbored hatred for so long, and for what? Why didn't I question more, seek answers about what happened? Why did I settle for not remembering the details of that fateful night?

"I'm so sorry," I cry, covering my face. "I'm sorry I hated you for so long."

Victoria shakes her head. "Hayley, you didn't know. Nobody knew the truth."

I choke on my words, struggling to breathe. "But I should've. I should've done something, at the very least, tried to talk to you again. I-I'm sorry. I don't know what to say."

"You don't need to say anything," Victoria reassures me. "None of that matters anymore. We can't change anything that happened. What matters is that you're here. We're together, and that's the only thing I really care about now."

I melt into her words and wrap my arms around Victoria again, not wanting to let go.

* * *

DAVID AND MIA ROSSI'S HOUSE– ANCHORAGE, ALASKA

VICTORIA

It's her, it's really Hayley.

Hayley exhales sharply. "Hi."

Victoria's gaze remains fixed on her daughter, who sits nervously at the kitchen table. Despite recognizing the twenty-two-year-old before her, all Victoria can see is the image of seven-year-old Hayley.

A whirlwind of emotions surges within Victoria, her heart warming and then chilling. She maintains eye contact with Hayley until tears fill her own eyes.

"I think it's best if we give them a moment if you're both comfortable with that," Leanne suggests, ushering David, Mia, and Kate out of the kitchen.

Alone at last, the two of them share a space that harkens back to their last encounter in Chugach State Park. *What is she thinking? Is she still harboring resentment?*

Then, Victoria cries. She chokes on her words. "Can I please hug you?"

Hayley instantly stands up and reaches for Victoria, who takes her into her arms. Their embrace is everything and more than Victoria could need at the moment.

This is really, Hayley. This is my daughter. Victoria whispers, "Hayley, I am so sorry."

"I know."

A sigh of relief escapes Victoria as her shoulders drop. Tenderness colors her actions as she affectionately brushes a strand of hair from

Hayley's face. "I love you so much, baby. Not once did I not think of you. I've always been with you."

Hayley covers her face. "I'm so sorry. I'm sorry I hated you for so long."

Victoria's heart aches. "Hayley, you didn't know. Nobody knew the truth."

"But I should've. I should've done something, at the very least, tried to talk to you again. I-I'm sorry. I don't know what to say."

"You don't need to say anything," Victoria reassures Hayley. "None of that matters anymore. We can't change anything that happened. What matters is that you're here. We're together, and that's the only thing I really care about now."

Surprisingly, Hayley embraces Victoria once again, wrapping her mother in a tight hold that refuses to let go.

Chapter 41

DAVID AND MIA ROSSI'S HOUSE– ANCHORAGE, ALASKA

ME

Still in our embrace, eventually, Victoria and I gently pull away from each other. My eyes remain fixed on hers, still filled with awe.

Victoria is really here. I've touched her. This is not a figment of my imagination, as it was before.

"Can we talk?" Victoria asks, taking a seat in the chair she pulled out.

I nod. "Yes, please."

I gradually resume my place in the kitchen chair. Despite sitting side by side, an overwhelming sense of distance lingers between us. "I can't believe you're here. When did you get out of the hospital?" I inquire.

Has she been out that long? Have David and Kate known for that duration? Why haven't I seen anything in the news? "Honestly,

I can't remember. I think it was a few months ago. It's been a while," she replies.

My eyebrows raise.

"So you've been staying here?" I ask, brushing my hair back.

"Yes. The entire time."

Guilt tugs at me, but I force it aside. "I'm just surprised I never heard anything about this since you've been out for months. Our case was all over the news."

"Yeah, I'm not sure why either, but it must be because the video tape isn't public knowledge yet. It's nice, though, having some privacy."

I nod, reflecting on the times when privacy seemed like an elusive luxury. "So do you know what happens next? Can we file a wrongful civil case against the police? Someone involved in the trial? It's not right. It's not fair that you were wrongly convicted and held in the hospital for so long."

"I know. I think we can file that soon. Right now, the focus is on finding out who dropped off the videotape—more than anything."

I exhale sharply, shaking my head in disbelief. "I just can't believe it. You were put away for something you didn't do," I say. "Somebody has to be held responsible."

Victoria looks at me gently and briefly closes her eyes. "It'll happen. I trust that it will. At this point, I'm just trying to move forward. I've lost years of my life because of this... What I can do now is focus on rebuilding."

How can she be the bigger person in this situation? I wouldn't be able to do this.

Silence envelops us, and my thoughts shift to the videotape. I had just been at the property where the little blue house used to live, and the idea that someone planted that disturbing footage there turns my stomach. How was that night even captured on film? Does Victoria remember any of it?

I clear my throat. "Did they tell you about the videotape?"

She nods. "Yes, I actually chose not to watch it."

"They gave you the option?"

Victoria continues to nod. "Yes, all of us, actually. David, Kate, Michael, and Mia."

"So it really shows a man killing Emma? He was wearing a black ski mask apparently?"

"Yes, there were actually three of them that night," Victoria says. "Do you remember?"

I shake my head regrettably. "Not much, honestly. I really wish I did, though. Paul did tell me that there were three men there that night. Do you remember anything?"

"Yes, parts of what happened. But I didn't remember much for years. A little memory would come into my mind here and there, but I blocked a lot of it out. Since being here, I've remembered more."

I nod. "I guess I remember running through the woods with you. That's about it."

"You were only seven," Victoria smiles sadly. "It's understandable why you don't remember much."

I nod, breaking her eye contact. "Can I ask you another question?"

"Of course. You can ask as many as you'd like."

"I'm really nervous to ask it."

"Don't be," Victoria says. "Go ahead. What is it?"

It takes a few moments, but eventually, the words emerge. "Why didn't you choose me that night?"

Chapter 42

DAVID AND MIA ROSSI'S HOUSE– ANCHORAGE, ALASKA

ME

I'm breathless, shaking my head in amazement after hearing Victoria's answer. "Is it really that simple?"

Victoria reaches for my hand, her gaze tender "Yes, it is."

"So you didn't choose me because you just…panicked? You picked the first one of us who you saw?"

Victoria nods, tears pooling in her eyes. "Yes. I promise. That's the only reason. Please believe me," she says, almost pleading. "I know it may be hard to believe because it feels so personal, but I promise you this: I just panicked. I wasn't thinking clearly. I was being tortured by this man… thrown around the room, pushed, and hit. Trust me, I know none of that is an excuse—"

"But you were being tortured," I interrupt, nodding.

Victoria didn't choose Emma over me to be cruel or because she was her favorite. She ultimately didn't have a choice.

"Still it's no excuse." Tears form in Victoria's eyes. "I don't want you to think I chose Emma because of any other reason than it was random. I didn't love her more than you. I didn't like her more than you. It's none of that. It's my biggest regret, as in saying a name in general. I wish they just would've killed me instead."

I nod, allowing her words to sink in. "I believe you."

Victoria unravels at my affirmation, reaching out and embracing me. I yield to her touch, feeling the weight of regret dissipate from her shoulders.

A few seconds later, I pull away, gazing off in thought. "I have so many questions. Now that I'm thinking about it… This had to have been targeted. I know a lot of people don't think that it was, but it has to be. They must've known us, right? I mean, how could they tell Emma and me apart? If you said Emma, but they shot her, they must've done that on purpose."

Victoria nods. "You're probably onto something. Right now, nobody knows anything. That's what they're trying to figure out."

I shake my head again, lost in thought. None of this makes sense, or at least, a lot of it doesn't make sense. Why would these men just kill Emma and not me? We were innocent in all of this. And why didn't they kill Victoria? How was what happened recorded when a fire burned down the house? Did the men take the gun with them? How much does the tape show about what happened that night?

I take a deep breath, turning to face Victoria. "You know… even after hearing all of this, I still want to see this tape."

"You do?"

"I do… So, I know you already said you don't want to watch it, but if you change your mind, I think it could be good for us to watch it together."

"You and me?"

"Yes."

Victoria nods, gently taking my hand. "I can do that for you."

"Are you sure?" I ask.

"Yes. I'll be with you," Victoria reassures, squeezing my hand tighter. "It'll be okay. We'll be okay."

Chapter 43

DAVID AND MIA ROSSI'S HOUSE– ANCHORAGE, ALASKA

ME

It's been hours, and I'm officially emotionally burned out after today. It feels as though I've been in Alaska for weeks, despite it being the day my flight landed. The adrenaline and highs from all the new information and stimuli are subsiding, and I'm finally descending from the intense spectrum of emotions.

Before heading to bed, Mia graciously brings me a woven basket of toiletries, complete with a hotel-style robe, water bottles, snacks, tissues, toothbrush, and toothpaste. I express my gratitude, dropping my luggage near the floor in their guest room.

As Mia quietly exits, she asks me quietly about how I'm doing. Her eyes radiate empathy, devoid of any mischievous curiosity. I offer her a soft smile and nod. "I'm okay. Today has just been a lot. How are you doing?"

Mia quietly laughs. "I'm the last person you should ask that. I'm fine. I was mostly upstairs today. I wanted to give you guys some space."

"I appreciate that."

What I'm realizing is that everyone in our family is grappling with their own struggles. It's not just me who has suffered, clearly. Truthfully, I'm not sure how well Mia is handling all of this. I doubt I could manage it if I were in her shoes. Mia married a man with a complicated and dark past, and while she's involved somewhat with our family at times, I bet she often feels like an outsider. How does Mia seem okay with Victoria, her husband's ex-wife, staying at their home and taking up some of their space? How can it not be a lot for her to handle?

I clear my throat. "Mia, can I ask you something before you go?"

"Sure," she says softly, leaning against the doorframe.

Our eyes meet, and I continue, "How are you handling this?"

Mia lightly laughs, looking at me in confusion. "I think I should be the one asking you that."

I shake my head. "Sure, but this isn't just about me. This is also a lot for you to take on. I don't know how you're doing this."

Mia smiles gently. "You do what you have to do for the ones you love."

Before I can respond, there's a knock at the door. Kate stands in the doorway. "Hi, can I come in?" she asks gently.

Mia looks at me, then steps away from the door. "I'll see you tomorrow morning. Sleep well."

I wave at Mia and then turn towards Kate. "Hey, I thought you left already. It's late."

My body tenses as Kate enters the room. I reflect on our earlier conversation and the hurtful words I had spoken.

"I wanted to check in," Kate says. "Can we talk?"

"Sure, about what exactly?"

"Our conversation from earlier."

An exhale slips from my nostrils. I don't think this day is ever going to end. "Sure, I guess."

Slowly, Kate looks away and avoids making eye contact. Her words are quiet, almost inaudible. "I want to say... that I really wish you'd appreciate me more."

My heart drops to my stomach. I was expecting her to ask me how I'm doing, not this.

"What do you mean? You know I appreciate you. Today was—"

Kate interrupts me, frowning. "I don't think you do. You know, you're not the only one who's had to go through this."

Her words sting, just like my words had stung her earlier.

Kate clears her throat before speaking again. "Listen, Hayley. I know you've gone through a lot. So much actually. And I'm not comparing by any means, but sometimes...it seems like you forget you're not the only one going through this."

"Kate, I get that but after today—"

"Please let me finish," she says quietly. "After everything happened, I really tried my best to step up. Sure, I know I'll never be your mother or even somebody who's maybe really important to you, but you had nobody left. Only David. Not your grandparents, *my* mom and dad, Victoria, or Emma. In less than a year, everything changed. I wanted you to be protected, from the news, police, and the truth. I know you never asked me to do this and I'm not trying to guilt trip you, but I gave up so much to move in with David and help raise you. Yes, I wanted to do that, but it doesn't take away how much of a sacrifice it was."

Tears swim in my eyes as Kate speaks and I don't interrupt. I let her speak her truth.

Kate continues, "I mean, I felt partially responsible for what happened, Hayley. When I heard what Victoria—allegedly—

did, it broke me. I blamed myself for missing the warning signs, which in reality, were never there. Just like everyone else, I blamed everything on Victoria's schizophrenia. Of course, now I know the truth…about what actually happened. But at the time, I didn't. I thought she was the one who did it, and I blamed myself."

Kate continues, "I don't think you know this, but Victoria didn't talk to me or anybody for years, Hayley. Years. I tried desperately to get answers from her when I'd visit, but all I got was silence. Just from that behavior alone, of course I believed she did it. I thought Victoria was sitting in her remorse for killing Emma. So, years later, when she tried telling me the few memories she had, I didn't believe her.

"I wanted to protect you. You lost so much in such a short period of time. Remember how you had nightmares for years, at least until middle school? You also refused to talk for years, which is ironic since that's what was happening with Victoria. So that's why I agreed with David to keep her away from you. I made sure no phone calls, letters, or–"

"Letters?"

Kate meets my eye contact again. "Victoria wrote you letters. She'd give them to me when I'd visit her at the hospital. I never opened them or gave them to you because your father didn't want me to. Yes, I should've overruled that and just let you make that decision for yourself. But it's what I felt like I had to do."

"You have to be kidding me? Great, another thing to be upset with David about." What did Victoria write in those letters? Did she write memories in them? What if I would've read the letters; could I have figured out she was innocent?

Kate takes a deep breath in. "I know… it continues to be more and more for you to take in. I just really hope you can look back and see how much I was there for you, Hayley. How I did everything in my power to protect you. Again, I know I'll never be your mom, but I treated you like my sister. I was always there."

Tears roll down my cheeks as I watch Kate relive her pain, and I forget about the letters. Her pain feels like my pain.

I sit up from the bed, stand, and wrap my arms around Kate. "Kate, I'm sorry. I never thought of what it must've been like for you to go through this. I really didn't, selfishly."

She sinks further into my touch. "I just want you to know I tried. That I always looked out for your best interest."

"I finally see that now, Kate. Again, I'm sorry for making you feel this way."

Kate half-smiles. "Thank you. That means a lot. Clean slate?"

"Yes," I say, embracing her once more. "Deal."

Chapter 44

DAVID AND MIA ROSSI'S HOUSE– ANCHORAGE, ALASKA

ME

The next morning, reality shakes me awake. Not an alarm clock. No noise throughout the house. Just my reality. As I awake, my eyelids burn from all the tears I cried yesterday.

Groggily, I glance up at the ceiling. It's nearly ten in the morning here in Alaska; back home, it's almost one in the afternoon. For a few minutes, I sit in silence, reflecting on the past twenty-four hours. The memories replay in my mind like a movie, akin to a psychological thriller where I'm on the edge of my seat, unable to look away. So much has changed. The truth is out, and I can finally see perspectives beyond my own

When I head downstairs, the house remains quiet, even though it's midmorning. Entering the kitchen, I find Victoria near the coffee maker. She's dressed in a hotel-like robe, identical to mine, and her dark hair is pulled back in a high ponytail, reminiscent of how she looked when I was a kid in the mornings.

I jump slightly at the sight of her, reminding myself that Victoria is real, not just a hallucination like the ones in my art studio's mirror.

Victoria turns around, smiling softly. "Good morning."

"Morning," I greet, walking further into the kitchen.

Victoria smiles and then stirs creamer into her coffee. "How did you sleep?"

I shrug, reflecting on my conversation with Kate and Mia from last night. "Pretty good, considering yesterday."

Victoria nods, seemingly understanding, taking a sip of her coffee. Her face lights up as she observes me. "Want me to make you some coffee?"

"I'm okay," I decline. "I'm not much of a coffee drinker."

"Well, you didn't get that from me," she laughs. "Want to sit with me on the back porch? I do this every morning and have been out there for a while."

That sounds nice. "Sure."

Victoria leads me to the back porch door. Stepping outside, the mid-morning air is cool. Beautiful, towering trees blanket the land in front of us, reminding me again of fall. Brilliant colors of reds, oranges, and yellows decorate the branches.

"It's beautiful, isn't it?" Victoria remarks, watching me take in the view. "This time of year really is my favorite."

"Yes. I always forget how beautiful it is here."

Victoria and I take a seat, looking out at the trees again. The silence is nice between us, and yet it still feels awkward. Even though we're sitting next to one another, it still feels like there's so much distance between us. As I continue to observe the trees and sit in the silence, I'm reminded of my hallucinations. What if

I have one here? Should I bring this up to Victoria, especially now that the two of us are alone again?

"Hey, I want to talk to you about something."

Victoria nods, setting down her coffee. "Anything."

"So, this is really hard for me to talk about, but I-I think something is going on with me."

Victoria's head turns slightly, and she looks at me with gentle concern. "As in potentially having schizophrenia?"

She knows? My eyes widen. "What? How did you know?"

"I overheard Kate mention it before you came here."

Well, this makes things a bit easier. "Oh. Okay. Well, for the past few months, I've been having a lot of symptoms." I pause, observing her worried facial expression. "I understand if this is difficult for you to talk about."

Victoria shakes her head. "Don't worry, it's not." There's no disappointment in her voice. "What are your symptoms exactly?"

I sigh, reflecting on everything that's transpired over the past few months. It takes me a few seconds until I finally admit the truth. "I've been seeing and hearing things."

I observe the changes in Victoria's face. At first, her expression is focused and nervous, then her head tilts with curiosity.

"Like what?" she asks.

"Things that aren't there. Noises that just disappear. I've seen you."

"Me?"

That's when I recall seeing Victoria in the mirror, how her thin lips turned upward, giving me a small but relieved smile as she stared at me.

"Yes. You... Emma... and this figure that I've been seeing since I was a kid." I gulp, feeling my blood run cold. "It's this weird floating figure with a black hood. I saw it a lot growing up, standing in my doorway at night mostly. I saw it recently again in Minnesota."

"Wow, I'm speechless," Victoria responds. "How are you doing with this?"

"Not well."

Victoria notes, "You know what's really interesting? That you're seeing me and Emma?"

"Why? What did you usually hallucinate?"""

"Before, I'd see faces and hear laughing, crying, screaming, or random talking. I never saw anyone that I knew personally. You know what it felt like, though? Like the room was breathing. Like my eyes would see my reality but I'd experience a different parallel reality beyond it. We all have different experiences with it?"

"So do you think it was strange that I was seeing you and Emma?"

Victoria nods. "Not really, because what even is normal? Sure, a lot of what you're experiencing isn't what I did, but that doesn't mean you should compare. You're *you*. And you don't even know if you have schizophrenia. You just have some symptoms."

As a soft smile forms on my face from her words; safeness finally doesn't feel so far away anymore.

Chapter 45

The day passes by as Victoria and Hayley continue chatting on the back porch. The moment is precious as Victoria and Hayley talk for hours, diving into story after story. Hayley shares what she remembers from her childhood and her life back in Minnesota, giving Victoria the details she's always yearned to learn. *It finally feels like I'm starting to get to know Hayley.*

Victoria remembers how Kate would describe Hayley as logical, cold, and assertive to her as they sat in the hospital together. Deep down, Victoria always knew that none of those characteristics sounded right, and now Hayley could prove that.

On the other hand, Victoria shares more about her experiences with schizophrenia and what it was like to go through her diagnosis. For Victoria, it feels so good to finally let her side of the truth out, to set the details free. To be seen, heard, and encouraged. And surprisingly it's with her daughter.

As Victoria is about to talk about the night of the murder, the screen door slides open. Out pops Kate. Her smile is a little forced, but it's bright for the afternoon. A couple of decorated boxes are in Kate's hands. Instantly, Victoria's heart races—she recognizes the pattern on the boxes. *Wow, she finally brought them over.*

"Hi! Good morning," Kate says, closing the screen door behind her.

Victoria watches as Hayley's eyebrows turn inward, looking at the boxes. "Hey, whatcha got there?"

Kate looks at Victoria and then back to Hayley. "Well, I thought I'd bring these over since we talked about them last night. They're for you." She hands Hayley the boxes, who takes them into her lap.

Victoria clears her throat. "While I was...away at the hospital, I wrote you letters. They're the ones we were talking about."

Hayley's eyebrows turn inward again. Slowly, she lifts the lid off of the box and inside rests dozens of faded envelopes.

Victoria continues. "I always believed maybe one day you would read them when you were ready. A lot of them are similar because there were only so many updates I had for you, but I tried to write at least one letter per week. Sometimes more depending on how I was feeling and if I heard any news about you from Kate."

Hayley's shoulders drop as she combs through the pile of letters. Carefully, she inspects each one—as if they could rip in half at her touch.

It's surreal for Victoria to watch her daughter look through the letters she wrote years ago. They're filled with so many emotions, longing for connection, and genuine curiosity in Hayley's life. Yes, it pains Victoria that Kate hid these letters from Hayley for years. Yet, as more and more time goes on, Victoria starts to let go of the situation. *How can I hate someone who was indoctrinated with false information and who was so young?* There's softness and understanding when Victoria thinks of Kate now versus the feelings of frustration and disappointment she used to feel.

Kate sits down next to Victoria, watching as Hayley goes through the letters. "There's more boxes, by the way. I just brought over what I could find at my house. I'm missing quite a few, which is strange, so I'll have to search for them in the house." She looks at Victoria with a slight smile. "But trust me when I say there's a lot more."

Hayley nods, still combing through the pile of letters. She stares at them anxiously, clearly wanting to open the letters right there and then. "How many do you think you wrote in total?"

Victoria shrugs. "Probably hundreds."

"Wow," Hayley says, shaking her head in disbelief and looking back down at the letters. "Just in this box there's a lot. I'll read them later," Hayley says quietly, closing the lid.

Silence fills the space between the three of them until Kate says, "So, what's the plan for today?"

Hayley looks at Victoria and doesn't say anything.

"I'm going to call Paul soon. To tell him we want to watch the tape tomorrow," Victoria says. "I'm thinking the rest of the time we can just all spend time together."

Kate batted her eyelashes. "Wow, when did you decide that you wanted to watch it? I thought you weren't going to?"

Victoria looks at Hayley with a smile, feeling safe and proud to have her daughter near her side. "Change of plans, I guess. We decided that we're going to watch it...together."

"Wow, I'm proud of you both," Kate says, leaning in closer. "I think that's a really great idea actually." She turns to Hayley. "Do you want any information about what's on the tape? Not sure if that would be helpful or not."

Hayley shakes her head. "No, I think I'm okay actually. I already know what I need to know from yesterday. Any more information will just cause me to overthink more. I'd rather just go in and see."

Kate nods, "I totally get that. It'll be a lot to take in."

Hayley clears her throat and looks down nervously. "Oh, by the way, speaking of tomorrow. I know this may not be the best time," she says, "but I have an update."

Both Kate and Victoria glance at each other.

"What's that?" Kate asks.

Hayley grimaces slightly. "I know I should've mentioned this sooner, but my boyfriend is flying in tomorrow."

Victoria's eyebrows raise. Since when does Hayley have a boyfriend?

Kate's face drops in confusion. "Here to Alaska? Since when do you have a boyfriend?"

Hayley nods. "It's been awhile."

"Um, does he know what's going on?" Kate asks suspiciously.

"Most of it," Hayley says quietly but confidently. "That's why he's coming here. To support me and just honestly be here."

"Okay…When is he flying in tomorrow?"

Victoria clears her throat. "Late morning. Maybe we can pick him up before we go to the police station to watch the tape?"

Kate nods, looking impressed and simultaneously shocked by Hayley. "Sure. Well, looks like we're gonna have a full house around here."

Chapter 46

HIM (MIKE)

The three of them are in the first cabin. He, also known as Mike, sits across from his friends, Max and Charles.

"Are you sure about tomorrow?" Charles asks, clearing his throat and nervousness slips through his lips as she speaks. "I mean, it's just been awhile since we've done this. I know we're gonna do it no matter what, but…"

Tomorrow's going to happen even if the execution of it all kills Mike. *Why is he questioning things? He better not back out. He can't.*

A gentle smile forms on Mike's face, surprising Charles and Max. Slowly, Mike sets down the gun that was in his hand but is now on the folding table.

"Yes. I am sure," Mike says. "You know that this is the plan." Like always, Mike's voice is soft. Kind. But this time, there's a hint of frustration in it.

It's the first time the three of them have seen each other since Mike made the 54 hour drive from Minneapolis to Anchorage. Charles and Max were responsible for watching the cabins as Mike road tripped the scenic and epic drive through Canada to Anchorage, starting from Minneapolis.

With only his carry on and Hayley's canvas in the back of his vehicle, Mike made the trek home in about a week. It's something he's always wanted to do, especially as a park ranger. Mike spent all his time exploring Alaska, he wanted to include exploring Canada as part of their plan. Since Mike was the one who picked up the canvas, he didn't need to have it shipped somewhere in Alaska, which would've come across as suspicious and set off a red flag in Hayley's brain.

Now that Mike was home and Hayley was finally in Alaska, staying at the Rossi household according to Charles, they needed to move quickly if their plan was going to be executed smoothly by tomorrow. Who knew how much time the three of them had left before things would start getting more complicated?

Since yesterday morning, Mike had followed David to the hospital to continue to observe his work routine, Max watched Mia leave her for workout class, and Charles broke into Kate's house to steal the last of the boxes with Victoria's letters. Nothing went wrong and nobody saw them. Thankfully.

Things were finally wrapping up and today was the last day they'd have to get their plan in order. The only thing left was to get everything ready for Hayley here in the second cabin.

Slowly, Mike pulls out a gold key and passes it to Charles. "Here, be sure to lock the door when you're done organizing down there."

"Sure thing," Charles says, nodding.

As Mike puts his hand back in his pocket, his fingers against the photograph. He thinks of her again, Rebecca. A softness touches him but it doesn't last for long.

Mike takes a deep breath. "It's been fun boys. We're finally doing this again, and it feels great. Early this year, Max's execution went far beyond what we could imagine, mine will go well tomorrow, and later on in the New Year, Charles' will go excellent. I'm happy we get to do this again together." Mike says, setting his gun on the kitchen table.

And that's what the three of the men had in common: an animalistic need for constant, painful, and unimaginable revenge. Fifteen years ago only seemed like yesterday when they first met. This was their time again for another round of revenge. They'd been working together for over a decade and a half to grieve, heal, but also plot more revenge. It was a brotherhood that nobody would ever be able to understand nor be a part of.

Mike heads out the door, leaving the gun on the kitchen table and making his way to the second cabin only yards away. Mike thinks back to David. *David makes a living playing the role of God. Soon, he'll meet me—the man who has centered his life around playing the Devil.*

He presses his hand against his pocket, feeling the photograph through his clothes. "This is all for you, Rebecca."

Chapter 47

DAVID AND MIA ROSSI'S HOUSE– ANCHORAGE, ALASKA

ME

The afternoon unfolds peacefully, effortlessly slipping away. Victoria, Kate, and I share stories throughout most of the day, taking turns amidst a leisurely lunch. It's only as evening settles in that I manage to slip away for some alone time. In my hands, I carry the adorned boxes as I climb the stairs, making my way to my bedroom. Finally, I can enjoy the privacy to read them.

Seated on my bed, I open one of the lids and reach for the first envelope my fingers come into contact with. This particular one sports a red kiss-mark on the front. With slow and delicate movements, I unseal the envelope and immerse myself in the letter.

Dear Hayley,

I miss you very much, my dear. Guess what? Kate came the other day and showed me new pictures of you. You've gotten so big and have already started fourth grade?! I'm so excited for you! I wish I was there to see it all, sweet pea. I hear fourth grade is a great year, and I know you'll have a great time. Did you know that I still remember when I was in fourth grade? That was a long time ago, huh? I bet you can't imagine your mom being that little. I hope your daddy is doing well and that you and Kate are staying busy. Remember you always have Kate if you need anything. I can't wait to see all of the things you do this school year, baby. I love you very much. Please remember that.

Love, Mommy

As I finish reading, a teardrop lands on the letter, darkening and expanding the ink. Slowly, I wipe away the remnants of the tear from my face and set the letter down. I take a deep breath, feeling my emotions overwhelm me.

It hits me that Victoria truly wrote me letters, expressing genuine care. Shaking my head, I'm reminded of how Kate and David kept these from me for years. What if I had read these letters sooner? Would I have wanted to build a relationship with Victoria? I believe so. Could I have discerned her innocence earlier? Maybe.

The letters consistently remind me of Victoria's care and unwavering hope for me. Despite Kate and David withholding them, Victoria's calm demeanor when Kate handed over the letters stands out. How can she remain so composed? Victoria's incredible strength and resilience continue to leave me in awe. I honestly don't know how she does it. Just as Victoria often emphasizes, dwelling on the what-ifs doesn't serve me well.

I grab the next letter and my eyes read through each word carefully.

Dear Hayley,

How are you? How are your classes? Are you enjoying them so far? I'm not sure if you know this, but when I was your age, I loved art class. I remember we always had that class on Mondays and Thursdays. I remember making and designing puppets for a puppet show. Now that was fun. My second favorite class was music class, which we only had one day a week unfortunately. I always wished we could go more often. I love you very much.

Love, Mommy

Taking a deep breath, I open the next envelope. And the next one. And the next one after that. Throughout the night, I read and reread the letters. They vary in length, some brief and others long and elaborate, just as Victoria had warned.

After reading nearly half of the letters in one box, I resist the urge to go to Victoria's bedroom to discuss them. Even though I really want to, I hold back. I recognize the importance of being alone, especially after a full day of conversations with both Victoria and Kate.

Moreover, tomorrow is supposed to be busy as we plan to watch the tape, so getting some sleep is important. Plus, Brandon arrives in town tomorrow, and I'm looking forward to seeing him.

I lay my head on the pillow. Though it takes a few minutes, eventually, my eyes close. As I drift off to sleep, the image of the red lipstick kiss marks lingers in my mind. The color red stays vivid in my thoughts.

Chapter 48

ASLEEP AND DREAMING – ANCHORAGE, ALASKA

ME

Blood. There was so much blood that night.

It happened almost fifteen years ago. Normally I never remember the details from that haunting night. Yet, this time I do. It's as if a scalpel permanently carved the memory into my brain—it replays constantly like a broken reel.

The memory is a nightmare—feeling more like déjà vu on acid than anything. In it, I'm in my childhood home in Alaska; inside the little blue house. The only time I return here is when my head hits the pillow and my eyes close.

Everything is the same from that night, yet demonically and dramatically heightened. The hues of the living room are vibrant, shining like a social media filter. The smell of ashy smoke overwhelms my nostrils to the point where I wince—probably looking like I'm about to sneeze. The sound of the clock echoes in the empty room like a slow-beating drum, reminding me I'm alone.

I look down at my hands. They're tied tightly to the sides of a raggedy kitchen chair.

My throat tightens.

I push against the rope, feeling as if I'm an animal caught in a trap. The sound of the clock grows louder and picks up pace.

I give a final, aggressive push. Nothing budges, and I give up.

Then, to the left of me appears another kitchen chair. No one's sitting in it.

"Hello?" I call out.

My eyes scan the living room. I wait, pause, and then try again. This time, I call out her name. "Emma, where are—"

Immediately, I stop. My voice—the one that just spoke—doesn't belong to the twenty-two-year-old me. It belongs to a child.

Drops of sweat slip down my neck towards the middle of my back.

Looking down again, I see a pair of two short legs instead of my adult legs. They don't reach the floor, and white tights and a red checkered dress cover them.

The ticking of the clock speeds faster.

I stare at the other kitchen chair.

Suddenly, a fiery heat engulfs me, the intense sensation overwhelming my body. It becomes more and more painful as each second passes, but my eyes never look away from the kitchen chair.

Then, everything goes black.

I'm awake—just like all the other times before. The covers from my bed fall to the floor as my gasp startles me, but then the relief comes, just like it does every time.

"Thank God."

Upon hearing my current-day voice, I let tears fall from my eyes. They always do when I awaken from this recurring nightmare.

Darkness overcomes me until my eyes adjust. Slowly, I lay back down in my bed, leaving the covers on the floor. I'm too hot, trying not to think of the fire from the nightmare. Placing a hand on top of my heart, I feel it beat against my palm: it's the only noise in the room, and it reminds me of the clock.

I think of Victoria, who's in the room across from me. Maybe I should go to her and tell her about the dream. It's when I start to sit up that I realize I can't. I'm frozen, as if straight-jacketed to the bed.

The ticking grows louder and louder.

My chest tightens as I think of all the times before what's to come. "Don't think about it." Only a whisper escapes me. "Don't think about it. You're stronger than this, Hayley."

But I do. I do think about it—just like all the times before when I've thought of Victoria.

That's when *it* appears.

The shadow in the doorway.

And, suddenly, the ticking stops.

Yet, standing in the doorway is not the Phantom, but someone else.

Chapter 49

AWAKE FROM NIGHTMARE – ANCHORAGE, ALASKA

ME

A figure appears in the doorway. This time it has no hooded cloak, and its skin isn't gray or stained with blood. It's a person, but dressed in all black and the face is covered by a ski mask. Is it one of the three men who wore ski masks the night of the murder?

Memories from the night of the murder surge through my mind. Suddenly, the entire room plunges into darkness, and I can no longer discern the figure in the doorway. Initially, a memory unfolds—Victoria, Emma, and I together, visiting Malibu Beach—a tradition we upheld every winter during visits to my grandparents. We'd revel in the water, feed seagulls day-old bread, and gather seashells.

Next, I envision the times I'd sit outside David's bedroom door at night, listening to him seclude himself in his room and weep in our rental home since the little blue house had succumbed to the fire. Then, I see the dozens of reporters camped outside the rental home. How the flashing lights reminded me of gunshots, provoking my screams to echo constantly inside the walls of the house.

In the next wave of recollection, I vividly see the night of the murder, clearer than ever. The memory breaks free in my mind, revealing the presence of three men with black ski masks in our house, just as Paul had described. They seized Victoria, hurling and assaulting her, creating pools of blood on the floor, while Emma and I were bound to kitchen chairs by ropes, mirroring the scenes from my nightmares. A gunshot rang out, igniting a fire.

The scene goes dark, only to be replaced by Victoria waking me up in the woods, specifically in Chugach State Park. My breaths were shallow and noisy as Victoria clung to my hand, pulling me in every direction as we fled through the darkness and through the woods.

The memory persists, and finally, I remember.

* * *

DAVID AND MIA ROSSI'S HOUSE– ANCHORAGE, ALASKA

ME

The next morning, sunlight sneaks through the windows, casting playful dances across the room. My eyes flutter open, startled by the sound of my cell phone ringing. Still immersed in the intensity of last night's nightmare, I answer reluctantly, without bothering to check the caller ID.

"Hello?"

It's Brandon. His voice, which usually calms me, doesn't this time. "Good morning."

I blink away the lingering memories. "Hey, good morning. What time is it? Are you at the airport?"

"Yes, waiting at my gate now. How did you sleep?"

His question doesn't register. Instead, an overwhelming urge to rush into Victoria's room and share the details of my nightmare consumes me. Was the Phantom the man in the black ski mask? Did I really remember the night of the incident?

Brandon repeats his question.

I respond hastily, "Good. Hey, listen. We'll pick you up at the airport and head straight to the police station. I, uh, I've got to go."

"Is everything okay–"

"I'll call you back. I'm sorry, I've gotta take care of something quick."

The urge to tell Victoria only grows inside of me more. She's probably sitting on the porch by now, waiting for me downstairs.

I hang up my cell phone and wrap myself in my robe before walking out of the bedroom. Desperately, I want to run, but I remind myself there's no need. Mia is near, heading towards the stairs, and I don't want to alarm her.

"Good morning, sunshine," she says with a smile. "How'd you sleep?"

If only she knew.

"Good," I say, forcing myself to sound enthusiastic. "How'd you sleep?"

"Great!" Mia smiles larger. "Heading out to pilates. I'll be back later."

"Have a good time," I smile, and continue to walk. As I head towards the staircase to follow Mia, something catches my attention in the corner of my eyes.

I turn. Down the hallway stands a familiar figure.

It's Emma.

My mouth drops, but screams don't leave my mouth.

Emma stands and looks at me, warmly and curiously. She looks different from what I'm used to seeing her. Typically, Emma's long dark hair is in two messy braids, and she's wearing jean shorts and a white top with a puppy printed on it. However, this time, she's wearing the exact clothing from my nightmare last night.

Instead of disappearing as Emma normally does, she continues to stand in place as if challenging me. Frozen in place.

My throat is tight but her name is able to escape my mouth. "Emma?"

At the sound of her name, Emma runs. But instead of disappearing and vanishing at once—like she's done so many times before—I see her rush into Victoria's open bedroom ahead of me.

She calls my name from the bedroom. "Hayley?"

A pit in my stomach forms.

Without hesitation, I run to Victoria's bedroom. Once inside, I scan the room, realizing that I've never been in here before. Nobody is here, including Emma. For a few seconds, I examine the tall bookshelves in front of me filled with medical journals and expensive coffee-table books, king-sized bed, fireplace, and the abstract, gold light fixture in the middle of the ceiling. Near Victoria's nightstand by the bed, there lies a photograph. It's of me and Emma when we were younger, holding onto each other and wearing matching pink one-piece swimsuits.

Where is Emma?

Desperately, I search the bedroom, but she's nowhere to be found. It's not until I pass the large bay window that I see movement again. Emma is standing outside, looking up at me. Her blue eyes melt into mine, and one of her hands extends, pointing at something in front of her.

My eyes turn inward.

What's she doing?

I move closer to the window and look further downwards to see what she's pointing at. I can't see anything. What does she want me to see?

Then, I turn, racing out of the bedroom and down the stairs. Frantically, I open the front door and run outside to where Emma was standing. The late morning is cool, and the wind brushes against my neck. Emma's gone, disappeared again. I run towards the spot where she was standing, curious about what she was pointing at.

"Emma–"

Suddenly, something hits me. A sharp pain in my back causes me to fall forward onto my knees. The pain is excruciating. I try to scream, but a swift hand covers my mouth, stifling any sound. Darkness engulfs my vision as my eyes are covered.

I feel myself being carried away.

Chapter 50

DAVID AND MIA ROSSI'S HOUSE– ANCHORAGE, ALASKA

VICTORIA

It's morning and Victoria waits for Hayley to join her on the back porch. She expects Hayley will since she did so yesterday. These are the kind of mornings Victoria used to only dream about, never imagining she'd actually get to share them with her daughter. As she patiently waits for Hayley to wake up, Victoria immerses herself in *The Anchorage Daily News,* savoring the quiet moments with her morning coffee.

Victoria's eager to talk with Hayley about how she's feeling about watching the tape. She's very well aware that Hayley needs this closure, and, truthfully, so does Victoria. As mother and daughter, they'll embark on this journey together, seeking the answers they crave, not just for themselves but also for Emma.

Fond memories of Emma flood Victoria's thoughts, especially her infectious, gummy smile. A gentle chuckle escapes as Victoria reminisces about the playful days when Emma affectionately dubbed Hayley as 'Lee,' playfully navigating the challenge of pronouncing the elusive 'H.' As time unfolded, Emma effortlessly mastered the art, leaving behind a tapestry of heartwarming memories.

Victoria's lost in thought then as if gone with the wind. She wonders what Emma would be like if she were alive today. Would she and Hayley be close? Would Emma have also moved to Minnesota or gone somewhere else? Would the three of them get along into adulthood?

Suddenly, a scream pierces the air. Startled, Victoria jumps in her seat, the newspaper slipping from her hands, and the coffee cup shattering on the porch floor.

Her blood runs cold as the familiar scream echoes around her. Victoria stands and races inside the house. "Hello?" she calls frantically. "Hayley? Mia?"

Silence.

Victoria hurries through the kitchen and darts towards the entryway. Peering out the front window, she's greeted by an unexpected sight: a large man with his face concealed by a black ski mask. In mere moments, he's pulling Hayley toward the nearby street where a black van awaits.

Fear flashes in Victoria's eyes as her mind floods with memories. *Is this real? Am I truly witnessing this? It's been years since I experienced hallucinations.*

"This must be happening," Victoria says and places a hand against the wall to steady herself.

Move. You need to move. This has to be real.

Then, the man forcefully drags Hayley into the black van, and Victoria's heart plummets as if it were sinking into the ground.

"NO!" she shrieks, flinging open the door and sprinting outside, but it's useless. The vehicle speeds away down the street and fades into the distance.

In that moment, Victoria experiences a surreal detachment, as if she's an observer in the balcony of a theater. *Move! You have to follow them.* Adrenaline jolts her back to reality, and Victoria rushes back inside the house, seizing a pair of car keys. Sprinting toward the nearest vehicle outside, she vows to do whatever it takes to get her daughter back.

Chapter 51

BRANDON

The plane ride from Minneapolis to Anchorage is the longest flight
Brandon has ever been on. It's around six hours, but it feels longer.
During the flight, he occupies himself by working on a paper for a
graduate school class and listening to music.

As Brandon works on his graduate paper, he finds himself
thinking back to when Hayley first opened up to him about her
past. How she explained nervously that she hadn't shared it with
anyone before. Her vulnerability meant a lot to Brandon. It's
something he's never been good at doing. Even though it's only
been days since he last saw her, he already misses Hayley.

While Brandon has experienced various relationships in the
past, none have held his attention like the connection he shares

with Hayley. Despite her dark past, she somehow radiates a unique light, a quality Brandon finds both intriguing and effortless on her part.

Now more than ever, Brandon is committed to being there for Hayley when she needs support the most. He is determined to stand by her side in any way possible, acknowledging the challenges she has faced and appreciating the remarkable person she is.

After hours in the air, the plane finally touches down, prompting Brandon to switch off airplane mode on his cell phone. Surprisingly, there are no incoming messages from Hayley. His brows furrow as he gazes at the screen, a sense of anticipation tinged with curiosity.

"That's odd," he grumbles to himself.

Brandon quickly sends Hayley another message as he walks off the plane's ramp and into the terminal. While he waits for the sound of his phone to ring, Brandon walks through the airport, slightly entertained. To him, the Ted Stevens Anchorage International Airport is everything an Alaska airport should be: naturistic and with a small-town feel.

As he makes his way to baggage claim, he finally receives a call. However, it's not from Hayley like expected but rather from her aunt, Kate.

"Hello?"

"Is this Brandon?" the voice asks breathlessly.

"Yes, this is Kate, right?"

Kate exhales in relief. "Yes. Brandon, hi. I'm sorry you're meeting me under these circumstances but I'm calling to see if you've heard from Hayley? I know we are supposed to be there already to pick you up, but I can't find either Hayley or her mom, Victoria."

"I haven't heard from her since this morning before my flight. She said she was going to call me back but she never did."

"What did she say to you?"

"That you guys were going to pick me up and then we'd head to the police station," Brandon says.

Kate groans, a hint of distress in her voice. . "Oh no, is that it? She didn't say anything else or where she is?"

"No." *Where is she?*

Kate sighs. "Okay, well I'm at the house now and they're not here *and* not picking up their phone—both Hayley and Victoria. I doubt they're watching the videotape already. They would've let me know. What do you think?"

Brandon is speechless. His heart races as he listens to Kate while also basking in the weirdness of their conversation since this is the first time they've spoken.

"I'm not sure. It doesn't seem like her. Have you tried calling the police station? I'm sure they can let you know if they're there."

"Good idea! I'll call them now. Hang tight, I'll come pick you up now. Just wait there."

"I don't mind ubering. Let me do that so it's easier."

"Are you sure?"

"Yes, definitely." As Brandon inputs the address, a strange sensation gnaws at his stomach, adding an unsettling layer to the unfolding situation.

Chapter 52

SOMEWHERE DARK AND COLD– ANCHORAGE, ALASKA

ME

Survival mode. That's where my body is right now. I'm frozen, uncertain if it's been days or just hours since I last saw seven-year-old Emma. All I comprehend in this moment is the engulfing darkness, and I'm too scared to move—fearful of what might lurk in the shadows, afraid of being taken again.

I remember being forcibly dragged away. Now, I lie on a cold, concrete floor, goosebumps covering my arms and legs.

Tears well up as the harsh reality sets in—I am alone. Who took me? Why? Did anyone witness it? Did Victoria hear my screams? We were supposed to watch the tape today—Victoria and I. Surely, if she can't find me, she'll realize something is wrong, won't she? As I grapple with these questions, negativity and dread flood my mind. What awaits me? Who awaits me? Is this actually reality, or am I trapped in one of my nightmares?

Then, Victoria pops into my mind, right on cue. Sadness washes over me as I envision her face.

I'll never get to fix my relationship with her now. What if something happens to me, and now she has to go her whole life not knowing what happened to me?

I blink back tears, and they trace a path down my cheeks. "Today was supposed to be a good day," I whisper.

I need to try–try and figure out where I am. Don't lose faith.

That's when I sit up and start crawling around the space again. Stretching out my hand in front of me, I reach for something, anything. Finally, my fingers graze against a wall. I feel paper and what seems like tacks.

Why is there so much paper on the wall?

Then, a sound comes from above me.

Thump. Thump. Thump.

Instinctively, I look up even though my eyes only see darkness. The sound suggests that I'm beneath something—am I in a basement or on the first floor? Regardless of where I am, what I do know is that the person above me is the person who took me. It has to be.

My jaw starts quivering.

Please, God. Please, get me out of this alive. I'm begging you.

I hold my breath, attuned to the footsteps above me. Then, they stop, and it feels as if my heart stops too.

Suddenly, light bursts into the space around me, and my eyes instinctively close from the intensity. Gradually, they adjust, and I find myself gazing upward toward the source. A small opening in the ceiling reveals someone looking down at me—a figure concealed by a black ski mask.

My eyes widen as I fixate on the black ski mask—a memory all too familiar.

My eyes widen, locked on the black ski mask—a hauntingly familiar memory. Swiftly, I retreat against the wall, memories from the night of the murder casting a shadow over my vision. Words spill from my mouth before I can process them: "Please, please don't hurt me."

Certainly, this is connected.

The person, likely a man, remains silent. The sound is deafening.

"I'm begging you. Please don't hurt me!"

He reaches for something at his side, and my mind immediately conjures the image of a gun.

"No, no, no!"

Instead, it's long and black, hitting the ground with a resounding noise. Before I can react or say anything more, he closes the door, snuffing out the light, and once again, I find myself surrounded in darkness.

Quickly, I scurry away from the wall and in the direction of whatever he threw down. My hands guide me, and eventually I find the object. My fingers trace it, feeling the long aluminum structure. It takes me a few minutes to figure out what it is as I feel the texture.

A flashlight?

My fingers push down on its side, and it clicks. Golden light explodes into the darkness. I lift it up, observing the trap door at the very top where the man was standing. Then, I swing it around towards the walls.

When I realize what's surrounding me, a loud shriek escapes from my lungs.

Chapter 53

DRIVING TOWARDS CHUGACH STATE PARK–ANCHORAGE, ALASKA

VICTORIA

Behind the wheel for the first time in nearly fifteen years, Victoria follows the black van. Surprisingly, the muscle memory of driving returns, though fear takes hold of the wheel, propelling her down the road like a maniac.

Notably, Victoria is taken aback to find Mia's vehicle in the driveway. Mia usually carpooling with her workout buddy means she must have already left for pilates. Victoria shudders at the thought of what might have occurred had Mia's car not been there.

The man who abducted Hayley wore a black ski mask. That's what stand out over and over again in Victoria's mind.

Is this nightmare happening all over again?

Driving anxiously, Victoria scans and searches Mia's vehicle, desperately seeking anything useful. It finally dawns on her that she doesn't have a cell phone, never called the police, and has no idea where the man is heading. Still in her robe and slippers, Victoria feels utterly unprepared for the unfolding situation, causing guilt and shame to rush over her.

However, Victoria continues on. She follows the black van, remaining vigilant. *Does the man know I'm tailing him? How far should I stay back? Where are they taking Hayley?* The questions weigh on her mind as she presses on.

I'll do whatever it takes to get Hayley back. No matter what it is.

After navigating through Anchorage, the van now heads toward the outskirts of town. In mere moments, Victoria discerns its destination—Chugach State Park.

Memories from the night of the murder explode in her mind. The last time Victoria set foot here was when she and Hayley were wandering and running through the woods after waking up. Hayley's fear was palpable in the darkness, illuminated only by the moon and stars that shone brightly that night.

"We're reliving this all over again?" Victoria whispers, grappling with the surrealness of the situation. *This can't be happening. It just can't!*

As the black van enters the State Park, it accelerates, disappearing like a vanishing act. Victoria, trailing too far behind, loses sight of it.

Driving into the State Park, Victoria's body is drenched in sweat, and panic grips her.

Where did it go?!

Victoria pushes down on the accelerator and drives maniacally through the State Park, the memories bubbling up to the service in her mind again.

Keep driving! You have no choice!

Her chest tightens, making it difficult to breathe as Victoria tries to focus on the road, which is becoming smaller and smaller.

"Black ski masks," Victoria whispers. "He's wearing a black ski mask."

It has to be the men from that night. There's no other explanation.

"I'm not imagining this. I'm not imagining this," Victoria reminds herself. *This part of our lives was supposed to be over and here it is happening all over again.*

Again, the memories paint the inside of her eyes, distracting Victoria's focus on the road. She remembers how the men in ski masks grabbed her from the kitchen while she was cooking dinner, covered her mouth, and dragged her by the hair into the living room. Emma and Hayley's screams were loud, echoing throughout the entire blue house.

As if right out of a movie, the men made Victoria choose between the two of them— a memory that Victoria could never get herself to face and forced her mind to forget for so many years. It's a moment beyond comprehension, particularly for any mother. The men, their faces hidden behind ski masks, pointed a gun at Victoria, coercing her into choosing which of her daughters' lives she wanted to spare.

Victoria could only pick one—Emma or Hayley. Now, as if all at once, Victoria remembers clearly. Just thinking about this memory makes Victoria gasp out loud, bringing her back to reality. Tears stream down her face, obstructing her view of the road.

"I'm sorry, I'm sorry, I wasn't a better mom!" Victoria screams. "I'm sorry I chose Emma when I shouldn't have said anything."

In desperation, Victoria presses down harder on the accelerator, and then, a sudden burst of pressure strikes her body. After what feels like an eternity, Victoria eventually realizes she's been hit by an airbag, and the car has come to a halt. Peering out the window, she sees the front of the car mangled by a tree.

* * *

SOMEWHERE DARK AND COLD– ANCHORAGE, ALASKA

MIKE

He closes the trap door in the first cabin and stares down at it momentarily. *It's finally happening. The moment is finally here.*

Mike's face warms, and he consciously avoids dwelling on how scared Hayley must be. He vividly recalls the red flush on her face, a manifestation of fear and overwhelm. Calmly, Mike repeats to himself that this is a part of the plan. Succumbing to emotions and sympathy for Hayley would be foolish. It's not apart of the plan.

"Stop it. You need to do this."

As if on repeat, Mike reminds himself that he's doing this for Rebecca, for himself, and for his late child. There's a reason behind all of this, once again.

Suddenly, Hayley's screams echo down in the cellar. The noise startles Mike at first but then it intrigues him. *She's finally seeing what I left for her, visible all over the walls.*

What's on the walls serves as another reminder of why tonight needed to happen. More revenge is necessary because Hayley remains unaware of the truth. She needs to understand what really happened, and the walls will aid in that revelation.

Just as Mike is about to turn around, something touches his back. He pivots, only to find Max. How hadn't Mike heard him?

"Yes?" Mike says.

Max clears his throat, resembling a kid in a candy shop. "We're ready for phase two now. Charles is waiting in the car."

Mike nods, reminiscing on how far the three of them have come since meeting on that online community so many years ago. Finally, they are doing this again, united and in the name of justice.

"And you guys have everything? You know where the security cameras are at the hospital? David parks on the ground floor in the garage."

"Of course, we do," Max says. "He's going to take his lunch in less than an hour. We'll be parked close by and grab him."

"Perfect," Mike says. Everything needs to be in perfect order if we're going to pull this off successfully.

Mike nods proudly, heading towards the cabin door. "Let the games officially begin."

Chapter 54

SOMEWHERE DARK AND COLD– ANCHORAGE, ALASKA

ME

My shriek echoes as the flashlight slips from my hand, hitting the ground with a bang. Hastily, I retrieve it and direct its beam back onto the walls. Each of the four surfaces is plastered with hundreds, if not thousands, of printed pictures and newspaper clippings—no inch of bare space remains.

Drawing closer to one of the walls, my mouth hangs open in awe. The pictures predominantly feature me, creating a surreal collage that envelops the entire space. How did he get these pictures?

The walls narrate the story of my entire life, a montage capturing moments from my younger years at nine or ten to more recent ones. For instance, there's a picture of Emma and me being baptized at our family church, another from our time at the beach in Malibu, and dozens more from our grade school days—every photograph tells the story of my existence.

For a few extra seconds, I fixate on a picture of Emma and me playing in the sandbox outside our small blue house. This must have been only weeks or months before the murder.

Next, I come across a few images of me working in my art studio. These pictures stand out, appearing different from the rest, as if captured by something other than a cell phone or camera.

There are pictures of me sitting in my artist's chair, completing an invoice, and even one where I'm peering through the door keyhole—all clearly taken from within my apartment. My stomach drops. How is this possible?

"There's no way," I whisper. "There's no way he's been watching me this entire time."

How did he install a camera in my studio apartment? How did he find out where I lived? How is this happening again?

I reflect on the times when I accidentally left the studio door unlocked. Could that be it? Is that how he gained access to my place? Then, I recall the black van that followed me after work many weeks ago. Was that him, or did I hallucinate at that moment? Surely, that must have been him?

What was real and what wasn't—I honestly don't know at this point.

With a shaky hand, I guide the flashlight's beam toward the newspaper clippings. As I inch closer to the wall, I realize they mostly feature stories about the night of the murder.

Specifically, they're coverings of the investigation status, theories on where Emma's body was located, and detailed opinion pieces from strangers who clearly had too much time on their hands. Most of them ridiculed and villainized Victoria, using words and theories to cast ill will on her. Reading them confirms that my childhood memories of Victoria were, indeed, taken from these news clips rather than my actual reality.

Tears swell in my eyes as I read the hurtful headlines and see the dark and unpleasant photos of Victoria.

This isn't the truth. She never did it.

Continuing to move the flashlight across the walls, reading the articles, I eventually realize I'm no longer reading stories about the night of the murder. No. Instead, I'm surprisingly reading stories about the deaths of three women.

What are these? Why would he include these? What do these stories have to do with me?

I read the stories carefully and calculatedly. From what the articles say, all three women died from surgery complications in one way or another. When I get to the article towards the middle of the wall, my mouth drops wide open.

That's when I see her. "Oh my God," I gasp.

The article shows a picture of one of the women who was killed.

It's Beks. In the picture, she's smiling brightly. Her green eyes stare back at me warmly, and she's wearing a casual, summer dress and silver earrings.

"How? How is that Beks?" I whisper.

I think back to the night I met Beks for the first time.

'Hello, dear. My name's Rebecca, but you can call me Beks.'

But she's supposed to be dead? It clearly shows here that she's dead. So I imagined her, as well, at my apartment? Why? How?

'I apologize for just dropping over, but I heard a scream coming from your place.'

I back away from the wall, letting the flashlight drop to my side. My chest tightens, and I can no longer breathe. Shaking, I desperately search for an exit or anything that can help me escape.

"No, no, no!" I scream, pressing my hands against the wall. "This isn't happening. This isn't real."

Suddenly, I trip over something, losing my balance and falling to the ground. After sitting up and reclaiming the flashlight again, I direct its beam to see what caused the stumble. Boxes are stacked in the corner, and a thin sheet covers a sizable object behind them.

Taking a deep breath, I shine the light again. Nervously, I open the first box. I pull the lid off and inside are letters, all addressed to me. A profound sense of heartbreak washes over me.

"No," I whisper, dropping the lid down. Is this why Kate couldn't find the rest of Victoria's letters? How did he take them from her?

I recall what Kate said. *"I have all of them, too. Again, I just need to find them."*

Then, I remember the thin sheet. So far, everything in this space has a purpose, so what is behind the sheet?

Carefully, I move a few boxes out of my way and grab the delicate fabric. I pull it aggressively, and it falls to the floor, bunching at the bottom.

Glancing up, recognition overwhelms me immediately. My heart plummets to my stomach like a triggered avalanche.

"Impossible."

Chapter 55

CHUGACH STATE PARK– ANCHORAGE, ALASKA

VICTORIA

"No!" Victoria screams, her voice piercing through the tense air. "No, no, no!"

Her gaze fixates on the wisps of smoke emerging from the hood of the vehicle, panic gripping her like a chokehold. *What have I done? How am I going to find Hayley now?*

Victoria springs out of the car, slamming the door behind her. The twin headlights cast sharp beams into the surrounding trees, accentuating her isolation in the dark woods.

"I'll find her. I have to find Hayley."

Victoria repeats the mantra until it becomes a lifeline. She opens the car door, turns off the engine, retrieves the keys, and searches the back seat once more, hoping to find anything that could help her. Despite her earlier inspection, nothing new reveals itself. Plastic cups and water bottles clutter the car floor, offering no potential weapons.

Giving up on the vehicle, Victoria starts walking, still wearing her robe and slippers. The Fall morning gradually slips into afternoon, but Victoria persists. She doesn't stop walking, not even once.

A bald eagle circles above, casting a menacing shadow. Familiar feelings of vulnerability engulf Victoria, yet determination fuels her.

"I'll find her. I'll find Hayley."

She forges ahead through the branches until a trail appears. After hours of walking, a distant reflective light catches Victoria's attention. She halts for the first time, turning toward the glimmer through the trees. It appears to emanate from some sort of structure. A cabin?

Could Hayley be inside?

Without hesitation, Victoria navigates through the trees, pushing past branches, and hopes that the light holds answers.

Chapter 56

SOMEWHERE DARK AND COLD– ANCHORAGE, ALASKA

ME

"Impossible," I say again, my voice cracking.

In a state of awe, I stand before what was once concealed by the thin sheet. It's the canvas I toiled on all summer, adorned with blue and white abstracts and the golden chariot—a project into which I poured every ounce of energy, even during my hallucinations.

"No, no, no," I whisper, still looking up at the painting. "This can't be real."

I exhale sharply, dropping to my knees.

So, he bought it? This man was my client?

The man with the black ski mask's name is Mike? This is a game to him. He inquired and paid for my painting to infiltrate my life and mentally torment me. That's why the letters are here, as well. The pictures. The news articles. Everything has a purpose.

But what is it?

Why is he doing this again?

Then the realization hits me: I need to figure out how to play his game if I'm going to survive.

Quickly, I revisit the articles on the walls, taking my time to absorb the information. It takes a while, but I gradually piece together more details. As far as I understand, Beks and the other two women, Kari and Jordan, all passed away due to surgery or birth complications. That information is clearly accurate, as it was the main focus of the articles. However, Kari and Jordan were not from Alaska, unlike Beks, who hailed from Memphis and a small town in Connecticut, respectively. What stands out the most is that when Beks died during labor, along with her baby son, she was in an Anchorage hospital.

Specifically, the hospital where David works at.

Thump. Thump. Thump.

The sound of footsteps returns, indicating that the man—Mike—must be back. I lift my gaze from the newspaper clipping, flashing the light above and toward the trapdoor.

Seconds later, the trapdoor opens. I lean against the wall adorned with pictures and newspaper articles. Light bursts from below. It takes my eyes a few seconds to adjust, but when they do, the first thing I see is the ski mask covering his face.

My jaw quivers before I speak. "What do you want?"

Silence envelops the space between us. As I've always believed, Victoria taught me that silence often speaks more than words can, and Mike is proving that to be true at this moment.

Despite the danger, I understand the necessity and the importance of saying something. I need a response from him. "Your name is Mike, right? You bought my painting."

Silence lingers, but I continue anyway.

"What am I doing here?" Tears well up in my eyes. "Please, please tell me!"

The man shifts, lowering himself into a crouch position above the trapdoor. He clears his throat. "I'm sorry you have to be in the middle of this."

The familiarity of his voice hits me. I heard that voice only days ago. It belongs to Mike, the man standing over six feet tall with deep-set wrinkles on his forehead and whiskers above his lip. The day he picked up the canvas was the same day he acted strangely—looking up towards my ceiling as he was about to leave and then standing outside my studio door, eerily gazing through the eyehole.

I recall his words. 'I'm sorry'?

Why is he apologizing?

"In the middle of what?" I ask. "What do you mean?"

He pauses before responding, "Hayley, did you look at the walls?"

Goosebumps ripple across my body as he utters my name. "Yes, I saw all the pictures. I read every article. You bought my painting."

"Everything?"

"Yes, I read everything."

He nods, still crouching down. "So, you should know why you're here then."

No, I don't. But I need to keep him talking. "No. But I know that you're the man who broke into my house when I was little. The man who killed my sister, aren't you?"

Silence.

"Tell me! Please!" I scream.

Triggered by my scream, Mike stands up and shakes his head. "Hayley, you deserve to know the truth. The reason why you're here is because of your evil and conniving father, David. He killed my wife, Rebecca. Rebecca Martin."

Beks.

My mouth drops open.

Mike continues before I can say anything. "You should know this from the walls already, but let me remind you: she died of cardiac arrest while delivering our son, Matthew. Your pathetic excuse of a father didn't give my wife the right amount of oxygen and medication when the epidural was administered. And she died, along with my son who also during childbirth. David did this."

I shake my head back and forth.

Is this true? Did David actually do this or is Mike lying? Either way, the conviction in his voice is scaring me.

He continued, "I tried going to the authorities and the hospital to report him... his malpractice, but they didn't believe me. They didn't do anything."

Slowly, Mike pulls something from his pocket. Again, I imagine it's a gun but it's not. It's a photograph. At least that's what it looks like it is. He moves it only inches from his face.

I need to keep him talking. "So it is you. You're the person who killed my sister, aren't you? You're the one who broke in and killed her?"

The man pauses before speaking. "And David is the one who killed my wife."

He admitted it. The man loosely admitted he's the person who broke into our home and killed Emma. Not Victoria.

Tears slide down my cheeks. "Why? Why us? Why did you have to do this to us?"

"You really want to know?"

"Yes!"

Mike doesn't hesitate, and the words cut deep. "To break up your father's family like he broke mine. If he's going to play God, I can play the Devil."

Mike steps away and the trap door closes.

Chapter 57

CHUGACH STATE PARK– ANCHORAGE, ALASKA

VICTORIA

Rushing through the trees, Victoria pushes past the branches, getting closer and closer to the light in the distance. Every second counts, and she knows it.

As Victoria pushes past the last set of branches, she realizes the light is coming from a post. It shines brightly, highlighting the small, run-down cabin, which looks like it could cave in after one snowfall this winter.

"Is she in there?" Victoria whispers.

Steadying her breath, Victoria approaches the cabin, walks up the steps, and reaches for the doorknob slowly, discovering it's locked.

Victoria sighs, wiggling the doorknob again.

"What if Hayley's in there?"

Victoria races down the steps and then runs around the cabin, looking for something that will help her get inside. As she searches, she thinks about the men in ski masks and how they were able to break into their blue home through the glass sliding door—just like how she's breaking into this cabin now.

Hurry, I must hurry.

At the rear of the cabin, a porch comes into view. Victoria rushes up the stairs, noting a glass sliding door. She shakes her head at the irony, and to her surprise, the door is unlocked and opens easily. Silently, Victoria steps inside, greeted by darkness. The wooden floor beneath her feels unsteady, as if it might collapse at any moment.

Victoria gulps, extending her hands to touch the wall, searching for a light switch. *What if someone is in here?* At this point, it doesn't matter. Eventually, she finds one, feeling its outline.

Despite the danger, Victoria quiets her worrisome mind and flips the light switch. White light floods the cabin.

She freezes, waiting for a sound. A presence. Anything.

But there's only silence.

When she realizes the cabin is empty, Victoria begins to search. A 1970's refrigerator and freezer occupy what might pass for a kitchen. The entire cabin is tiny, so her search doesn't take long. In the center of the kitchen and living room, there's a red and white rug, a folding table strewn with piles of papers and beer cans, and a recliner in the corner.

Heading toward the one-bedroom, Victoria finds it empty, with only a mattress on the floor. As she rushes back into the kitchen, her foot snags on the red and white rug, and in one quick motion, she falls, hitting the floor with a loud bang.

"Ow!"

It takes her a few seconds, but Victoria gets back on her feet, ignoring the pain overwhelming her body. Then, she hears something.

Thump. Thump. Thump.

It's coming from underneath her.

"What was that?" she whispers.

Victoria hears the sound again, a staccato tapping. Slowly, she drops to her knees and brings her ear down towards the wooden floor, listening carefully.

Looking up, Victoria notices the red and white rug snagged in front of her. Hidden underneath the rug is a trapdoor with a keyhole.

Hayley must be down there!

Crawling toward the trapdoor, Victoria reaches for the handle and lock. She pulls on the door, but it doesn't budge.

"Find the key," Victoria whispers to herself. "There has to be a key around here somewhere."

Again, Victoria races throughout the cabin, checking every corner and pile of junk for the key. As she searches, her memory is on fire. She tries to focus on her search, but all she can see are the memories in her mind from that night.

Sliding glass door. Men in black ski masks. Chugach State Park.

As Victoria races back into the kitchen, she slams into the folding table. A dingle and a bang echo throughout the cabin, causing Victoria to snap out of it. She looks down at the wooden floor, piles of papers on the floor from the table along with the gold key and a gun.

The gun makes her stomach churn.

Quickly, Victoria reaches and grabs the gold key and the gun. In swift motions, she drops to her knees at the trapdoor. With a shaky hand, she pushes the key inside the lock, and it immediately clicks when turning it.

"I'm coming, Hayley," Victoria whispers.

In one swift motion, Victoria swings the trapdoor open. She looks down below at the space beneath her. It's mostly dark, except for a few faint spots where the light creeps into the picture.

Then, a figure approaches the opening below Victoria. Almost immediately, she recognizes the figure, who is now looking up at her.

Victoria lets out a gasp.

* * *

CABIN 1 IN CHUGACH STATE PARK – ANCHORAGE, ALASKA

MIKE

Once more, Mike seals the trapdoor, leaving Hayley to the shadows of both darkness and truth. He exhales sharply, reminding himself that he isn't the one inflicting pain upon her. It's David who's been causing Hayley's suffering, the same David who took Rebecca's life. If only David hadn't murdered Rebecca, Mike wouldn't be compelled to enact this harrowing scenario once again.

David Rossi, an anesthesiologist turned murderer.

The truth, a dream Mike had harbored for years, is now laid bare before Hayley.

Taking a deep breath, Mike places the gold key gently on the folded kitchen table, deviating from his usual practice of stashing it in his pocket. After Rebecca's tragic death, Mike had sought justice tirelessly, repeatedly approaching the authorities. Even without concrete proof of David's culpability, Mike sensed the presence of something deeply unethical in the fate that befell his wife.

Predictably, nobody believed Mike; there was no investigation, no one willing to lend an ear—except for Charles and Max. Mike had connected with them through an online grief community years later. They not only listened but also empathized, understanding the profound loss each had endured.

Within weeks, the trio discovered a shared bond of wrongful deaths in their families, a cosmic sign that they were destined to unite for a purpose—vengeance, a pursuit of justice that was long overdue. After years of friendship, they solidified their plan for retribution against those who had wronged them, starting with the Rossi family, and then targeting Kari and Jordan for Max and Charles.

It had to unfold this way. David, with his fatal mistakes and a myopic worldview, saw the world in stark black and white. Mike, fueled by the desire to destroy David's perfectly controlled world, aimed to shatter the illusions surrounding that fateful night and expose the truth.

Now, Mike thinks back to the times when he'd watched David from afar. For years, Mike studied him as if Mike were the doctor and David were the patient. Following the night of the murder, David underwent severe emotional and mental distress. He transformed into a single father overnight, lost a daughter, and saw his marriage crumble.

But it wasn't enough. Mike knew the night of the incident would never be enough. Fifteen years ago, he crafted a plan that transcended them all, encompassing tonight's actions.

Mike places a hand over his pocket, above the photograph, dismissing any sympathy gnawing at his conscience for Hayley.

"Soon, it'll be done, Beks. Very soon."

David wanted to play God, so I became his Devil. Now, it's time to be his Rumpelstiltskin.

Chapter 58

ME

The trapdoor opens once more. I find myself in the same position, sitting and leaning against the wall. Time seems indeterminate, whether hours or minutes have slipped away remains uncertain. All that envelops me is overwhelm, confusion, and fear.

Mike stands above me once again, and I nervously gaze up at him. In a swift motion, he reaches for something behind him. A flexible rope ladder cascades down, dangling from the trapdoor. I watch as the ladder swings back and forth until it steadies, triggering a memory from the night of the murder: a man grabs seven-year-old me and two kitchen chairs, tying me to one of them with a rope.

Quickly, I stand up, pressing my body against the wall, my eyes fixed on the ladder.

Mike's voice is unemotional and harsh. "Climb."

I glance back and forth between him and the ladder.

"No, please!" I scream, shaking my head vehemently. What awaits me at the top?

Suddenly, my thoughts are interrupted by a stampede of commotion above me. More footsteps hit the floorboards, and muffled screams echo throughout the space above me. What's going on? Who else is here?

Again, I look at the ladder. "Please don't make me do this."

"I'm not going to keep asking you." Mike slowly reaches down to his side. I expect him to pull out the photograph, the one he was looking at previously. But he doesn't. This time, my intuition was right all along. Mike pulls out a gun and points the trigger right at me.

"No, please. Don't!" I scream, pushing back against the wall again. This is it. This is the end.

"Climb!" Mike yells, shaking the gun at me. "Don't make me keep asking!"

The sound of his scream echoes through the space around me, causing me to instantly jump. Without thinking, I walk toward the ladder, shaking and nearly falling to the ground as I put one foot in front of the other.

Approaching the ladder, I observe the rope again. Placing a hand on top of my heart, I feel it beat against my palm. It's the only noise in the room, and it reminds me of the clock.

I look up at Mike at the top of the trap door. With the gun still pointing at me, he catches my glance and then yells, "WHAT DID I JUST SAY?! Climb!"

I jump again, feeling tears fall down my face. It's at this moment when I realize that nobody is going to know what happened to me. Victoria. Kate. David. Mia. They'll all think I ran off, not wanting to face reality or heal our relationships.

Slowly, I climb the ladder and do what I'm told—heading towards the unimaginable. As I climb, Victoria pops into my mind, and I feel immense burning in my stomach. All she wanted was to start over with me. And we're never going to get to do that.

I'm never going to get to see her again.

We're never going to rebuild our relationship.

Then, I think of David. Even though he apparently is the reason for what's happening, I don't know if it's the truth or not. For all I know, this could be a complete lie. Regardless, David is still my dad. I'm never going to know if what Mike's telling me is true.

Mike yells, "Keep climbing!"

I must've slowed down. I keep climbing even though every step makes me feel more terrified to know what's at the very top. Eventually, I arrive near the top of the ladder. Before I can see what's above, hands grab me. Immediately, my body is picked up, just like what had happened outside at David and Mia's house.

I scream, kicking and punching, but it doesn't do any good. My eyes adjust to the light, and I see two figures restraining me. Just like Mike, they both have black ski masks covering their eyes, and I can't make out their faces.

This is happening again, and it's just like the night of the murder. It's happening again.

Within seconds, the rush of adrenaline in my body subsides, replaced by an overwhelming sense of fear. The realization hits me as my mouth is covered by something, and I scream through the tape, "Please don't do this!"

In a matter of moments, I'm lowered and forcefully dropped into a chair. My gaze falls, and I find myself bound to the chair. As I glance downward, I catch sight of a pair of long legs, but my thoughts harken back to the days of my own shorter legs, adorned in white tights and a red checkered dress so many years ago.

It's a haunting echo of the past—a cruel déjà vu.

"No, no, no!" I scream through the duct tape, pushing aggressively against the rope. Just like that night so long ago, I don't budge.

A movement catches my eye, and I look up to see David, trapped and tied to a chair like me, but across the room, far away.

"Oh my God!" I scream through the tape.

His mouth is also covered, and he's looking at me. Tears stream down his red face.

'*To break up your father's family like he broke mine.*'

Is all of this true? Of course, I want to ask David if it is but does it really matter now? Everything feels as if it's too late.

Suddenly, one of the three men in ski masks seizes another chair and positions it beside me. My heart drops to my stomach as I watch him fix its position.

Then, Mike strides toward me with the gun still in his hand, but it's pointed to the ground now. As he gets closer, he eventually faces me. His eyes are brown, and unexpectedly, they're also filled with tears.

Mike clears his throat as he looks down at me. "I'm sorry. I have to do this."

Before I can respond, I'm distracted by more movement in the corner of my eyes. I turn and that's when I see her. One of the men in the ski masks is holding onto someone. Her face is elongated, but not as much as mine. She's leaner than me, almost too lean, and our hair, skin, and eyes are all perfect matches.

I gasp through the duct tape covering my mouth.

"Emma?!"

Chapter 59

I gasp loudly through the duct tape, pushing against the rope, feeling like an animal ensnared in a trap. And there she is—Emma. Standing before me, her chest rises and falls with each breath, confusion swimming in her eyes as she stares at me, and her footsteps echo loudly. It's not the seven-year-old Emma I've been envisioning for months in my hallucinations, but a reflection of the present twenty-two-year-old me.

She's alive?! How is she alive?

Emma's arms are duct-taped together in front of her, and she holds my gaze, watching me with a mix of fear and urgency. It's then that I notice the absence of fingers on one of her hands. I shift my attention to David, who stands frozen and awestruck.

After what feels like an eternity, our eyes meet, silently exchanging thoughts about the surreal scene unfolding before us. He remains speechless, yet I grasp the unspoken words hanging between us.

This is undeniably real—no room for second-guessing. Emma has been alive all this time, and now she's here. The question lingers, hanging in the air: how?

I turn my gaze back to Mike, the gun now aimed at me, causing my heart to plummet into my stomach once more. His finger hovers over the trigger, prompting a gasp through the duct tape, momentarily taking my attention from Emma. Fear widens my eyes.

In the midst of this, a man in a ski mask seizes Emma, guiding her towards the vacant chair beside me. She struggles to settle into it–flaring her body left and right. My mind echoes over and over again with the memory of seven-year-old Emma's words in the storage closet, "Are we going to be okay, Hayley?"

The surrealness of the situation deepens as I come to the realization that Emma's body isn't scattered across Chugach State Park as we all previously assumed. This initial assumption, unsettling as it was, turns out it wasn't true. In a somewhat disoriented state, I find myself grappling with this unexpected truth. How is this even possible?

I force myself to remember that law enforcement only found some of Emma's fingers and not other parts of her body. With a heightened sense of vigilance, I carefully scrutinize Emma's hands, a mix of awe and disbelief rushing through me. Witnessing her, observing Emma, is truly astonishing. The assumptions everyone made were wrong; her entire body wasn't scattered across Chugach State Park. She is here. She is alive.

In this moment, Emma maintains eye contact, her bright blue eyes still filled with fear. Time seems to slow down, as if questioning its own existence. I'm caught in the convergence of two realms: one where I confront my present-day sister, and another where I see my seven-year-old sibling, clad in white tights and a red checkered dress.

As Emma is secured to the chair alongside me all three of the men advance towards David.

In a matter of seconds, Mike aggressively rips the tape off David's mouth, who coughs aggressively, trying to catch his breath. A moment later, David unleashes a scream, uttering, "Hayley and Emma, I am so sorry."

His words break me, leaving me emotionally shattered.

"Shut up!" Mike yells, slapping David across the face.

I gasp, watching the relentless barrage of blows on David, each strike painting his face a dark crimson color. Memories flash of Victoria enduring similar violence—slapped, thrown, and kicked to the ground. Here we are again, Emma and I, bound to kitchen chairs by rough rope. The impending dread hangs heavy; it's only a matter of time before the sharp crack of a gun, the roar of fire, and nothingness consume us.

Then, when David catches his breath, Mike leans in closer to David and asks. "How does it feel? How does it feel to lose your family again?"

David vigorously shakes his head, his breath escaping in urgent gasps as he pleads, "I've told you, I didn't kill your wife. Please, you have to believe me!"

"QUIET!" Mike roars, slapping David's face again. Blood spills, tracing down like an icicle melting. "You killed her! You know you did. You hid it for years. Say their names! My wife and son!" Mike bellows.

David remains silent, prompting Mike to persist in his assault. Blood keeps pooling on David's face, his tears mixing with the crimson, creating a macabre tableau resembling a bloody Halloween mask rather than my father's face.

Mike relentlessly pounds David until, at last, he breaks. The words slid out of his mouth in a desperate state. "Rebecca. Rebecca Martin. And Matthew Martin."

The revelation hangs in the air like shattered glass slipping through my fingers. Did David really kill Rebecca and Matthew, or did David just give up and say their names? Either way, the apparent truth leaves me breathless—shattered, just like the glass slipping through my fingers.

Then, gradually, Mike raises the gun, aiming it directly between Emma and me. I'm paralyzed, unable to force my gaze from his finger on the trigger.

Mike then turns back to David, the gun still pointed towards us. He clears his throat. "Choose."

My heart stops. It's as if the ticking clock inside of me explodes.

I think about Victoria again at this point. But this time, I remind myself of her explanation for choosing Emma. *'I don't want you to think I chose Emma because of any other reason than it was random. I didn't love her more than you. I didn't like her more than you. It's none of that. It's my biggest regret, as in saying a name in general. I wish they just would've killed me."*

The realization hits me: One of us is going to die this time. He's making David pick between Emma and me.

David looks up at Mike in terror and then back at Emma and me, trapped in the raggedy kitchen chairs.

David shakes his head and cries, "No! Don't make me do this!"

Mike rumbles loudly. "Just like what your wife had to do, choose who you want to save. Choose who will be your sacrifice. You can only pick one. Hayley or Emma." He looks at me as the man says my name and then at Emma once he says hers.

It's happening again.

My head drops, and I stare down at the floor, not wanting to see what comes next. As impossible as it seems like to do, I accept my fate. What choice do I have? I acknowledge that the answers and healing I so desperately crave may forever elude me.

"Choose!" Mike's scream echoes through the tense air once more.

David spits out a mouthful of blood before uttering, "I can't. I just can't do that."

"Come on, you understand the rules," Mike insists. "If you don't make a choice, they'll both die. That's a guarantee. Now you know exactly how your wife felt when she had to choose Emma."

I steal a quick glance upward, meeting David's eyes as he shakes his head in refusal. His gaze is filled with remorse, and in that charged moment, an unspoken understanding passes between us.

"You have ten seconds," Mike announces. "Ten…"

David mouths the words, 'I love you,' and my heart shatters. Though I know he can't see, I reciprocate the sentiment through the duct tape binding my mouth. Despite the immense pain he's inflicted upon me—hiding the letters from me, keeping me away from Victoria, and hiding this unspeakable truth of killing two innocent people— a twinge of empathy still lingers within me for him. He's my dad. How could it not?

Mike's countdown continues. "Nine…eight…"

In desperation, David screams, turning towards Mike. "No! Please. Please just take me. Please kill me."

"Seven…six…"

David's screams intensify, his frantic struggle against the chair growing more manic. My gaze shifts to Emma one last time; she hasn't averted her eyes from me. I attempt a smile, but the muscles in my face no longer cooperate under the tight grip of the duct tape.

At the very least, I find solace in the fact that Emma's been alive and survived after all of this time. At least I got to be reunited with Victoria again and discover the truth about her innocence.

"Five...four..."

My eyes lower again towards the ground one last time.

"Three...two..."

We know the truth now. I can find rest and solace in that.

"One."

I hold my breath, and the resounding gunshots pierce the air.

Chapter 60

SOMEWHERE DARK AND COLD– ANCHORAGE, ALASKA

ME

Darkness surrounds me. I can't tell if I'm dead or alive, or if my eyes are opened or closed. It's like I'm trapped in my own body, a hauntingly familiar sensation that refuses to release its grip from me.

After a brief moment, a realization dawns on me –there's no sensation of pain. Am I still alive? Then, my eyes snap open, and the first sight that greets me is Emma. She's alive, staring back at me with an elongated face, ghostly pale, and hollow eyes. Remarkably, there's no trace of blood on her; she remains untouched.

She's alive, and so am I? What happened?

I turn, scanning the cabin, and then I see it – the blood. Three men lie in pools of it on the wooden floor, resembling dismembered dolls smeared with red paint. The sight triggers a gasp of horror.

Amid the blood, a photograph of a woman with ashy blonde hair and bright green eyes, blood-stained, lies near Mike. It's a picture of Beks.

Glancing forward, I catch sight of David, still bound to his chair, miraculously alive. His entire body appears as though it has been immersed in a pool of blood, yet he persists. Despite the surreal scene, he's remarkably alert, moving within the confines of his seat, and barely clinging to each breath.

He survived, too?

David's gaze locks onto mine in an instant. Spotting me, he shouts urgently, gesturing towards the front door, "Look, girls!"

I follow his gaze and pivot. In the cabin doorway stands Victoria—wrapped in a robe, her hair tousled, and a firm grip on a gun, aimed unwaveringly at the trio of masked men. Her disheveled hair seems almost electrically charged, standing on end, while dirt and leaves cling to her clothes.

Victoria's gaze shifts between Emma and me, lingering for several heartbeats. Tears well up in her eyes, and her arms tremble, causing the gun to lower to her side. Finally, her eyes lock onto mine. "You're alive, Hayley. And Emma's alive, too—she's been held here the entire time." Victoria's words rush out with urgency as if she can't convey them quickly enough. "She was in the other cabin nearby. I saw her before they brought her here. I-I followed them here."

The truth reignites the pulse in my heart, as if her words are mending the shattered and ticking clock within me. A surge of questions floods my mind, yet they yield to an overwhelming sense of peace. The intricacies, logistics, and inquiries—they can all be addressed later. It doesn't matter right now. What matters in this moment is the relief that this nightmare is done, at least for now.

Victoria gasps in relief, dropping to her knees in overwhelm. Her entire body shakes with the intensity of the moment. "It's over. It's finally over."

She takes several moments, glancing towards the space between Emma and me. Eventually, a gentle smile covers Victoria's face, and, shockingly, a calmness begins to well up inside me—a feeling I never thought possible.

In a moment I never thought possible, we, as a family, hold the truth before the rest of the world, together. Before the media, the police, or any outsider, our story remains ours alone to understand and to reveal–something we were never able to do before.

Now, we stand at the brink of a second chance. In this moment, it hits me—the truth is finally out and acknowledgment has begun, giving us the freedom to finally move forward.

Epilogue

Ready to find out more? Visit lindsayjcampbell.com to read the epilogue for *The Space Between Them* and join Lindsay's newsletter to be the first to know about new releases and receive exclusive reading content.

Discussion Questions

Spoiler alert: Please note that the discussion questions below contain spoilers to the book.

1. Why does the author choose to create a mythical confusion on what may or may not be hallucinations or reality for Hayley? Does she or doesn't she have schizophrenia?

2. Throughout the novel, we can see that Hayley and Victoria's lives have many parallel moments–along with many other characters. What are some examples of this throughout the novel and what purpose does this serve?

3. Brandon creates feelings of calmness, safety, and centeredness in Hayley. Why is it important for her to experience these emotions? What purpose does Brandon serve as a character?

4. As a character, Beks juxtaposes the story's realism as she is a dead character. What is the purpose of this? Is Beks a hallucination, paranormal, or something else?

5. What does the Phantom symbolize, and why did Hayley finally see the hallucinatory figure that night at the bar?

6. Stigma is often associated with discussions around mental health and mental illness, specifically illnesses like depression and anxiety. However, it's generally not as often focused on schizophrenia, and throughout the novel, we see the consequences of this. How would the novel have been different if Victoria was never diagnosed with schizophrenia?

7. If you had to choose, who or what is to blame for Victoria being falsely accused and indicted?

8. Even after many years, Mike is still in the bargaining stage of grief and an entire family has to suffer for it. What do you think of him as a character?

9. It's a known secret that many failed hospital operations are caused by human errors. What do you think of David's dark secret, according to Mike?

10. Mike says 'David wanted to play God, so I became his Devil. Now it's time to be his Rumpelstiltskin.' What does Mike mean by this?

11. The choice of being forced to kill a family member is a harsh cost in the name of Mike's so-called 'justice.' With that being said, what does Emma's survival at the end represent?

12. Forgiveness, accountability, mental health stigma, and vengeance are themes throughout the novel. How is each exemplified?

Review
The Space Between Them

We want to hear from you. Let us know what you think about The Space Between Them by leaving a review on Amazon and Goodreads. Your feedback is highly appreciated!

Acknowledgments

To Jesus Christ, my Lord and Savior, who planted the idea in my mind.

To my parents and my sister who have always believed in me.

To my grandparents who embraced my love for writing and let child-me write dozens of stories on their typewriter.

To the family and friends who have supported me during every stage of my writing journey.

To my friend, Shelby, who has always championed me since draft one.

To my husband who pushed me when I needed it the most.

To my dedicated ARC readers who provided helpful feedback.

To my editor, Jennifer Collins, and format editor, Mirajul Kayal, for working their magic.

To my book designer, William Ntim, for designing a dream cover.

Again, to my mother, who I couldn't have done this without. This book is dedicated to you. Thank you.